P9-DMI-611

GREAT RUSSIAN SHORT STORIES

DOVER THRIFT EDITIONS

Edited by
Paul Negri

DOVER PUBLICATIONS, INC.
MINEOLA, NEW YORK

DOVER THRIFT EDITIONS

GENERAL EDITOR: PAUL NEGRI
EDITOR OF THIS VOLUME: JENNY BAK

Copyright

Copyright © 2003 by Dover Publications, Inc.
All rights reserved.

Bibliographical Note

This Dover edition, first published in 2003, is a new selection of twelve short stories reprinted from standard texts. A new introductory Note has been specially prepared for this edition.

Library of Congress Cataloging-in-Publication Data

Great Russian short stories / edited by Paul Negri.
    p. cm. — (Dover thrift editions)
    Contents: The queen of spades / Alexander Pushkin —The overcoat / Nikolai Gogol — The district doctor / Ivan Turgenev — White nights / Fyodor Dostoyevsky — How much land does a man need? / Leo Tolstoy — The clothes mender / Nicholas Leskov — The signal / Vsevolod Garshin — The lady with the toy dog / Anton Chekhov — The white mother / Fedor Sologub — Twenty-six men and a girl / Maxim Gorky — The outrage / Alexander Kuprin — Lazarus / Leonide Andreyev.
   ISBN-13: 978-0-486-42992-2 (pbk.)
   ISBN-10: 0-486-42992-X (pbk.)
    1. Short stories, Russian—Translations into English. 2. Russian fiction—19th century—Translations into English. 3. Russian fiction—20th century—Translations in English. I. Negri, Paul. II. Series.

PG3286.G74 2003
891.73'0108—dc21
2003046070

Manufactured in the United States by LSC Communications
42992X12   2020
www.doverpublications.com

For

Claire Wingfield

&

"The vocation of every man and woman
is to serve other people."
Leo Tolstoy

Note

THE AUTHORS that contributed to Russia's Golden Age of literature are credited with bringing the rich literary tradition of their then-obscure nation to the forefront of Western European interest. Viewed as primitive and backward during the late eighteenth century, czarist Russia was shunned from the European collective and hovered between Asian and Western sensibilities. By that time, however, the educated gentry in Russia had already begun to absorb aspects of Western lifestyle into their own. By the 1800s, French was the preferred language of the elite, and small factions were calling for a more Western-style monarchy to replace the centuries-old autocratic czarist system.

This European influence—and the predictable backlash from purists—succeeded in inspiring the emergence of the greatest of Russian authors. From poetry to fiction, their writings drew from a wealth of topics springing from the turbulent social and political landscape of the country, as well as from the bottomless well of human flaws and virtues. The prevailing theme of the downtrodden proletariat, sometimes juxtaposed with the privileged and idle bourgeoisie, was particularly relevant and common in that era of Realist writing.

Beginning with Pushkin, often considered Russia's greatest poet and a pioneer of its modern literature, this selection of short stories features an illustrious and formidable roster of writers. These authors—including Tolstoy, Chekhov, and Dostoyevsky—are perhaps better known for their longer works, but were equally adept at meeting the minimalist limitations of short story writing, in which every word must bear weight. From the allegorical "How Much Land Does a Man Need?" to the ironic "The Clothesmender," these works are excellent examples of this difficult craft, in which extraneous descriptions must be carefully whittled away to reveal core ideas without sacrificing substance.

The stories in this collection represent a varied range of style and subject matter, but each offers a fascinating glimpse of the factors that shaped modern Russia. These insights offer an unvarnished portrait of the pre-Stalinist Russian character—painfully conflicted by greed, self-destruction, love, and hope. It is clear why these evocative tales have become classics in the short story genre, and why these authors have been immortalized as the masters of modern Russian literature.

Contents

THE QUEEN OF SPADES

Alexander Pushkin

I

THERE WAS a card party at the rooms of Naroumoff of the Horse Guards. The long winter night passed away imperceptibly, and it was five o'clock in the morning before the company sat down to supper. Those who had won, ate with a good appetite; the others sat staring absently at their empty plates. When the champagne appeared, however, the conversation became more animated, and all took a part in it.

"And how did you fare, Sourin?" asked the host.

"Oh, I lost, as usual. I must confess that I am unlucky: I play mirandole,[1] I always keep cool, I never allow anything to put me out, and yet I always lose!"

"And you did not once allow yourself to be tempted to back the red? . . . Your firmness astonishes me."

"But what do you think of Hermann?" said one of the guests, pointing to a young Engineer: "He has never had a card in his hand in his life, he has never in his life laid a wager, and yet he sits here till five o'clock in the morning watching our play."

"Play interests me very much," said Hermann: "but I am not in the position to sacrifice the necessary in the hope of winning the superfluous."

---

[1] [Not increasing the stakes.]

1

"Hermann is a German: he is economical—that is all!" observed Tomsky. "But if there is one person that I cannot understand, it is my grandmother, the Countess Anna Fedorovna."

"How so?" inquired the guests.

"I cannot understand," continued Tomsky, "how it is that my grandmother does not punt."[2]

"What is there remarkable about an old lady of eighty not punting?" said Naroumoff.

"Then you do not know the reason why?"

"No, really; haven't the faintest idea."

"Oh! then listen. You must know that, about sixty years ago, my grandmother went to Paris, where she created quite a sensation. People used to run after her to catch a glimpse of the 'Muscovite Venus.' Richelieu made love to her, and my grandmother maintains that he almost blew out his brains in consequence of her cruelty. At that time ladies used to play at faro. On one occasion at the Court, she lost a very considerable sum to the Duke of Orleans. On returning home, my grandmother removed the patches from her face, took off her hoops, informed my grandfather of her loss at the gaming-table, and ordered him to pay the money. My deceased grandfather, as far as I remember, was a sort of house-steward to my grandmother. He dreaded her like fire; but, on hearing of such a heavy loss, he almost went out of his mind; he calculated the various sums she had lost, and pointed out to her that in six months she had spent half a million of francs, that neither their Moscow nor Saratoff estates were in Paris, and finally refused point blank to pay the debt. My grandmother gave him a box on the ear and slept by herself as a sign of her displeasure. The next day she sent for her husband, hoping that this domestic punishment had produced an effect upon him, but she found him inflexible. For the first time in her life, she entered into reasonings and explanations with him, thinking to be able to convince him by pointing out to him that there are debts and debts, and that there is a great difference between a Prince and a coachmaker. But it was all in vain, my grandfather still remained obdurate. But the matter did not rest there. My grandmother did not know what to do. She had shortly before become acquainted with a very remarkable man. You have heard of Count St. Germain,[3] about whom so many marvelous stories are told. You know that he represented himself as the Wandering Jew, as the discoverer of the elixir of life, of the philosopher's stone, and so forth. Some

---

[2] [To play against the banker, in faro.]
[3] [Famous adventurer, died 1784.]

laughed at him as a charlatan; but Casanova, in his memoirs, says that he was a spy. But be that as it may, St. Germain, in spite of the mystery surrounding him, was a very fascinating person, and was much sought after in the best circles of society. Even to this day my grandmother retains an affectionate recollection of him, and becomes quite angry if anyone speaks disrespectfully of him. My grandmother knew that St. Germain had large sums of money at his disposal. She resolved to have recourse to him, and she wrote a letter to him asking him to come to her without delay. The queer old man immediately waited upon her and found her overwhelmed with grief. She described to him in the blackest colors the barbarity of her husband, and ended by declaring that her whole hope depended upon his friendship and amiability.

"St. Germain reflected.

"'I could advance you the sum you want,' said he; 'but I know that you would not rest easy until you had paid me back, and I should not like to bring fresh troubles upon you. But there is another way of getting out of your difficulty: you can win back your money.'

"'But, my dear Count,' replied my grandmother, 'I tell you that I haven't any money left.'

"'Money is not necessary,' replied St. Germain: 'be pleased to listen to me.'

"Then he revealed to her a secret, for which each of us would give a good deal . . ."

The young officers listened with increased attention. Tomsky lit his pipe, puffed away for a moment and then continued:

"That same evening my grandmother went to Versailles to the *jeu de la reine*.[4] The Duke of Orleans kept the bank; my grandmother excused herself in an off-handed manner for not having yet paid her debt, by inventing some little story, and then began to play against him. She chose three cards and played them one after the other: all three won *sonika*,[5] and my grandmother recovered every farthing that she had lost."

"Mere chance!" said one of the guests.

"A tale!" observed Hermann.

"Perhaps they were marked cards!" said a third.

"I do not think so," replied Tomsky gravely.

"What!" said Naroumoff, "you have a grandmother who knows how to hit upon three lucky cards in succession, and you have never yet succeeded in getting the secret of it out of her?"

---

[4] [The Queen's card party.]
[5] [Breaking the bank.]

"That's the deuce of it!" replied Tomsky: "she had four sons, one of whom was my father; all four were determined gamblers, and yet not to one of them did she ever reveal her secret, although it would not have been a bad thing either for them or for me. But this is what I heard from my uncle, Count Ivan Ilitch, and he assured me, on his honor, that it was true. The late Chaplitsky—the same who died in poverty after having squandered millions—once lost, in his youth, about three hundred thousand rubles—to Zoritch,[6] if I remember rightly. He was in despair. My grandmother, who was always very severe upon the extravagance of young men, took pity, however, upon Chaplitsky. She gave him three cards, telling him to play them one after the other, at the same time exacting from him a solemn promise that he would never play at cards again as long as he lived. Chaplitsky then went to his victorious opponent, and they began a fresh game. On the first card he staked fifty thousand rubles and won *sonika*; he doubled the stake and won again, till at last, by pursuing the same tactics, he won back more than he had lost . . .

"But it is time to go to bed: it is a quarter to six already."

And indeed it was already beginning to dawn: the young men emptied their glasses and then took leave of each other.

II

The old Countess A—— was seated in her dressing-room in front of her looking-glass. Three waiting-maids stood around her. One held a small pot of rouge, another a box of hair-pins, and the third a tall cap with bright red ribbons. The Countess had no longer the slightest pretensions to beauty, but she still preserved the habits of her youth, dressed in strict accordance with the fashion of seventy years before, and made as long and as careful a toilette as she would have done sixty years previously. Near the window, at an embroidery frame, sat a young lady, her ward.

"Good morning, grandmamma," said a young officer, entering the room. "*Bonjour, Mademoiselle Lise.* Grandmamma, I want to ask you something."

"What is it, Paul?"

"I want you to let me introduce one of my friends to you, and to allow me to bring him to the ball on Friday."

---

[6] [A favorite of Catherine the Great.]

"Bring him direct to the ball and introduce him to me there. Were you at B——'s yesterday?"

"Yes; everything went off very pleasantly, and dancing was kept up until five o'clock. How charming Eletskaia was!"

"But, my dear, what is there charming about her? Isn't she like her grandmother, the Princess Daria Petrovna? By the way, she must be very old, the Princess Daria Petrovna."

"How do you mean, old?" cried Tomsky thoughtlessly; "she died seven years ago."

The young lady raised her head and made a sign to the young officer. He then remembered that the old Countess was never to be informed of the death of any of her contemporaries, and he bit his lips. But the old Countess heard the news with the greatest indifference.

"Dead!" said she; "and I did not know it. We were appointed maids of honor at the same time, and when we were presented to the Empress . . ."

And the Countess for the hundredth time related to her grandson one of her anecdotes.

"Come, Paul," said she, when she had finished her story, "help me to get up. Lizanka,[7] where is my snuff-box?"

And the Countess with her three maids went behind a screen to finish her toilette. Tomsky was left alone with the young lady.

"Who is the gentleman you wish to introduce to the Countess?" asked Lizaveta Ivanovna in a whisper.

"Naroumoff. Do you know him?"

"No. Is he a soldier or a civilian?"

"A soldier."

"Is he in the Engineers?"

"No, in the Cavalry. What made you think that he was in the Engineers?"
The young lady smiled, but made no reply.

"Paul," cried the Countess from behind the screen, "send me some new novel, only pray don't let it be one of the present day style."

"What do you mean, grandmother?"

"That is, a novel, in which the hero strangles neither his father nor his mother, and in which there are no drowned bodies. I have a great horror of drowned persons."

"There are no such novels nowadays. Would you like a Russian one?"

"Are there any Russian novels? Send me one, my dear, pray send me one!"

---

[7] Diminutive of Lizaveta (Elizabeth).

"Good-bye, grandmother: I am in a hurry. . . . Good-bye, Lizaveta Ivanovna. What made you think that Naroumoff was in the Engineers?"

And Tomsky left the boudoir.

Lizaveta Ivanovna was left alone: she laid aside her work and began to look out of the window. A few moments afterwards, at a corner house on the other side of the street, a young officer appeared. A deep blush covered her cheeks; she took up her work again and bent her head down over the frame. At the same moment the Countess returned completely dressed.

"Order the carriage, Lizaveta," said she; "we will go out for a drive."

Lizaveta arose from the frame and began to arrange her work.

"What is the matter with you, my child, are you deaf?" cried the Countess. "Order the carriage to be got ready at once."

"I will do so this moment," replied the young lady, hastening into the ante-room.

A servant entered and gave the Countess some books from Prince Paul Alexandrovitch.

"Tell him that I am much obliged to him," said the Countess. "Lizaveta! Lizaveta! where are you running to?"

"I am going to dress."

"There is plenty of time, my dear. Sit down here. Open the first volume and read to me aloud."

Her companion took the book and read a few lines.

"Louder," said the Countess. "What is the matter with you, my child? Have you lost your voice? Wait—give me that footstool—a little nearer—that will do!"

Lizaveta read two more pages. The Countess yawned.

"Put the book down," said she: "what a lot of nonsense! Send it back to Prince Paul with my thanks. . . . But where is the carriage?"

"The carriage is ready," said Lizaveta, looking out into the street.

"How is it that you are not dressed?" said the Countess: "I must always wait for you. It is intolerable, my dear!"

Liza hastened to her room. She had not been there two minutes, before the Countess began to ring with all her might. The three waiting-maids came running in at one door and the valet at another.

"How is it that you cannot hear me when I ring for you?" said the Countess. "Tell Lizaveta Ivanovna that I am waiting for her."

Lizaveta returned with her hat and cloak on.

"At last you are here!" said the Countess. "But why such an elaborate toilette? Whom do you intend to captivate? What sort of weather is it? It seems rather windy."

"No, Your Ladyship, it is very calm," replied the valet.

"You never think of what you are talking about. Open the window. So it is: windy and bitterly cold. Unharness the horses. Lizaveta, we won't go out—there was no need for you to deck yourself like that."

"What a life is mine!" thought Lizaveta Ivanovna.

And, in truth, Lizaveta Ivanovna was a very unfortunate creature. "The bread of the stranger is bitter," says Dante, "and his staircase hard to climb." But who can know what the bitterness of dependence is so well as the poor companion of an old lady of quality? The Countess A—— had by no means a bad heart, but she was capricious, like a woman who had been spoilt by the world, as well as being avaricious and egotistical, like all old people who have seen their best days, and whose thoughts are with the past and not the present. She participated in all the vanities of the great world, went to balls, where she sat in a corner, painted and dressed in old-fashioned style, like a deformed but indispensable ornament of the ball-room; all the guests on entering approached her and made a profound bow, as if in accordance with a set ceremony, but after that nobody took any further notice of her. She received the whole town at her house, and observed the strictest etiquette, although she could no longer recognize the faces of people. Her numerous domestics, growing fat and old in her ante-chamber and servants' hall, did just as they liked, and vied with each other in robbing the aged Countess in the most bare-faced manner. Lizaveta Ivanovna was the martyr of the household. She made tea, and was reproached with using too much sugar; she read novels aloud to the Countess, and the faults of the author were visited upon her head; she accompanied the Countess in her walks, and was held answerable for the weather or the state of the pavement. A salary was attached to the post, but she very rarely received it, although she was expected to dress like everybody else, that is to say, like very few indeed. In society she played the most pitiable rôle. Everybody knew her, and nobody paid her any attention. At balls she danced only when a partner was wanted, and ladies would only take hold of her arm when it was necessary to lead her out of the room to attend to their dresses. She was very self-conscious, and felt her position keenly, and she looked about her with impatience for a deliverer to come to her rescue; but the young men, calculating in their giddiness, honored her with but very little attention, although Lizaveta Ivanovna was a hundred times prettier than the bare-faced and cold-hearted marriageable girls around whom they hovered. Many a time did she quietly slink away from the glittering but wearisome drawing-room, to go and cry in her own poor little room, in which stood a screen, a chest of drawers, a looking-glass and a painted bedstead, and where a tallow candle burnt feebly in a copper candle-stick.

One morning—this was about two days after the evening party

described at the beginning of this story, and a week previous to the scene at which we have just assisted—Lizaveta Ivanovna was seated near the window at her embroidery frame, when, happening to look out into the street, she caught sight of a young Engineer officer, standing motionless with his eyes fixed upon her window. She lowered her head and went on again with her work. About five minutes afterwards she looked out again—the young officer was still standing in the same place. Not being in the habit of coquetting with passing officers, she did not continue to gaze out into the street, but went on sewing for a couple of hours, without raising her head. Dinner was announced. She rose up and began to put her embroidery away, but glancing casually out of the window, she perceived the officer again. This seemed to her very strange. After dinner she went to the window with a certain feeling of uneasiness, but the officer was no longer there—and she thought no more about him.

A couple of days afterwards, just as she was stepping into the carriage with the Countess, she saw him again. He was standing close behind the door, with his face half-concealed by his fur collar, but his dark eyes sparkled beneath his cap. Lizaveta felt alarmed, though she knew not why, and she trembled as she seated herself in the carriage.

On returning home, she hastened to the window—the officer was standing in his accustomed place, with his eyes fixed upon her. She drew back, a prey to curiosity and agitated by a feeling which was quite new to her.

From that time forward not a day passed without the young officer making his appearance under the window at the customary hour, and between him and her there was established a sort of mute acquaintance. Sitting in her place at work, she used to feel his approach; and raising her head, she would look at him longer and longer each day. The young man seemed to be very grateful to her: she saw with the sharp eye of youth, how a sudden flush covered his pale cheeks each time that their glances met. After about a week she commenced to smile at him. . . .

When Tomsky asked permission of his grandmother the Countess to present one of his friends to her, the young girl's heart beat violently. But hearing that Naroumoff was not an Engineer, she regretted that by her thoughtless question, she had betrayed her secret to the volatile Tomsky.

Hermann was the son of a German who had become a naturalized Russian, and from whom he had inherited a small capital. Being firmly convinced of the necessity of preserving his independence, Hermann did not touch his private income, but lived on his pay, without allowing himself the slightest luxury. Moreover, he was reserved and ambitious, and his companions rarely had an opportunity of making merry at the expense of his extreme parsimony. He had strong passions and an ardent imagination, but his firmness of disposition preserved him from the ordinary errors of young men. Thus, though a gamester at heart, he never touched a card, for he considered his position did not allow him—as he said—"to risk the necessary in the hope of winning the superfluous," yet he would sit for nights together at the card table and follow with feverish anxiety the different turns of the game.

The story of the three cards had produced a powerful impression upon his imagination, and all night long he could think of nothing else. "If," he thought to himself the following evening, as he walked along the streets of St. Petersburg, "if the old Countess would but reveal her secret to me! if she would only tell me the names of the three winning cards. Why should I not try my fortune? I must get introduced to her and win her favor—become her lover. . . . But all that will take time, and she is eighty-seven years old: she might be dead in a week, in couple of days even! . . . But the story itself: can it really be true? . . . No! Economy, temperance and industry: those are my three winning cards; by means of them I shall be able to double my capital—increase it sevenfold, and procure for myself ease and independence."

Musing in this manner, he walked on until he found himself in one of the principal streets of St. Petersburg, in front of a house of antiquated architecture. The street was blocked with equipages; carriages one after the other drew up in front of the brilliantly illuminated doorway. At one moment there stepped out on to the pavement the well-shaped little foot of some young beauty, at another the heavy boot of a cavalry officer, and then the silk stockings and shoes of a member of the diplomatic world. Furs and cloaks passed in rapid succession before the gigantic porter at the entrance.

Hermann stopped. "Whose house is this?" he asked of the watchman at the corner.

"The Countess A——'s," replied the watchman.

Hermann started. The strange story of the three cards again presented itself to his imagination. He began walking up and down before the house, thinking of its owner and her strange secret. Returning late to his modest lodging, he could not go to sleep for a long time, and when at last he did doze off, he could dream of nothing but cards, green tables, piles of banknotes and heaps of ducats. He played one card after the other, winning uninterruptedly, and then he gathered up the gold and filled his pockets with the notes. When he woke up late the next morning, he sighed over the loss of his imaginary wealth, and then sallying out into the town, he found himself once more in front of the Countess's residence. Some unknown power seemed to have attracted him thither. He stopped and looked up at the windows. At one of these he saw a head with luxuriant black hair, which was bent down probably over some book or an embroidery frame. The head was raised. Hermann saw a fresh complexion and a pair of dark eyes. That moment decided his fate.

III

Lizaveta Ivanovna had scarcely taken off her hat and cloak, when the Countess sent for her and again ordered her to get the carriage ready. The vehicle drew up before the door, and they prepared to take their seats. Just at the moment when two footmen were assisting the old lady to enter the carriage, Lizaveta saw her Engineer standing close beside the wheel; he grasped her hand; alarm caused her to lose her presence of mind, and the young man disappeared—but not before he had left a letter between her fingers. She concealed it in her glove, and during the whole of the drive she neither saw nor heard anything. It was the custom of the Countess, when out for an airing in her carriage, to be constantly asking such questions as: "Who was that person that met us just now? What is the name of this bridge? What is written on that signboard?" On this occasion, however, Lizaveta returned such vague and absurd answers, that the Countess became angry with her.

"What is the matter with you, my dear?" she exclaimed. "Have you taken leave of your senses, or what is it? Do you not hear me or understand what I say? . . . Heaven be thanked, I am still in my right mind and speak plainly enough!"

Lizaveta Ivanovna did not hear her. On returning home she ran to her room, and drew the letter out of her glove: it was not sealed. Lizaveta read it. The letter contained a declaration of love; it was tender, respectful, and copied word for word from a German novel. But Lizaveta did not know anything of the German language, and she was quite delighted.

For all that, the letter caused her to feel exceedingly uneasy. For the first time in her life she was entering into secret and confidential relations with a young man. His boldness alarmed her. She reproached herself for her imprudent behavior, and knew not what to do. Should she cease to sit at the window and, by assuming an appearance of indifference towards him, put a check upon the young officer's desire for further acquaintance with her? Should she send his letter back to him, or should she answer him in a cold and decided manner? There was nobody to whom she could turn in her perplexity, for she had neither female friend nor adviser. . . . At length she resolved to reply to him.

She sat down at her little writing-table, took pen and paper, and began to think. Several times she began her letter, and then tore it up: the way she had expressed herself seemed to her either too inviting or too cold and decisive. At last she succeeded in writing a few lines with which she felt satisfied.

"I am convinced," she wrote, "that your intentions are honorable, and that you do not wish to offend me by any imprudent behavior, but our acquaintance must not begin in such a manner. I return you your letter, and I hope that I shall never have any cause to complain of this undeserved slight."

The next day, as soon as Hermann made his appearance, Lizaveta rose from her embroidery, went into the drawing-room, opened the ventilator and threw the letter into the street, trusting that the young officer would have the perception to pick it up.

Hermann hastened forward, picked it up and then repaired to a confectioner's shop. Breaking the seal of the envelope, he found inside it his own letter and Lizaveta's reply. He had expected this, and he returned home, his mind deeply occupied with his intrigue.

Three days afterwards, a bright-eyed young girl from a milliner's establishment brought Lizaveta a letter. Lizaveta opened it with great uneasiness, fearing that it was a demand for money, when suddenly she recognized Hermann's handwriting.

"You have made a mistake, my dear," said she: "this letter is not for me."

"Oh, yes, it is for you," replied the girl, smiling very knowingly. "Have the goodness to read it."

Lizaveta glanced at the letter. Hermann requested an interview.

"It cannot be," she cried, alarmed at the audacious request, and the manner in which it was made. "This letter is certainly not for me."

And she tore it into fragments.

"If the letter was not for you, why have you torn it up?" said the girl. "I should have given it back to the person who sent it."

"Be good enough, my dear," said Lizaveta, disconcerted by this remark, "not to bring me any more letters for the future, and tell the person who sent you that he ought to be ashamed. . . ."

But Hermann was not the man to be thus put off. Every day Lizaveta received from him a letter, sent now in this way, now in that. They were no longer translated from the German. Hermann wrote them under the inspiration of passion, and spoke in his own language, and they bore full testimony to the inflexibility of his desire and the disordered condition of his uncontrollable imagination. Lizaveta no longer thought of sending them back to him: she became intoxicated with them and began to reply to them, and little by little her answers became longer and more affectionate. At last she threw out of the window to him the following letter:

"This evening there is going to be a ball at the Embassy. The Countess will be there. We shall remain until two o'clock. You have now an opportunity of seeing me alone. As soon as the Countess is gone, the servants will very probably go out, and there will be nobody left but the Swiss, but he usually goes to sleep in his lodge. Come about half-past eleven. Walk straight upstairs. If you meet anybody in the ante-room, ask if the Countess is at home. You will be told 'No,' in which case there will be nothing left for you to do but to go away again. But it is most probable that you will meet nobody. The maidservants will all be together in one room. On leaving the ante-room, turn to the left, and walk straight on until you reach the Countess's bedroom. In the bedroom, behind a screen, you will find two doors: the one on the right leads to a cabinet, which the Countess never enters; the one on the left leads to a corridor, at the end of which is a little winding staircase; this leads to my room."

Hermann trembled like a tiger, as he waited for the appointed time to arrive. At ten o'clock in the evening he was already in front of the Countess's house. The weather was terrible; the wind blew with great violence; the sleety snow fell in large flakes; the lamps emitted a feeble light, the streets were deserted; from time to time a sledge, drawn by a sorry-looking hack, passed by, on the look-out for a belated passenger. Hermann was enveloped in a thick overcoat, and felt neither wind nor snow.

At last the Countess's carriage drew up. Hermann saw two footmen carry out in their arms the bent form of the old lady, wrapped in sable fur, and immediately behind her, clad in a warm mantle, and with her head ornamented with a wreath of fresh flowers, followed Lizaveta. The door was closed. The carriage rolled away heavily through the yielding snow. The porter shut the street-door; the windows became dark.

Hermann began walking up and down near the deserted house; at length he stopped under a lamp, and glanced at his watch: it was twenty minutes past eleven. He remained standing under a lamp, his eyes fixed upon the watch, impatiently waiting for the remaining minutes to pass. At half-past eleven precisely, Hermann ascended the steps of the house, and made his way into the brightly-illuminated vestibule. The porter was not there. Hermann hastily ascended the staircase, opened the door of the ante-room and saw a footman sitting asleep in an antique chair by the side of a lamp. With a light firm step Hermann passed by him. The drawing-room and dinning-room were in darkness, but a feeble reflection penetrated thither from the lamp in the ante-room.

* * *

Hermann reached the Countess's bedroom. Before a shrine, which was full of old images, a golden lamp was burning. Faded stuffed chairs and divans with soft cushions stood in melancholy symmetry around the room, the walls of which were hung with China silk. On one side of the room hung two portraits painted in Paris by Madame Lebrun.[8] One of these represented a stout, red-faced man of about forty years of age in a bright-green uniform and with a star upon his breast; the other— a beautiful young woman, with an aquiline nose, forehead curls and a rose in her powdered hair. In the corners stood porcelain shepherds and shepherdesses, dining-room clocks from the workshop of the celebrated Leroy, bandboxes, roulettes, fans and the various playthings for the amusement of ladies that were in vogue at the end of the last century, when Montgolfier's balloons and Mesmer's magnetism were the rage. Hermann stepped behind the screen. At the back of it stood a little iron bedstead; on the right was the door which led to the cabinet; on the left—the other which led to the corridor. He opened the latter, and saw the little winding staircase which led to the room of the poor companion. . . . But he retraced his steps and entered the dark cabinet.

The time passed slowly. All was still. The clock in the drawing-room struck twelve; the strokes echoed through the room one after the other, and everything was quiet again. Hermann stood leaning against the cold stove. He was calm; his heart beat regularly, like that of a man resolved upon a dangerous but inevitable undertaking. One o'clock in the morning struck; then two; and he heard the distant noise of carriage-wheels. An involuntary agitation took possession of him. The carriage drew near and stopped. He heard the sound of the carriage-steps being let down. All was bustle within the house. The servants were running hither and thither, there was a confusion of voices, and the rooms were lit up. Three antiquated chamber-maids entered the bedroom, and they were shortly afterwards followed by the Countess who, more dead than alive, sank into a Voltaire armchair.[9] Hermann peeped through a chink. Lizaveta Ivanovna passed close by him, and he heard her hurried steps as she hastened up the little spiral staircase. For a moment his heart was assailed by something like a pricking of conscience, but the emotion was only transitory, and his heart became petrified as before.

The Countess began to undress before her looking-glass. Her rose-bedecked cap was taken off, and then her powdered wig was removed

---

[8] [Elisabeth Vigée-Lebrun, 1755–1842.]
[9] [Soft armchair with high back and low seat.]

from off her white and closely-cut hair. Hairpins fell in showers around her. Her yellow satin dress, brocaded with silver, fell down at her swollen feet.

Hermann was a witness of the repugnant mysteries of her toilette; at last the Countess was in her night-cap and dressing-gown, and in this costume, more suitable to her age, she appeared less hideous and deformed.

Like all old people in general, the Countess suffered from sleeplessness. Having undressed, she seated herself at the window in a Voltaire armchair and dismissed her maids. The candles were taken away, and once more the room was left with only one lamp burning in it. The Countess sat there looking quite yellow, mumbling with her flaccid lips and swaying to and fro. Her dull eyes expressed complete vacancy of mind, and, looking at her, one would have thought that the rocking of her body was not a voluntary action of her own, but was produced by the action of some concealed galvanic mechanism.

Suddenly the death-like face assumed an inexplicable expression. The lips ceased to tremble, the eyes became animated: before the Countess stood an unknown man.

"Do not be alarmed, for Heaven's sake, do not be alarmed!" said he in a low but distinct voice. "I have no intention of doing you any harm, I have only come to ask a favor of you."

The old woman looked at him in silence, as if she had not heard what he had said. Hermann thought that she was deaf, and, bending down towards her ear, he repeated what he had said. The aged Countess remained silent as before.

"You can insure the happiness of my life," continued Hermann, "and it will cost you nothing. I know that you can name three cards in order——"

Hermann stopped. The Countess appeared now to understand what he wanted; she seemed as if seeking for words to reply.

"It was a joke," she replied at last: "I assure you it was only a joke."

"There is no joking about the matter," replied Hermann angrily. "Remember Chaplitsky, whom you helped to win."

The Countess became visibly uneasy. Her features expressed strong emotion, but they quickly resumed their former immobility.

"Can you not name me these three winning cards?" continued Hermann.

The Countess remained silent; Hermann continued:

"For whom are you preserving your secret? For your grandsons? They are rich enough without it; they do not know the worth of money. Your cards would be of no use to a spendthrift. He who cannot preserve his paternal inheritance, will die in want, even though he had a demon at his service. I am not a man of that sort; I know the value of money. Your three cards will not be thrown away upon me. Come!" . . .

He paused and tremblingly awaited her reply. The Countess remained silent; Hermann fell upon his knees.

"If your heart has ever known the feeling of love," said he, "if you remember its rapture, if you have ever smiled at the cry of your new-born child, if any human feeling has ever entered into your breast, I entreat you by the feelings of a wife, a lover, a mother, by all that is most sacred in life, not to reject my prayer. Reveal to me your secret. Of what use is it to you? . . . May be it is connected with some terrible sin, with the loss of eternal salvation, with some bargain with the devil. . . . Reflect,—you are old; you have not long to live—I am ready to take your sins upon my soul. Only reveal to me your secret. Remember that the happiness of a man is in your hands, that not only I, but my children, and grandchildren will bless your memory and reverence you as a saint. . . ."

The old Countess answered not a word.

Hermann rose to his feet.

"You old hag!" he exclaimed, grinding his teeth, "then I will make you answer!"

With these words he drew a pistol from his pocket.

At the sight of the pistol, the Countess for the second time exhibited strong emotion. She shook her head and raised her hands as if to protect herself from the shot . . . then she fell backwards and remained motionless.

"Come, an end to this childish nonsense!" said Hermann, taking hold of her hand. "I ask you for the last time: will you tell me the names of your three cards, or will you not?"

The Countess made no reply. Hermann perceived that she was dead!

IV

Lizaveta Ivanovna was sitting in her room, still in her ball dress, lost in deep thought. On returning home, she had hastily dismissed the chambermaid who very reluctantly came forward to assist her, saying that she would undress herself, and with a trembling heart had gone up to her own room, expecting to find Hermann there, but yet hoping not to find him. At the first glance she convinced herself that he was not there, and she thanked her fate for having prevented him keeping the appointment. She sat down without undressing, and began to recall to mind all the circumstances which in so short a time had carried her so far. It was not three weeks since the time when she first saw the young officer from the window—and yet she was already in correspondence with him, and he had succeeded in inducing her to grant him a nocturnal interview! She

knew his name only through his having written it at the bottom of some
of his letters; she had never spoken to him, had never heard his voice,
and had never heard him spoken of until that evening. But, strange to
say, that very evening at the ball, Tomsky, being piqued with the young
Princess Pauline N——, who, contrary to her usual custom, did not flirt
with him, wished to revenge himself by assuming an air of indifference:
he therefore engaged Lizaveta Ivanovna and danced an endless mazurka
with her. During the whole of the time he kept teasing her about her par-
tiality for Engineer officers; he assured her that he knew far more than
she imagined, and some of his jests were so happily aimed, that Lizaveta
thought several times that her secret was known to him.

"From whom have you learnt all this?" she asked, smiling.

"From a friend of a person very well known to you," replied Tomsky,
"from a very distinguished man."

"And who is this distinguished man?"

"His name is Hermann."

Lizaveta made no reply; but her hands and feet lost all sense of feeling.

"This Hermann," continued Tomsky, "is a man of romantic personality. He has the profile of a Napoleon, and the soul of a
Mephistopheles. I believe that he has at least three crimes upon his
conscience . . . How pale you have become!"

"I have a headache . . . But what did this Hermann—or whatever his
name is—tell you?"

"Hermann is very much dissatisfied with his friend: he says that in
his place he would act very differently . . . I even think that Hermann
himself has designs upon you; at least, he listens very attentively to all
that his friend has to say about you."

"And where has he seen me?"

"In church, perhaps; or on the parade—God alone knows where. It
may have been in your room, while you were asleep, for there is nothing that he——"

Three ladies approaching him with the question: *"oubli ou regret?"*[10]
interrupted the conversation, which had become so tantalizingly interesting to Lizaveta.

The lady chosen by Tomsky was the Princess Pauline herself. She
succeeded in effecting a reconciliation with him during the numerous
turns of the dance, after which he conducted her to her chair. On
returning to his place, Tomsky thought no more either of Hermann or
Lizaveta. She longed to renew the interrupted conversation, but the

---

[10] ["Forgetfulness or regret?": conventional words cloaking the identity of ladies requesting
a dance; the man would choose a word and then dance with the corresponding lady.]

mazurka came to an end, and shortly afterwards the old Countess took her departure.

Tomsky's words were nothing more than the customary small talk of the dance, but they sank deep into the soul of the young dreamer. The portrait, sketched by Tomsky, coincided with the picture she had formed within her own mind, and thanks to the latest romances, the ordinary countenance of her admirer became invested with attributes capable of alarming her and fascinating her imagination at the same time. She was now sitting with her bare arms crossed and with her head, still adorned with flowers, sunk upon her uncovered bosom. Suddenly the door opened and Hermann entered. She shuddered.

"Where were you?" she asked in a terrified whisper.

"In the old Countess's bedroom," replied Hermann: "I have just left her. The Countess is dead."

"My God! What do you say?"

"And I am afraid," added Hermann, "that I am the cause of her death."

Lizaveta looked at him, and Tomsky's words found an echo in her soul: "This man has at least three crimes upon his conscience!" Hermann sat down by the window near her, and related all that had happened.

Lizaveta listened to him in terror. So all the passionate letters, those ardent desires, this bold obstinate pursuit—all this was not love! Money—that was what his soul yearned for! She could not satisfy his desire and make him happy! The poor girl had been nothing but the blind tool of a robber, of the murderer of her aged benefactress! . . . She wept bitter tears of agonized repentance. Hermann gazed at her in silence: his heart, too, was a prey to violent emotion, but neither the tears of the poor girl, nor the wonderful charm of her beauty, enhanced by her grief, could produce any impression upon his hardened soul. He felt no pricking of conscience at the thought of the dead old woman. One thing only grieved him: the irreparable loss of the secret from which he had expected to obtain great wealth.

"You are a monster!" said Lizaveta at last.

"I did not wish for her death," replied Hermann: "my pistol was not loaded."

Both remained silent.

The day began to dawn. Lizaveta extinguished her candle: a pale light illumined her room. She wiped her tear-stained eyes and raised them towards Hermann: he was sitting near the window, with his arms crossed and with a fierce frown upon his forehead. In this attitude he bore a striking resemblance to the portrait of Napoleon. This resemblance struck Lizaveta even.

"How shall I get you out of the house?" said she at last. "I thought of conducting you down the secret staircase, but in that case it would be necessary to go through the Countess's bedroom, and I am afraid."

"Tell me how to find this secret staircase—I will go alone."

Lizaveta arose, took from her drawer a key, handed it to Hermann and gave him the necessary instructions. Hermann pressed her cold, powerless hand, kissed her bowed head, and left the room.

He descended the winding staircase, and once more entered the Countess's bedroom. The dead old lady sat as if petrified; her face expressed profound tranquillity. Hermann stopped before her, and gazed long and earnestly at her, as if he wished to convince himself of the terrible reality; at last he entered the cabinet, felt behind the tapestry for the door, and then began to descend the dark staircase, filled with strange emotions. "Down this very staircase," thought he, "perhaps coming from the very same room, and at this very same hour sixty years ago, there may have glided, in an embroidered coat, with his hair dressed *à l'oiseau royal*[11] and pressing to his heart his three-cornered hat, some young gallant who has long been moldering in the grave, but the heart of his aged mistress has only to-day ceased to beat. . . ."

At the bottom of the staircase Hermann found a door, which he opened with a key, and then traversed a corridor which conducted him into the street.

V

Three days after the fatal night, at nine o'clock in the morning, Hermann repaired to the Convent of ——, where the last honors were to be paid to the mortal remains of the old Countess. Although feeling no remorse, he could not altogether stifle the voice of conscience, which said to him: "You are the murderer of the old woman!" In spite of his entertaining very little religious belief, he was exceedingly superstitious; and believing that the dead Countess might exercise an evil influence upon his life, he resolved to be present at her obsequies in order to implore her pardon.

The church was full. It was with difficulty that Hermann made his way through the crowd of people. The coffin was placed upon a rich catafalque beneath a velvet baldachin. The deceased Countess lay within it, with her hands crossed upon her breast, with a lace cap upon her head and dressed in a white satin robe. Around the catafalque stood the mem-

---

[11] ["In the manner of the royal bird," the name of a contemporary hair style.]

bers of her household: the servants in black *caftans*, with armorial ribbons upon their shoulders, and candles in their hands; the relatives—children, grandchildren, and great-grandchildren—in deep mourning.

Nobody wept; tears would have been *une affectation*. The Countess was so old, that her death could have surprised nobody, and her relatives had long looked upon her as being out of the world. A famous preacher pronounced the funeral sermon. In simple and touching words he described the peaceful passing away of the righteous, who had passed long years in calm preparation for a Christian end. "The angel of death found her," said the orator, "engaged in pious meditation and waiting for the midnight bridegroom."

The service concluded amidst profound silence. The relatives went forward first to take farewell of the corpse. Then followed the numerous guests, who had come to render the last homage to her who for so many years had been a participator in their frivolous amusements. After these followed the members of the Countess's household. The last of these was an old woman of the same age as the deceased. Two young women led her forward by the hand. She had not strength enough to bow down to the ground—she merely shed a few tears and kissed the cold hand of her mistress.

Hermann now resolved to approach the coffin. He knelt down upon the cold stones and remained in that position for some minutes; at last he arose, as pale as the deceased Countess herself; he ascended the steps of the catafalque and bent over the corpse. . . . At that moment it seemed to him that the dead woman darted a mocking look at him and winked with one eye. Hermann started back, took a false step and fell to the ground. Several persons hurried forward and raised him up. At the same moment Lizaveta Ivanovna was borne fainting into the porch of the church. This episode disturbed for some minutes the solemnity of the gloomy ceremony. Among the congregation arose a deep murmur, and a tall thin chamberlain, a near relative of the deceased, whispered in the ear of an Englishman who was standing near him, that the young officer was a natural son of the Countess, to which the Englishman coldly replied: "Oh!"

During the whole of that day, Hermann was strangely excited. Repairing to an out-of-the-way restaurant to dine, he drank a deal of wine, contrary to his usual custom, in the hope of deadening his inward agitation. But the wine only served to excite his imagination still more. On returning home, he threw himself upon his bed without undressing, and fell into a deep sleep.

When he woke up it was already night, and the moon was shining into the room. He looked at his watch: it was a quarter to three. Sleep had left him; he sat down upon his bed and thought of the funeral of the old Countess.

At that moment somebody in the street looked in at his window, and immediately passed on again. Hermann paid no attention to this incident. A few moments afterwards he heard the door of his ante-room open. Hermann thought that it was his orderly, drunk as usual, returning from some nocturnal expedition, but presently he heard footsteps that were unknown to him: somebody was walking softly over the floor in slippers. The door opened, and a woman dressed in white, entered the room. Hermann mistook her for his old nurse, and wondered what could bring her there at that hour of the night. But the white woman glided rapidly across the room and stood before him——and Hermann recognized the Countess!

"I have come to you against my wish," she said in a firm voice: "but I have been ordered to grant your request. Three, seven, ace, will win for you if played in succession, but only on these conditions: that you do not play more than one card in twenty-four hours, and that you never play again during the rest of your life. I forgive you my death, on condition that you marry my companion, Lizaveta Ivanovna."

With these words she turned round very quietly, walked with a shuffling gait towards the door and disappeared. Hermann heard the street-door open and shut, and again he saw someone look in at him through the window.

For a long time Hermann could not recover himself. He then rose up and entered the next room. His orderly was lying asleep upon the floor, and he had much difficulty in waking him. The orderly was drunk as usual, and no information could be obtained from him. The street-door was locked. Hermann returned to his room, lit his candle, and wrote down all the details of his vision.

VI

Two fixed ideas can no more exist together in the moral world than two bodies can occupy one and the same place in the physical world. "Three, seven, ace" soon drove out of Hermann's mind the thought of the dead Countess. "Three, seven, ace" were perpetually running through his head and continually being repeated by his lips. If he saw a young girl, he would say: "How slender she is! quite like the three of hearts." If anybody asked: "What is the time?" he would reply: "Five minutes to seven." Every stout man that he saw reminded him of the ace. "Three, seven, ace" haunted him in his sleep, and assumed all possible shapes. The threes bloomed before him in the forms of magnificent flowers, the sevens were represented by Gothic portals, and the aces became transformed into gigantic spiders. One thought alone occupied his whole mind—to make a profitable use of the secret which he had purchased so dearly. He thought of applying for a furlough so as to travel abroad. He wanted to go to Paris and tempt fortune in some of the public gambling-houses that abounded there. Chance spared him all this trouble.

There was in Moscow a society of rich gamesters, presided over by the celebrated Chekalinsky, who had passed all his life at the card-table and had amassed millions, accepting bills of exchange for his winnings and paying his losses in ready money. His long experience secured for him the confidence of his companions, and his open house, his famous cook, and his agreeable and fascinating manners gained for him the respect of the public. He came to St. Petersburg. The young men of the capital flocked to his rooms, forgetting balls for cards, and preferring the emotions of faro to the seductions of flirting. Naroumoff conducted Hermann to Chekalinsky's residence.

They passed through a suite of magnificent rooms, filled with attentive domestics. The place was crowded. Generals and privy counsellors were playing at whist; young men were lolling carelessly upon the velvet-covered sofas, eating ices and smoking pipes. In the drawing-room, at the head of a long table, around which were assembled about a score of players, sat the master of the house keeping the bank. He was a man of about sixty years of age, of a very dignified appearance; his head was covered with silvery-white hair; his full, florid countenance expressed good-nature, and his eyes twinkled with a perpetual smile. Naroumoff introduced Hermann to him. Chekalinsky shook him by the hand in a friendly manner, requested him not to stand on ceremony, and then went on dealing.

The game occupied some time. On the table lay more than thirty cards. Chekalinsky paused after each throw, in order to give the players time to arrange their cards and note down their losses, listened politely to their requests, and more politely still, put straight the corners of cards that some player's hand had chanced to bend. At last the game was finished. Chekalinsky shuffled the cards and prepared to deal again.

"Will you allow me to take a card?" said Hermann, stretching out his hand from behind a stout gentleman who was punting.

Chekalinsky smiled and bowed silently, as a sign of acquiescence. Naroumoff laughingly congratulated Hermann on his abjuration of that abstention from cards which he had practiced for so long a period, and wished him a lucky beginning.

"Stake!" said Hermann, writing some figures with chalk on the back of his card.

"How much?" asked the banker, contracting the muscles of his eyes; "excuse me, I cannot see quite clearly."

"Forty-seven thousand rubles," replied Hermann.

At these words every head in the room turned suddenly round, and all eyes were fixed upon Hermann.

"He has taken leave of his senses!" thought Naroumoff.

"Allow me to inform you," said Chekalinsky, with his eternal smile, "that you are playing very high; nobody here has ever staked more than two hundred and seventy-five rubles at once."

"Very well," replied Hermann; "but do you accept my card or not?"

Chekalinsky bowed in token of consent.

"I only wish to observe," said he, "that although I have the greatest confidence in my friends, I can only play against ready money. For my own part, I am quite convinced that your word is sufficient, but for the sake of the order of the game, and to facilitate the reckoning up, I must ask you to put the money on your card."

Hermann drew from his pocket a bank-note and handed it to Chekalinsky, who, after examining it in a cursory manner, placed it on Hermann's card.

He began to deal. On the right a nine turned up, and on the left a three.

"I have won!" said Hermann, showing his card.

A murmur of astonishment arose among the players. Chekalinsky frowned, but the smile quickly returned to his face.

"Do you wish me to settle with you?" he said to Hermann.

"If you please," replied the latter.

Chekalinsky drew from his pocket a number of bank-notes and paid at once. Hermann took up his money and left the table. Naroumoff could not recover his astonishment. Hermann drank a glass of lemonade and returned home.

The next evening he again repaired to Chekalinsky's. The host was dealing. Hermann walked up to the table; the punters immediately made room for him. Chekalinsky greeted him with a gracious bow.

Hermann waited for the next deal, took a card and placed upon it his forty-seven thousand rubles, together with his winnings of the previous evening.

Chekalinsky began to deal. A knave turned up on the right, a seven on the left.

Hermann showed his seven.

There was a general exclamation. Chekalinsky was evidently ill at ease, but he counted out the ninety-four thousand rubles and handed them over to Hermann, who pocketed them in the coolest manner possible and immediately left the house.

The next evening Hermann appeared again at the table. Everyone was expecting him. The generals and Privy Counsellors left their whist in order to watch such extraordinary play. The young officers quitted their sofas, and even the servants crowded into the room. All pressed round Hermann. The other players left off punting, impatient to see how it would end. Hermann stood at the table and prepared to play alone against the pale, but still smiling Chekalinsky. Each opened a pack of cards. Chekalinsky shuffled. Hermann took a card and covered it with a pile of bank-notes. It was like a duel. Deep silence reigned around.

Chekalinsky began to deal; his hands trembled. On the right a queen turned up, and on the left an ace.

"Ace has won!" cried Hermann, showing his card.

"Your queen has lost," said Chekalinsky, politely.

Hermann started; instead of an ace, there lay before him the queen of spades! He could not believe his eyes, nor could he understand how he had made such a mistake.

At that moment it seemed to him that the queen of spades smiled ironically and winked her eye at him. He was struck by her remarkable resemblance. . . .

"The old Countess!" he exclaimed, seized with terror.

Chekalinsky gathered up his winnings. For some time, Hermann remained perfectly motionless. When at last he left the table, there was a general commotion in the room.

"Splendidly punted!" said the players. Chekalinsky shuffled the cards afresh, and the game went on as usual.

* * *

Hermann went out of his mind, and is now confined in room Number 17 of the Oboukhoff Hospital. He never answers any questions, but he constantly mutters with unusual rapidity: "Three, seven, ace! Three, seven, queen!"

Lizaveta Ivanovna has married a very amiable young man, a son of the former steward of the old Countess. He is in the service of the State somewhere, and is in receipt of a good income. Lizaveta is also supporting a poor relative.

Tomsky has been promoted to the rank of captain, and has become the husband of the Princess Pauline.

THE OVERCOAT
Nikolai Gogol

IN THE department of . . . but it is better not to name the department.
There is nothing more irritable than all kinds of departments, regi-
ments, courts of justice and, in a word, every branch of public service.
Each separate man nowadays thinks all society insulted in his person.
They say that, quite recently, a complaint was received from a justice
of the peace, in which he plainly demonstrated that all the imperial
institutions were going to the dogs, and that his sacred name was being
taken in vain; and in proof he appended to the complaint a huge volume of some romantic composition, in which the justice of the peace
appears about once in every ten lines, sometimes in a drunken condition. Therefore, in order to avoid all unpleasantness, it will be better for
us to designate the department in question as *a certain department.*

So, *in a certain department* serves *a certain official*—not a very
prominent official, it must be allowed—short of stature, somewhat
pockmarked, rather red-haired, rather blind, judging from appearances, with a small bald spot on his forehead, with wrinkles on his
cheeks, with a complexion of the sort called sanguine. . . . How could
he help it? The Petersburg climate was responsible for that. As for his
rank—for with us the rank must be stated first of all—he was what is
called a perpetual titular councillor, over which, as is well known,
some writers make merry and crack their jokes, as they have the praise-
worthy custom of attacking those who cannot bite back.

His family name was Bashmachkin. It is evident from the name, that
it originated in *bashmak* (shoe); but when, at what time, and in what

manner, is not known. His father and grandfather, and even his brother-in-law, and all the Bashmachkins, always wore boots, and only had new heels two or three times a year. His name was Akakii Akakievich. It may strike the reader as rather singular and far-fetched; but he may feel assured that it was by no means far-fetched, and that the circumstances were such that it would have been impossible to give him any other name; and this was how it came about.

Akakii Akakievich was born, if my memory fails me not, towards night on the 23d of March. His late mother, the wife of an official, and a very fine woman, made all due arrangements for having the child baptized. His mother was lying on the bed opposite the door: on her right·stood the godfather, a most estimable man, Ivan Ivanovich Eroshkin, who served as presiding officer of the senate; and the godmother, the wife of an officer of the quarter, a woman of rare virtues, Anna Semenovna Byelobrushkova. They offered the mother her choice of three names—Mokiya, Sossiya or that the child should be called after the martyr Khozdazat. "No," pronounced the blessed woman, "all those names are poor." In order to please her, they opened the calendar at another place: three more names appeared—Triphilii, Dula and Varakhasii. "This is a judgment," said the old woman. "What names! I truly never heard the like. Varadat or Varukh might have been borne, but not Triphilii and Varakhasii!" They turned another page— Pavsikakhii and Vakhtisii. "Now I see," said the old woman, "that it is plainly fate. And if that's the case, it will be better to name him after his father. His father's name was Akakii, so let his son's be also Akakii." In this manner he became Akakii Akakievich.

They christened the child, whereat he wept, and made a grimace, as though he foresaw that he was to be a titular councillor. In this manner did it all come about. We have mentioned it, in order that the reader might see for himself that it happened quite as a case of necessity, and that it was utterly impossible to give him any other name. When and how he entered the department, and who appointed him, no one could remember. However much the directors and chiefs of all kinds were changed, he was always to be seen in the same place, the same attitude, the same occupation—the same official for letters; so that afterwards it was affirmed that he had been born in undress uniform with a bald spot on his head.

No respect was shown him in the department. The janitor not only did not rise from his seat when he passed, but never even glanced at him, as if only a fly had flown through the reception-room. His superiors treated him in a coolly despotic manner. Some assistant chief would thrust a paper under his nose without so much as saying, "Copy," or, "Here's a nice, interesting matter," or any thing else agreeable, as is customary in well-bred service. And he took it, looking only at the paper, and not observing who handed it to him, or whether he had the right to do so: he simply took it, and set about copying it.

The young officials laughed at and made fun of him, so far as their official wit permitted; recounted there in his presence various stories concocted about him, and about his landlady, an old woman of seventy; they said that she beat him; asked when the wedding was to be; and strewed bits of paper over his head, calling them snow. But Akakii Akakievich answered not a word, as though there had been no one before him. It even had no effect upon his employment: amid all these molestations he never made a single mistake in a letter.

But if the joking became utterly intolerable, as when they jogged his hand, and prevented his attending to his work, he would exclaim, "Leave me alone! Why do you insult me?" And there was something strange in the words and the voice in which they were uttered. There was in it a something which moved to pity; so that one young man, lately entered, who, taking pattern by the others, had permitted himself to make sport of him, suddenly stopped short, as though all had undergone a transformation before him, and presented itself in a different aspect. Some unseen force repelled him from the comrades whose acquaintance he had made, on the supposition that they were well-bred and polite men. And long afterwards, in his gayest moments, there came to his mind the little official with the bald forehead, with the heart-rending words, "Leave me alone! Why do you insult me?" And in these penetrating words, other words resounded—"I am thy brother." And the poor young man covered his face with his hand; and many a time afterwards, in the course of his life, he shuddered at seeing how much inhumanity there is in man, how much savage coarseness is concealed in delicate, refined worldliness and, O God! even in that man whom the world acknowledges as honorable and noble.

It would be difficult to find another man who lived so entirely for his duties. It is saying but little to say that he served with zeal: no, he served with love. In that copying, he saw a varied and agreeable world. Enjoyment was written on his face: some letters were favorites with him; and when he encountered them, he became unlike himself; he smiled and winked, and assisted with his lips, so that it seemed as though each letter might be read in his face, as his pen traced it. If his pay had been in proportion to his zeal, he would, perhaps, to his own surprise, have been made even a councillor of state. But he served, as his companions, the wits, put it, like a buckle in a buttonhole.

Moreover, it is impossible to say that no attention was paid to him. One director being a kindly man, and desirous of rewarding him for his long service, ordered him to be given something more important than mere copying; namely, he was ordered to make a report of an already concluded affair, to another court: the matter consisted simply in changing the heading, and altering a few words from the first to the third person. This caused him so much toil, that he was all in a perspiration, rubbed his forehead, and finally said, "No, give me rather something to copy." After that they let him copy on forever.

Outside this copying, it appeared that nothing existed for him. He thought not at all of his clothes: his undress uniform was not green, but a sort of rusty-meal color. The collar was narrow, low, so that his neck, in spite of the fact that it was not long, seemed inordinately long as it emerged from that collar, like the necks of plaster cats which wag their heads, and are carried about upon the heads of scores of Russian foreigners. And something was always sticking to his uniform—either a piece of hay or some trifle. Moreover, he had a peculiar knack, as he walked in the street, of arriving beneath a window when all sorts of rubbish was being flung out of it: hence he always bore about on his hat melon and watermelon rinds, and other such stuff.

Never once in his life did he give heed to what was going on every day in the street; while it is well known that his young brother official, extending the range of his bold glance, gets so that he can see when any one's trouser-straps drop down upon the opposite sidewalk, which always calls forth a malicious smile upon his face. But Akakii Akakievich, if he looked at anything, saw in all things the clean, even strokes of his written lines; and only when a horse thrust his muzzle, from some unknown quarter, over his shoulder, and sent a whole gust of wind down his neck from his nostrils, did he observe that he was not in the middle of a line, but in the middle of the street.

On arriving at home, he sat down at once at the table, supped his cabbage-soup quickly and ate a bit of beef with onions, never noticing their taste, ate it all with flies and anything else which the Lord sent at the moment. On observing that his stomach began to puff out, he rose from the table, took out a little vial with ink and copied papers which he had brought home. If there happened to be none, he took copies for himself, for his own gratification, especially if the paper was noteworthy, not on account of its beautiful style, but of its being addressed to some new or distinguished person.

Even at the hour when the grey Petersburg sky had quite disappeared, and all the world of officials had eaten or dined, each as he could, in accordance with the salary he received, and his own fancy; when all were resting from the departmental jar of pens, running to and fro, their own and other people's indispensable occupations and all the work that an uneasy man makes willingly for himself, rather than what is necessary; when officials hasten to dedicate to pleasure the time that is left to them—one bolder than the rest goes to the theater;

another, into the streets, devoting it to the inspection of some bonnets; one wastes his evening in compliments to some pretty girl, the star of a small official circle; one—and this is the most common case of all—goes to his comrades on the fourth or third floor, to two small rooms with an ante-room or kitchen, and some pretensions to fashion, a lamp or some other trifle which has cost many a sacrifice of dinner or excursion—in a word, even at the hour when all officials disperse among the contracted quarters of their friends, to play at whist, as they sip their tea from glasses with a kopek's worth of sugar, draw smoke through long pipes, relating at times some bits of gossip which a Russian man can never, under any circumstances, refrain from, or even when there is nothing to say, recounting everlasting anecdotes about the commandant whom they had sent to inform that the tail of the horse on the Falconet Monument[1] had been cut off—in a word, even when all strive to divert themselves, Akakii Akakievich yielded to no diversion.

No one could ever say that he had seen him at any sort of an evening party. Having written to his heart's content, he lay down to sleep, smiling at the thought of the coming day—of what God might send to copy on the morrow. Thus flowed on the peaceful life of the man, who, with a salary of four hundred rubles, understood how to be content with his fate; and thus it would have continued to flow on, perhaps, to extreme old age, were there not various ills sown among the path of life for titular councillors as well as for private, actual, court and every other species of councillor, even for those who never give any advice or take any themselves.

There exists in Petersburg a powerful foe of all who receive four hundred rubles salary a year, or thereabouts. This foe is no other than our Northern cold, although it is said to be very wholesome. At nine o'clock in the morning, at the very hour when the streets are filled with men bound for the departments, it begins to bestow such powerful and piercing nips on all noses impartially that the poor officials really do not know what to do with them. At the hour when the foreheads of even those who occupy exalted positions ache with the cold, and tears start to their eyes, the poor titular councillors are sometimes unprotected. Their only salvation lies in traversing as quickly as possible, in their thin little overcoats, five or six streets, and then warming their feet well in the porter's room, and so thawing all their talents and qualifications for official service, which had become frozen on the way.

Akakii Akakievich had felt for some time that his back and shoulders

---

[1] [The famous equestrian statue of Peter the Great, the work of the French sculptor Etienne-Maurice Falconet, 1716–1791.]

suffered with peculiar poignancy, in spite of the fact that he tried to traverse the legal distance with all possible speed. He finally wondered whether the fault did not lie in his overcoat. He examined it thoroughly at home, and discovered that in two places, namely, on the back and shoulders, it had become thin as mosquito-netting: the cloth was worn to such a degree that he could see through it, and the lining had fallen into pieces.

You must know that Akakii Akakievich's overcoat served as an object of ridicule to the officials: they even deprived it of the noble name of overcoat, and called it a kapota.[2] In fact, it was of singular make: its collar diminished year by year, but served to patch its other parts. The patching did not exhibit great skill on the part of the tailor, and turned out, in fact, baggy and ugly. Seeing how the matter stood, Akakii Akakievich decided that it would be necessary to take the overcoat to Petrovich, the tailor, who lived somewhere on the fourth floor up a dark staircase, and who, in spite of his having but one eye, and pock-marks all over his face, busied himself with considerable success in repairing the trousers and coats of officials and others; that is to say, when he was sober, and not nursing some other scheme in his head.

It is not necessary to say much about this tailor: but, as it is the custom to have the character of each personage in a novel clearly defined, there is nothing to be done; so here is Petrovich the tailor. At first he was called only Grigorii, and was some gentleman's serf: he began to call himself Petrovich from the time when he received his free papers, and began to drink heavily on all holidays, at first on the great ones, and then on all church festivals without discrimination, wherever a cross stood in the calendar. On this point he was faithful to ancestral custom; and, quarreling with his wife, he called her a low female and a German.

As we have stumbled upon his wife, it will be necessary to say a word or two about her; but, unfortunately, little is known of her beyond the fact that Petrovich has a wife, who wears a cap and a dress; but she cannot lay claim to beauty, it seems—at least, no one but the soldiers of the guard, as they pulled their moustaches, and uttered some peculiar sound, even looked under her cap when they met her.

Ascending the staircase which led to Petrovich—which, to do it justice, was all soaked in water (dishwater), and penetrated with the smell of spirits which affects the eyes, and is an inevitable adjunct to all dark stairways in Petersburg houses—ascending the stairs, Akakii Akakievich pondered how much Petrovich would ask, and mentally resolved not to give more than two rubles. The door was open; for the mistress, in cooking some fish, had raised such a smoke in the kitchen that not even the beetles were visible.

---

[2] A woman's cloak.

Akakii Akakievich passed through the kitchen unperceived, even by the housewife, and at length reached a room where he beheld Petrovich seated on a large, unpainted table, with his legs tucked under him like a Turkish pasha. His feet were bare, after the fashion of tailors as they sit at work; and the first thing which arrested the eye was his thumb, very well known to Akakii Akakievich, with a deformed nail thick and strong as a turtle's shell. On Petrovich's neck hung a skein of silk and thread, and upon his knees lay some old garment. He had been trying for three minutes to thread his needle, unsuccessfully, and so was very angry with the darkness, and even with the thread, growling in a low voice, "It won't go through, the barbarian! you pricked me, you rascal!"

Akakii Akakievich was displeased at arriving at the precise moment when Petrovich was angry: he liked to order something of Petrovich when the latter was a little downhearted, or, as his wife expressed it, "when he had settled himself with brandy, the one-eyed devil!" Under such circumstances, Petrovich generally came down in his price very readily, and came to an understanding, and even bowed and returned thanks. Afterwards, to be sure, his wife came, complaining that her husband was drunk, and so had set the price too low; but, if only a ten-kopek piece were added, then the matter was settled. But now it appeared that Petrovich was in a sober condition, and therefore rough, taciturn, and inclined to demand, Satan only knows what price. Akakii Akakievich felt this, and would gladly have beat a retreat, as the saying goes; but he was in for it. Petrovich screwed up his one eye very intently at him; and Akakii Akakievich involuntarily said, "How do you do, Petrovich!"

"I wish you a good-morning, sir," said Petrovich, and squinted at Akakii Akakievich's hands, wishing to see what sort of booty he had brought.

"Ah! I . . . to you, Petrovich, this"—It must be known that Akakii Akakievich expressed himself chiefly by prepositions, adverbs, and by such scraps of phrases as had no meaning whatever. But if the matter was a very difficult one, then he had a habit of never completing his sentences; so that quite frequently, having begun his phrase with the words, "This, in fact, is quite" . . . there was no more of it, and he forgot himself, thinking that he had already finished it.

"What is it?" asked Petrovich, and with his one eye scanned his whole uniform, beginning with the collar down to the cuffs, the back, the tails and button-holes, all of which were very well known to him, because they were his own handiwork. Such is the habit of tailors: it is the first thing they do on meeting one.

"But I, here, this, Petrovich, . . . an overcoat, cloth . . . here you see, everywhere, in different places, it is quite strong . . . it is a little dusty, and looks old, but it is new, only here in one place it is a little . . . on the back, and here on one of the shoulders, it is a little worn, yes, here on this shoulder it is a little . . . do you see? this is all. And a little work" . . .

Petrovich took the overcoat, spread it out, to begin with, on the table, looked long at it, shook his head, put out his hand to the window-sill after his snuff-box, adorned with the portrait of some general—just what general is unknown, for the place where the face belonged had been rubbed through by the finger, and a square bit of paper had been pasted on. Having taken a pinch of snuff, Petrovich spread the overcoat out on his hands, and inspected it against the light, and again shook his head; then he turned it, lining upwards, and shook his head once more; again he removed the general-adorned cover with its bit of pasted paper, and, having stuffed his nose with snuff, covered and put away the snuff-box, and said finally, "No, it is impossible to mend it: it's a miserable garment!"

Akakii Akakievich's heart sank at these words.

"Why is it impossible, Petrovich?" he said, almost in the pleading voice of a child: "all that ails it is, that it is worn on the shoulders. You must have some pieces." . . .

"Yes, patches could be found, patches are easily found," said Petrovich, "but there's nothing to sew them to. The thing is completely rotten: if you touch a needle to it—see, it will give way."

"Let it give way, and you can put on another patch at once."

"But there is nothing to put the patches on; there's no use in strengthening it; it is very far gone. It's lucky that it's cloth; for, if the wind were to blow, it would fly away."

"Well, strengthen it again. How this, in fact" . . .

"No," said Petrovich decisively, "there is nothing to be done with it. It's a thoroughly bad job. You'd better, when the cold winter weather comes on, make yourself some foot-bandages out of it, because stockings are not warm. The Germans invented them in order to make more money. [Petrovich loved, on occasion, to give a fling at the Germans.] But it is plain that you must have a new overcoat."

At the word new, all grew dark before Akakii Akakievich's eyes, and everything in the room began to whirl round. The only thing he saw clearly was the general with the paper face on Petrovich's snuff-box cover. "How a new one?" said he, as if still in a dream: "why, I have no money for that."

"Yes, a new one," said Petrovich, with a barbarous composure.

"Well, if it came to a new one, how, it" . . .

"You mean how much would it cost?"

"Yes."

"Well, you would have to lay out a hundred and fifty or more," said Petrovich, and pursed up his lips significantly. He greatly liked powerful effects, liked to stun utterly and suddenly, and then to glance sideways to see what face the stunned person would put on the matter.

"A hundred and fifty rubles for an overcoat!" shrieked poor Akakii Akakievich—shrieked perhaps for the first time in his life, for his voice had always been distinguished for its softness.

"Yes, sir," said Petrovich, "for any sort of an overcoat. If you have marten fur on the collar, or a silk-lined hood, it will mount up to two hundred."

"Petrovich, please," said Akakii Akakievich in a beseeching tone, not hearing, and not trying to hear, Petrovich's words, and all his "effects," "some repairs, in order that it may wear yet a little longer."

"No, then, it would be a waste of labor and money," said Petrovich; and Akakii Akakievich went away after these words, utterly discouraged. But Petrovich stood long after his departure, with significantly compressed lips, and not betaking himself to his work, satisfied that he would not be dropped, and an artistic tailor employed.

Akakii Akakievich went out into the street as if in a dream. "Such an affair!" he said to himself: "I did not think it had come to" . . . and then after a pause, he added, "Well, so it is! see what it has come to at last! and I never imagined that it was so!" Then followed a long silence, after which he exclaimed, "Well, so it is! see what already exactly, nothing unexpected that . . . it would be nothing . . . what a circumstance!" So saying, instead of going home, he went in exactly the opposite direction without himself suspecting it.

On the way, a chimney-sweep brought his dirty side up against him, and blackened his whole shoulder: a whole hatful of rubbish landed on him from the top of a house which was building. He observed it not; and afterwards, when he ran into a sentry, who, having planted his halberd beside him, was shaking some snuff from his box into his horny hand—only then did he recover himself a little, and that because the sentry said, "Why are you thrusting yourself into a man's very face? Haven't you the sidewalk?" This caused him to look about him, and turn towards home.

There only, he finally began to collect his thoughts, and to survey his position in its clear and actual light, and to argue with himself, not brokenly, but sensibly and frankly, as with a reasonable friend, with whom one can discuss very private and personal matters. "No," said Akakii Akakievich, "it is impossible to reason with Petrovich now: he is that . . . evidently, his wife has been beating him. I'd better go to him Sunday morning: after Saturday night he will be a little cross-eyed and sleepy, for he will have to get drunk, and his wife won't give him any money; and at such a time, a ten-kopek piece in his hand will—he will become more fit to reason with, and then the overcoat, and that." . . .

Thus argued Akakii Akakievich with himself, regained his courage, and waited until the first Sunday, when, seeing from afar that Petrovich's wife had gone out of the house, he went straight to him. Petrovich's eye was very much askew, in fact, after Saturday: his head drooped, and he was very sleepy; but for all that, as soon as he knew what the question was, it seemed as though Satan jogged his memory. "Impossible," said he: "please to order a new one." Thereupon Akakii Akakievich handed over the ten-kopek piece. "Thank you, sir; I will drink your good health," said Petrovich: "but as for the overcoat, don't trouble yourself about it; it is good for nothing. I will make you a new coat famously, so let us settle about it now."

Akakii Akakievich was still for mending it; but Petrovich would not hear of it, and said, "I shall certainly make you a new one, and please depend upon it that I shall do my best. It may even be, as the fashion goes, that the collar can be fastened by silver hooks under a flap."

Then Akakii Akakievich saw that it was impossible to get along without a new overcoat, and his spirit sank utterly. How, in fact, was it to be accomplished? Where was the money to come from? He might, to be sure, depend, in part, upon his present at Christmas; but that money had long been doled out and allotted beforehand. He must have some new trousers, and pay a debt of long standing to the shoemaker for putting new tops to his old boots, and he must order three shirts from the seamstress, and a couple of pieces of linen which it is impolite to mention in print—in a word, all his money must be spent; and even if the director should be so kind as to order forty-five rubles instead of forty, or even fifty, it would be a mere nothing, and a mere drop in the ocean towards the capital necessary for an overcoat: although he knew that Petrovich was wrong-headed enough to blurt out some outrageous price, Satan only knows what, so that his own wife could not refrain from exclaiming, "Have you lost your senses, you fool?"

At one time he would not work at any price, and now it was quite likely that he had asked a price which it was not worth. Although he knew that Petrovich would undertake to make it for eighty rubles, still, where was he to get the eighty rubles? He might possibly manage half; yes, a half of that might be procured: but where was the other half to come from? But the reader must first be told where the first half came from. Akakii Akakievich had a habit of putting, for every ruble he spent, a groschen into a small box, fastened with lock and key, and with a hole in the top for the reception of money. At the end of each half-year, he counted over the heap of coppers, and changed it into small silver coins. This he continued for a long time; and thus, in the course of some years, the sum proved to amount to over forty rubles.

Thus he had one half on hand; but where to get the other half? where to get another forty rubles? Akakii Akakievich thought and thought, and decided that it would be necessary to curtail his ordinary expenses, for the space of one year at least—to dispense with tea in the evening; to burn no candles, and, if there was anything which he must do, to go into his landlady's room, and work by her light; when he went into the street, he must walk as lightly as possible, and as cautiously, upon the stones and flagging, almost upon tiptoe, in order not to wear out his heels in too short a time; he must give the laundress as little to wash as possible; and, in order not to wear out his clothes, he must take them off as soon as he got home, and wear only his cotton dressing-gown, which had been long and carefully saved.

To tell the truth, it was a little hard for him at first to accustom himself to these deprivations; but he got used to them at length, after a fashion, and all went smoothly—he even got used to being hungry in the evening; but he made up for it by treating himself in spirit, bearing ever in mind the thought of his future coat. From that time forth, his existence seemed to become, in some way, fuller, as if he were married, as if some other man lived in him, as if he were not alone, and some charming friend had consented to go along life's path with him—and the friend was no other than that overcoat, with thick wadding and a strong lining incapable of wearing out. He became more lively, and his character even became firmer, like that of a man who has made up his mind, and set himself a goal. From his face and gait, doubt and indecision—in short, all hesitating and wavering traits—disappeared of themselves.

Fire gleamed in his eyes: occasionally, the boldest and most daring ideas flitted through his mind; why not, in fact, have marten fur on the collar? The thought of this nearly made him absent-minded. Once, in copying a letter, he nearly made a mistake, so that he exclaimed almost aloud, "Ugh!" and crossed himself. Once in the course of each month, he had a conference with Petrovich on the subject of the coat—where it would be better to buy the cloth, and the color, and the price—and he always returned home satisfied, though troubled, reflecting that the time would come at last when it could all be bought, and then the overcoat could be made.

The matter progressed more briskly than he had expected. Far beyond all his hopes, the director appointed neither forty nor forty-five rubles for Akakii Akakievich's share, but sixty. Did he suspect that Akakii Akakievich needed an overcoat? or did it merely happen so? at all events, twenty extra rubles were by this means provided. This circumstance hastened matters. Only two or three months more of hunger—and Akakii Akakievich had accumulated about eighty rubles. His heart, generally so quiet, began to beat.

On the first possible day, he visited the shops in company with Petrovich. They purchased some very good cloth—and reasonably, for they had been considering the matter for six months, and rarely did a month pass without their visiting the shops to inquire prices; and Petrovich said himself, that no better cloth could be had. For lining, they selected a cotton stuff, but so firm and thick, that Petrovich declared it to be better than silk, and even prettier and more glossy. They did not buy the marten fur, because it was dear, in fact; but in its stead, they picked out the very best of cat-skin which could be found in the shop, and which might be taken for marten at a distance.

Petrovich worked at the coat two whole weeks, for there was a great deal of quilting: otherwise it would have been done sooner. Petrovich charged twelve rubles for his work—it could not possibly be done for less: it was all sewed with silk, in small, double seams; and Petrovich went over each seam afterwards with his own teeth, stamping in various patterns.

It was—it is difficult to say precisely on what day, but it was probably the most glorious day in Akakii Akakievich's life, when Petrovich at length brought home the coat. He brought it in the morning, before the hour when it was necessary to go to the department. Never did a coat arrive so exactly in the nick of time; for the severe cold had set in, and it seemed to threaten increase. Petrovich presented himself with the coat as befits a good tailor. On his countenance was a significant expression, such as Akakii Akakievich had never beheld there. He seemed sensible to the fullest extent that he had done no small deed, and that a gulf had suddenly appeared, separating tailors who only put in linings, and make repairs, from those who make new things.

He took the coat out of the large pocket-handkerchief in which he had brought it. (The handkerchief was fresh from the laundress: he now removed it, and put it in his pocket for use.) Taking out the coat, he gazed proudly at it, held it with both hands, and flung it very skillfully over the shoulders of Akakii Akakievich; then he pulled it and fitted it down behind with his hand; then he draped it around Akakii Akakievich without buttoning it. Akakii Akakievich, as a man advanced in life, wished to try the sleeves. Petrovich helped him on with them, and it turned out that the sleeves were satisfactory also. In short, the coat appeared to be perfect, and just in season.

Petrovich did not neglect this opportunity to observe that it was only because he lived in a narrow street, and had no signboard, and because he had known Akakii Akakievich so long, that he had made it so cheaply; but, if he had been on the Nevsky Prospect, he would have charged seventy-five rubles for the making alone. Akakii Akakievich did not care to argue this point with Petrovich, and he was afraid of the large sums with which Petrovich was fond of raising the dust. He paid him, thanked him, and set out at once in his new coat for the department. Petrovich followed him, and, pausing in the street, gazed long at the coat in the distance, and went to one side expressly to run through a crooked alley, and emerge again into the street to gaze once more upon the coat from another point, namely, directly in front.

Meantime Akakii Akakievich went on with every sense in holiday mood. He was conscious every second of the time, that he had a new overcoat on his shoulders; and several times he laughed with internal satisfaction. In fact, there were two advantages—one was its warmth; the other, its beauty. He saw nothing of the road, and suddenly found himself at the department. He threw off his coat in the ante-room, looked it over well, and confided it to the especial care of the janitor. It is impossible to say just how every one in the department knew at once that Akakii Akakievich had a new coat, and that the "mantle" no longer existed. All rushed at the same moment into the ante-room, to inspect Akakii Akakievich's new coat. They began to congratulate him, and to say pleasant things to him, so that he began at first to smile, and then he grew ashamed.

When all surrounded him, and began to say that the new coat must be "christened," and that he must give a whole evening at least to it, Akakii Akakievich lost his head completely, knew not where he stood, what to answer, and how to get out of it. He stood blushing all over for several minutes, and was on the point of assuring them with great simplicity that it was not a new coat, that it was so and so, that it was the old coat. At length one of the officials, some assistant chief probably, in order to show that he was not at all proud, and on good terms with his inferiors, said, "So be it: I will give the party instead of Akakii Akakievich; I invite you all to tea with me to-night; it happens quite *apropos*, as it is my name-day."

The officials naturally at once offered the assistant chief their congratulations, and accepted the invitation with pleasure. Akakii Akakievich would have declined; but all declared that it was discourteous, that it was simply a sin and a shame, and that he could not possibly refuse. Besides, the idea became pleasant to him when he recollected that he should thereby have a chance to wear his new coat in the evening also.

That whole day was truly a most triumphant festival day for Akakii Akakievich. He returned home in the most happy frame of mind, threw off his coat, and hung it carefully on the wall, admiring afresh the cloth and the lining; and then he brought out his old, worn-out coat, for comparison. He looked at it, and laughed, so vast was the difference. And long after dinner he laughed again when the condition of the "mantle" recurred to his mind. He dined gayly, and after dinner wrote nothing, no papers even, but took his ease for a while on the bed, until it got dark. Then he dressed himself leisurely, put on his coat, and stepped out into the street.

Where the host lived, unfortunately we cannot say: our memory begins to fail us badly; and everything in St. Petersburg, all the houses and streets, have run together, and become so mixed up in our head, that it is very difficult to produce anything thence in proper form. At all events, this much is certain, that the official lived in the best part of the city; and therefore it must have been anything but near to Akakii Akakievich.

Akakii Akakievich was first obliged to traverse a sort of wilderness of deserted, dimly lighted streets; but in proportion as he approached the official's quarter of the city, the streets became more lively, more populous, and more brilliantly illuminated. Pedestrians began to appear; handsomely dressed ladies were more frequently encountered; the men had otter collars; peasant wagoners, with their grate-like sledges stuck full of gilt nails, became rarer; on the other hand, more and more coachmen in red velvet caps, with lacquered sleighs and bear-skin robes, began to appear; carriages with decorated coach-boxes flew swiftly through the streets, their wheels crunching the snow.

Akakii Akakievich gazed upon all this as upon a novelty. He had not been in the streets during the evening for years. He halted out of curiosity before the lighted window of a shop, to look at a picture representing a handsome woman, who had thrown off her shoe, thereby baring her whole foot in a very pretty way; and behind her the head of a man with side-whiskers and a handsome moustache peeped from the door of another room. Akakii Akakievich shook his head, and laughed, and then went on his way. Why did he laugh? Because he had met with a thing utterly unknown, but for which every one cherishes, nevertheless, some sort of feeling; or else he thought, like many officials, as follows: "Well, those French! What is to be said? If they like anything of that sort, then, in fact, that" . . . But possibly he did not think that. For it is impossible to enter a man's mind, and know all that he thinks.

At length he reached the house in which the assistant chief lodged. The assistant chief lived in fine style: on the staircase burned a lantern; his apartment was on the second floor. On entering the vestibule, Akakii Akakievich beheld a whole row of overshoes on the floor. Amid them, in the center of the room, stood a samovar, humming, and emitting clouds of steam. On the walls hung all sorts of coats and cloaks, among which there were even some with beaver collars or velvet facings. Beyond the wall the buzz of conversation was audible, which became clear and loud when the servant came out with a trayful of empty glasses, cream-jugs, and sugar-bowls. It was evident that the officials had arrived long before, and had already finished their first glass of tea.

Akakii Akakievich, having hung up his own coat, entered the room; and before him all at once appeared lights, officials, pipes, card-tables; and he was surprised by a sound of rapid conversation rising from all the tables, and the noise of moving chairs. He halted very awkwardly in the middle of the room, wondering, and trying to decide, what he ought to do. But they had seen him: they received him with a shout, and all went out at once into the ante-room, and took another look at his coat. Akakii Akakievich, although somewhat confused, was open-hearted, and could not refrain from rejoicing when he saw how they praised his coat. Then, of course, they all dropped him and his coat, and returned, as was proper, to the tables set out for whist. All this—the noise, talk, and throng of people—was rather wonderful to Akakii Akakievich. He simply did not know where he stood, or where to put his hands, his feet, and his whole body. Finally he sat down by the players, looked at the cards, gazed at the face of one and another, and after a while began to gape, and to feel that it was wearisome—the more so, as the hour was already long past when he usually went to bed. He wanted to take leave of the host; but they would not let him go, saying that he must drink a glass of champagne, in honor of his new garment, without fail.

In the course of an hour, supper was served, consisting of vegetable salad, cold veal, pastry, confectioner's pies, and champagne. They made Akakii Akakievich drink two glasses of champagne, after which he felt that the room grew livelier: still, he could not forget that it was twelve o'clock, and that he should have been at home long ago. In order that the host might not think of some excuse for detaining him, he went out of the room quietly, sought out, in the ante-room, his overcoat, which, to his sorrow, he found lying on the floor, brushed it, picked off every speck, put it on his shoulders, and descended the stairs to the street.

In the street all was still bright. Some petty shops, those permanent clubs of servants and all sorts of people, were open: others were shut, but, nevertheless, showed a streak of light the whole length of the door-crack, indicating that they were not yet free of company, and that probably domestics, both male and female, were finishing their stories and conversations, leaving their masters in complete ignorance as to their whereabouts.

Akakii Akakievich went on in a happy frame of mind: he even started to run, without knowing why, after some lady, who flew past like a flash of lightning, and whose whole body was endowed with an extraordinary amount of movement. But he stopped short, and went on very quietly as before, wondering whence he had got that gait. Soon there spread before him those deserted streets, which are not cheerful in the daytime, not to mention the evening. Now they were even more dim and lonely: the lanterns began to grow rarer—oil, evidently, had been less liberally supplied; then came wooden houses and fences: not a soul anywhere; only the snow sparkled in the streets, and mournfully darkled the low-roofed cabins with their closed shutters. He approached the place where the street crossed an endless square with barely visible houses on its farther side, and which seemed a fearful desert.

Afar, God knows where, a tiny spark glimmered from some sentry-box, which seemed to stand on the edge of the world. Akakii Akakievich's cheerfulness diminished at this point in a marked degree. He entered the square, not without an involuntary sensation of fear, as though his heart warned him of some evil. He glanced back and on both sides—it was like a sea about him. "No, it is better not to look," he thought, and went on, closing his eyes; and when he opened them, to see whether he was near the end of the square, he suddenly beheld, standing just before his very nose, some bearded individuals—of just what sort, he could not make out. All grew dark before his eyes, and his breast throbbed.

"But of course the coat is mine!" said one of them in a loud voice, seizing hold of the collar. Akakii Akakievich was about to shout for the watch, when the second man thrust a fist into his mouth, about the size of an official's head, muttering, "Now scream!"

Akakii Akakievich felt them take off his coat, and give him a push with a knee: he fell headlong upon the snow, and felt no more. In a few minutes he recovered consciousness, and rose to his feet; but no one was there. He felt that it was cold in the square, and that his coat was gone: he began to shout, but his voice did not appear to reach to the outskirts of the square. In despair, but without ceasing to shout, he started on a run through the square, straight towards the sentry-box, beside which stood the watchman, leaning on his halberd, and apparently curious to know what devil of a man was running towards him from afar, and shouting. Akakii Akakievich ran up to him, and began in a sobbing voice to shout that he was asleep, and attended to nothing, and did not see when a man was robbed. The watchman replied that he had seen no one; that he had seen two men stop him in the middle of the square, and supposed that they were friends of his; and that, instead of scolding in vain, he had better go to the captain on the morrow, so that the captain might investigate as to who had stolen the coat.

Akakii Akakievich ran home in complete disorder: his hair, which grew very thinly upon his temples and the back of his head, was entirely disarranged; his side and breast, and all his trousers, were covered with snow. The old woman, mistress of his lodgings, hearing a knocking, sprang hastily from her bed, and, with a shoe on one foot only, ran to open the door, pressing the sleeve of her chemise to her bosom out of modesty; but when she had opened it, she fell back on beholding Akakii Akakievich in such a state.

When he told the matter, she clasped her hands, and said that he must go straight to the superintendent, for the captain would turn up his nose, promise well, and drop the matter there: the very best thing to do, would be to go to the superintendent; that he knew her, because Finnish Anna, her former cook, was now nurse at the superintendent's; that she often saw him passing the house; and that he was at church every Sunday, praying, but at the same time gazing cheerfully at everybody; and that he must be a good man, judging from all appearances.

Having listened to this opinion, Akakii Akakievich betook himself sadly to his chamber; and how he spent the night there, any one can imagine who can put himself in another's place. Early in the morning, he presented himself at the superintendent's, but they told him that he was asleep. He went again at ten—and was again informed that he was asleep. He went at eleven o'clock, and they said, "The superintendent is not at home." At dinner-time, the clerks in the ante-room would not admit him on any terms, and insisted upon knowing his business, and what brought him, and how it had come about—so that at last, for once in his life, Akakii Akakievich felt an inclination to show some spirit, and said curtly that he must see the superintendent in person; that they should not presume to refuse him entrance; that he came from the department of justice, and, when he complained of them, they would see.

The clerks dared make no reply to this, and one of them went to call the superintendent. The superintendent listened to the extremely strange story of the theft of the coat. Instead of directing his attention to the principal points of the matter, he began to question Akakii Akakievich. Why did he return so late? Was he in the habit of going, or had he been, to any disorderly house? So that Akakii Akakievich got thoroughly confused, and left him without knowing whether the affair of his overcoat was in proper train, or not.

All that day he never went near the court (for the first time in his life). The next day he made his appearance, very pale, and in his old "mantle," which had become even more shabby. The news of the robbery of the coat touched many; although there were officials present who never omitted an opportunity, even the present, to ridicule Akakii Akakievich. They decided to take up a collection for him on the spot, but it turned out a mere trifle; for the officials had already spent a great deal in subscribing for the director's portrait, and for some book, at the suggestion of the head of that division, who was a friend of the author: and so the sum was trifling.

One, moved by pity, resolved to help Akakii Akakievich with some good advice at least, and told him that he ought not to go to the captain, for although it might happen that the police-captain, wishing to win the approval of his superior officers, might hunt up the coat by some means, still, the coat would remain in the possession of the police if he did not offer legal proof that it belonged to him: the best thing for him would be to apply to a certain *prominent personage*; that this *prominent personage*, by entering into relations with the proper persons, could greatly expedite the matter.

As there was nothing else to be done, Akakii Akakievich decided to go to the *prominent personage*. What was the official position of the *prominent personage*, remains unknown to this day. The reader must know that the *prominent personage* had but recently become a prominent personage, but up to that time he had been an insignificant person. Moreover, his present position was not considered prominent in comparison with others more prominent. But there is always a circle of people to whom what is insignificant in the eyes of others, is always important enough. Moreover, he strove to increase his importance by many devices; namely, he managed to have the inferior officials meet him on the staircase when he entered upon his service: no one was to presume to come directly to him, but the strictest etiquette must be observed; the "Collegiate Recorder" must announce to the government secretary, the government secretary to the titular councillor, or whatever other man was proper, and the business came before him in this manner. In holy Russia, all is thus contaminated with the love of imitation: each man imitates and copies his superior. They even say that a certain titular councillor, when promoted to the head of some little separate courtroom, immediately partitioned off a private room for himself, called it the *Audience Chamber*, and posted at the door a lackey with red collar and braid, who grasped the handle of the door, and opened to all comers; though the audience chamber would hardly hold an ordinary writing-table.

The manners and customs of the *prominent personage* were grand and imposing, but rather exaggerated. The main foundation of his system was strictness. "Strictness, strictness, and always strictness!" he generally said; and at the last word he looked significantly into the face of the person to whom he spoke. But there was no necessity for this, for the half-score of officials who formed the entire force of the mechanism of the office were properly afraid without it: on catching sight of him afar off, they left their work, and waited, drawn up in line, until their chief had passed through the room. His ordinary converse with his inferiors smacked of sternness, and consisted chiefly of three phrases: "How dare you?" "Do you know to whom you are talking?" "Do you realize who stands before you?"

Otherwise he was a very kind-hearted man, good to his comrades, and ready to oblige; but the rank of general threw him completely off his balance. On receiving that rank, he became confused, as it were, lost his way, and never knew what to do. If he chanced to be with his equals, he was still a very nice kind of man—a very good fellow in many respects, and not stupid: but just the moment that he happened to be in the society of people but one rank lower than himself, he was simply incomprehensible; he became silent; and his situation aroused sympathy, the more so, as he felt himself that he might have made an incomparably better use of the time. In his eyes, there was sometimes visible a desire to join some interesting conversation and circle; but he was held back by the thought, Would it not be a very great condescension on his part? Would it not be familiar? and would he not thereby lose his importance? And in consequence of such reflections, he remained ever in the same dumb state, uttering only occasionally a few monosyllabic sounds, and thereby earning the name of the most tiresome of men.

To this *prominent personage*, our Akakii Akakievich presented himself, and that at the most unfavorable time, very inopportune for himself, though opportune for the *prominent personage*. The prominent personage was in his cabinet, conversing very, very gayly with a recently arrived old acquaintance and companion of his childhood, whom he had not seen for several years. At such a time it was announced to him that a person named Bashmachkin had come. He asked abruptly, "Who is he?" "Some official," they told him. "Ah, he can wait! this is no time," said the important man. It must be remarked here, that the important man lied outrageously: he had said all he had to say to his friend long before; and the conversation had been interspersed for some time with very long pauses, during which they merely slapped each other on the leg, and said, "You think so, Ivan Abramovich!" "Just so, Stepan Varlamovich!" Nevertheless, he ordered that the official should wait, in order to show his friend—a man who had not been in the service for a long time, but had lived at home in the country—how long officials had to wait in his ante-room.

At length, having talked himself completely out, and more than that, having had his fill of pauses, and smoked a cigar in a very comfortable arm-chair with reclining back, he suddenly seemed to recollect, and told the secretary, who stood by the door with papers of reports, "Yes, it

seems, indeed, that there is an official standing there. Tell him that he
may come in." On perceiving Akakii Akakievich's modest mien, and his
worn undress uniform, he turned abruptly to him, and said, "What do
you want?" in a curt, hard voice, which he had practiced in his room
in private, and before the looking-glass, for a whole week before receiving his present rank.

Akakii Akakievich, who already felt betimes the proper amount of
fear, became somewhat confused: and as well as he could, as well as his
tongue would permit, he explained, with a rather more frequent addition than usual of the word *that*, that his overcoat was quite new, and
had been stolen in the most inhuman manner; that he had applied to
him, in order that he might, in some way, by his intermediation,
that . . . he might enter into correspondence with the chief superintendent of police, and find the coat.

For some inexplicable reason, this conduct seemed familiar to the
general. "What, my dear sir!" he said abruptly, "don't you know etiquette? Where have you come to? Don't you know how matters are
managed? You should first have entered a complaint about this at the
court: it would have gone to the head of the department, to the chief
of the division, then it would have been handed over to the secretary,
and the secretary would have given it to me." . . .

"But, your excellency," said Akakii Akakievich, trying to collect his
small handful of wits, and conscious at the same time that he was per-
spiring terribly, "I, your excellency, presumed to trouble you because
secretaries that . . . are an untrustworthy race." . . .

"What, what, what!" said the *important personage*. "Where did you
get such courage? Where did you get such ideas? What impudence
towards their chiefs and superiors has spread among the young genera-
tion!" The prominent personage apparently had not observed that
Akakii Akakievich was already in the neighborhood of fifty. If he could
be called a young man, then it must have been in comparison with
some one who was seventy. "Do you know to whom you speak? Do you
realize who stands before you? Do you realize it? do you realize it? I ask
you!" Then he stamped his foot, and raised his voice to such a pitch
that it would have frightened even a different man from Akakii
Akakievich.

Akakii Akakievich's senses failed him; he staggered, trembled in
every limb, and could not stand; if the porters had not run in to support
him, he would have fallen to the floor. They carried him out insensi-
ble. But the prominent personage, gratified that the effect should have
surpassed his expectations, and quite intoxicated with the thought that
his word could even deprive a man of his senses, glanced sideways at
his friend in order to see how he looked upon this, and perceived, not

without satisfaction, that his friend was in a most undecided frame of mind, and even beginning, on his side, to feel a trifle frightened.

Akakii Akakievich could not remember how he descended the stairs, and stepped into the street. He felt neither his hands nor feet. Never in his life had he been so rated by any general, let alone a strange one. He went on through the snow-storm, which was howling through the streets, with his mouth wide open, slipping off the sidewalk: the wind, in Petersburg fashion, flew upon him from all quarters, and through every cross-street. In a twinkling it had blown a quinsy into his throat, and he reached home unable to utter a word: his throat was all swollen, and he lay down on his bed. So powerful is sometimes a good scolding!

The next day a violent fever made its appearance. Thanks to the generous assistance of the Petersburg climate, his malady progressed more rapidly than could have been expected: and when the doctor arrived, he found, on feeling his pulse, that there was nothing to be done, except to prescribe a fomentation, merely that the sick man might not be left without the beneficent aid of medicine; but at the same time, he predicted his end in another thirty-six hours. After this, he turned to the landlady, and said, "And as for you, my dear, don't waste your time on him: order his pine coffin now, for an oak one will be too expensive for him."

Did Akakii Akakievich hear these fatal words? and, if he heard them, did they produce any overwhelming effect upon him? Did he lament the bitterness of his life?—We know not, for he continued in a raving, parching condition. Visions incessantly appeared to him, each stranger than the other: now he saw Petrovich, and ordered him to make a coat, with some traps for robbers, who seemed to him to be always under the bed; and he cried, every moment, to the landlady to pull one robber from under his coverlet: then he inquired why his old "mantle" hung before him when he had a new overcoat; then he fancied that he was standing before the general, listening to a thorough setting-down, and saying, "Forgive, your excellency!" but at last he began to curse, uttering the most horrible words, so that his aged landlady crossed herself, never in her life having heard anything of the kind from him—the more so, as those words followed directly after the words *your excellency*. Later he talked utter nonsense, of which nothing could be understood: all that was evident, was that his incoherent words and thoughts hovered ever about one thing—his coat.

At last poor Akakii Akakievich breathed his last. They sealed up neither his room nor his effects, because, in the first place, there were no heirs, and, in the second, there was very little inheritance; namely, a bunch of goose-quills, a quire of white official paper, three pairs of socks, two or three buttons which had burst off his trousers, and the "mantle" already known to the reader. To whom all this fell, God knows. I confess that the person who told this tale took no interest in the matter. They carried Akakii Akakievich out, and buried him. And Petersburg was left without Akakii Akakievich, as though he had never lived there. A being disappeared, and was hidden, who was protected by none, dear to none, interesting to none, who never even attracted to himself the attention of an observer of nature, who omits no opportunity of thrusting a pin through a common fly, and examining it under the microscope—a being who bore meekly the jibes of the department, and went to his grave without having done one unusual deed, but to whom, nevertheless, at the close of his life, appeared a bright visitant in the form of a coat, which momentarily cheered his poor life, and upon whom, thereafter, an intolerable misfortune descended, just as it descends upon the heads of the mighty of this world! . . .

Several days after his death, the porter was sent from the department to his lodgings, with an order for him to present himself immediately ("The chief commands it!"). But the porter had to return unsuccessful, with the answer that he could not come; and to the question, Why? he explained in the words, "Well, because: he is already dead! he was buried four days ago." In this manner did they hear of Akakii Akakievich's death at the department; and the next day a new and much larger official sat in his place, forming his letters by no means upright, but more inclined and slantwise.

But who could have imagined that this was not the end of Akakii Akakievich—that he was destined to raise a commotion after death, as if in compensation for his utterly insignificant life? But so it happened, and our poor story unexpectedly gains a fantastic ending.

A rumor suddenly spread throughout Petersburg that a dead man had taken to appearing on the Kalinkin Bridge, and far beyond, at night, in the form of an official seeking a stolen coat, and that, under the pretext of its being the stolen coat, he dragged every one's coat from his shoulders without regard to rank or calling—cat-skin, beaver, wadded, fox, bear, raccoon coats; in a word, every sort of fur and skin which men adopted for their covering. One of the department employés saw the dead man with his own eyes, and immediately recognized in him Akakii Akakievich: nevertheless, this inspired him with such terror, that he started to run with all his might, and therefore could not examine thoroughly, and only saw how the latter threatened him from afar with his finger.

Constant complaints poured in from all quarters, that the backs and shoulders, not only of titular but even of court councillors, were entirely exposed to the danger of a cold, on account of the frequent dragging off of their coats. Arrangements were made by the police to catch the corpse, at any cost, alive or dead, and punish him as an example to others, in the most severe manner: and in this they nearly succeeded; for a policeman, on guard in Kirushkin Alley, caught the corpse by the collar on the very scene of his evil deeds, for attempting to pull off the frieze coat of some retired musician who had blown the flute in his day.

Having seized hin by the collar, he summoned, with a shout, two of his comrades, whom he enjoined to hold him fast, while he himself felt for a moment in his boot, in order to draw thence his snuff-box, to refresh his six times forever frozen nose; but the snuff was of a sort which even a corpse could not endure. The policeman had no sooner succeeded, having closed his right nostril with his finger, in holding half a handful up to the left, than the corpse sneezed so violently that he completely filled the eyes of all three. While they raised their fists to wipe them, the dead man vanished utterly, so that they positively did not know whether they had actually had him in their hands at all. Thereafter the watchmen conceived such a terror of dead men, that they were afraid even to seize the living, and only screamed from a distance, "Hey, there! go your way!" and the dead official began to appear, even beyond the Kalinkin Bridge, causing no little terror to all timid people.

But we have totally neglected that *certain prominent personage,* who may really be considered as the cause of the fantastic turn taken by this true history. First of all, justice compels us to say, that after the departure of poor, thoroughly annihilated Akakii Akakievich, he felt something like remorse. Suffering was unpleasant to him: his heart was accessible to many good impulses, in spite of the fact that his rank very often prevented his showing his true self. As soon as his friend had left his cabinet, he began to think about poor Akakii Akakievich. And from that day forth, poor Akakii Akakievich, who could not bear up under an official reprimand, recurred to his mind almost every day. The thought of the latter troubled him to such an extent, that a week later he even resolved to send an official to him, to learn whether he really could assist him; and when it was reported to him that Akakii Akakievich had died suddenly of fever, he was startled, listened to the reproaches of his conscience, and was out of sorts for the whole day.

Wishing to divert his mind in some way, and forget the disagreeable impression, he set out that evening for one of his friends' houses, where he found quite a large party assembled; and, what was better, nearly every one was of the same rank, so that he need not feel in the least constrained. This had a marvellous effect upon his mental state. He expanded, made himself agreeable in conversation, charming: in short, he passed a delightful evening. After supper he drank a couple of glasses of champagne—not a bad recipe for cheerfulness, as every one knows. The champagne inclined him to various out-of-the-way adventures; and, in particular, he determined not to go home, but to go to see a certain well-known lady, Karolina Ivanovna, a lady, it appears, of German extraction, with whom he felt on a very friendly footing.

It must be mentioned that the prominent personage was no longer a young man, but a good husband, and respected father of a family. Two sons, one of whom was already in the service, and a good-looking, sixteen-year-old daughter, with a rather *retroussé* but pretty little nose, came every morning to kiss his hand, and say, "*Bonjour*, papa." His wife, a still fresh and good-looking woman, first gave him her hand to kiss, and then, reversing the procedure, kissed his. But the prominent personage, though perfectly satisfied in his domestic relations, considered it stylish to have a friend in another quarter of the city. This friend was hardly prettier or younger than his wife; but there are such puzzles in the world, and it is not our place to judge them.

So the important personage descended the stairs, stepped into his sleigh, and said to the coachman, "To Karolina Ivanovna's," and, wrapping himself luxuriously in his warm coat, found himself in that delightful position than which a Russian can conceive nothing better, which is, when you think of nothing yourself, yet the thoughts creep into your mind of their own accord, each more agreeable than the other, giving you no trouble to drive them away, or seek them. Fully satisfied, he slightly recalled all the gay points of the evening just passed, and all the *mots* which had made the small circle laugh. Many of them he repeated in a low voice, and found them quite as funny as before; and therefore it is not surprising that he should laugh heartily at them.

Occasionally, however, he was hindered by gusts of wind, which, coming suddenly, God knows whence or why, cut his face, flinging in it lumps of snow, filling out his coat-collar like a sail, or suddenly blowing it over his head with supernatural force, and thus causing him constant trouble to disentangle himself. Suddenly the important personage felt some one clutch him very firmly by the collar. Turning round, he perceived a man of short stature, in an old, worn uniform, and recognized, not without terror, Akakii Akakievich. The official's face was white as snow, and looked just like a corpse's. But the horror of the important personage transcended all bounds when he saw the dead man's mouth open, and, with a terrible odor of the grave, utter the following remarks:

"Ah, here you are at last! I have you, that . . . by the collar! I need your coat. You took no trouble about mine, but reprimanded me; now give up your own." The pallid prominent personage almost died. Brave as he was in the office and in the presence of inferiors generally, and although, at the sight of his manly form and appearance, every one said, "Ugh! how much character he has!" yet at this crisis, he, like many possessed of an heroic exterior, experienced such terror, that, not without cause, he began to fear an attack of illness.

He flung his coat hastily from his shoulders, and shouted to his coachman in an unnatural voice, "Home, at full speed!" The coachman, hearing the tone which is generally employed at critical moments, and even accompanied by something much more tangible, drew his head down between his shoulders in case of an emergency, flourished his knout, and flew on like an arrow. In a little more than six minutes the prominent personage was at the entrance of his own house.

Pale, thoroughly scared, and coatless, he went home instead of to Karolina Ivanovna's, got to his chamber after some fashion, and passed the night in the direst distress; so that the next morning over their tea, his daughter said plainly, "You are very pale to-day, papa." But papa remained silent, and said not a word to any one of what had happened to him, where he had been, or where he had intended to go.

This occurrence made a deep impression upon him. He even began to say less frequently to the under-officials, "How dare you? do you realize who stands before you?" and, if he did utter the words, it was after first having learned the bearings of the matter. But the most noteworthy point was, that from that day the apparition of the dead official quite ceased to be seen; evidently the general's overcoat just fitted his shoulders; at all events, no more instances of his dragging coats from people's shoulders were heard of.

But many active and apprehensive persons could by no means reassure themselves, and asserted that the dead official still showed himself in distant parts of the city. And, in fact, one watchman in Kolomna saw with his own eyes the apparition come from behind a house; but being rather weak of body—so much so, that once upon a time an ordinary full-grown pig running out of a private house knocked him off his legs, to the great amusement of the surrounding public coachmen, from whom he demanded a groschen apiece for snuff, as damages—being weak, he dared not arrest him, but followed him in the dark, until, at length, the apparition looked round, paused, and inquired, "What do you want?" and showed such a fist as you never see on living men. The watchman said, "It's of no consequence," and turned back instantly. But the apparition was much too tall, wore huge moustaches, and, directing its steps apparently towards the Obukhoff Bridge, disappeared in the darkness of the night.

THE DISTRICT DOCTOR

Ivan S. Turgenev

ONE DAY in autumn on my way back from a remote part of the country I caught cold and fell ill. Fortunately the fever attacked me in the district town at the inn; I sent for the doctor. In half-an-hour the district doctor appeared, a thin, dark-haired man of middle height. He prescribed me the usual sudorific, ordered a mustard-plaster to be put on, very deftly slid a five-ruble note up his sleeve, coughing drily and looking away as he did so, and then was getting up to go home, but somehow fell into talk and remained. I was exhausted with feverishness; I foresaw a sleepless night, and was glad of a little chat with a pleasant companion. Tea was served. My doctor began to converse freely. He was a sensible fellow, and expressed himself with vigor and some humor. Queer things happen in the world: you may live a long while with some people, and be on friendly terms with them, and never once speak openly with them from your soul; with others you have scarcely time to get acquainted, and all at once you are pouring out to him—or he to you—all your secrets, as though you were at confession. I don't know how I gained the confidence of my new friend—anyway, with nothing to leap up to it, he told me a rather curious incident; and here I will report his tale for the information of the indulgent reader. I will try to tell it in the doctor's own words.

"You don't happen to know," he began in a weak and quavering voice (the common result of the use of unmixed Berezov snuff); "you don't happen to know the judge here, Mylov, Pavel Lukich? . . . You don't know him? . . . Well, it's all the same." (He cleared his throat and rubbed his eyes.) "Well, you see, the thing happened, to tell you exactly without mistake, in Lent, at the very time of the thaws. I was sitting at his house—our judge's, you know—playing preference. Our judge is a good fellow, and fond of playing preference. Suddenly" (the doctor made frequent use of this word, suddenly) "they tell me, 'There's a servant asking for you.' I say, 'What does he want?' They say, 'He has brought a note—it must be from a patient.' 'Give me the note,' I say. So it is from a patient—well and good—you understand—it's our bread and butter. . . . But this is how it was: a lady, a widow, writes to me; she says, 'My daughter is dying. Come, for God's sake!' she says, 'and the horses have been sent for you.' . . . Well, that's all right. But she was twenty miles from the town, and it was midnight out of doors, and the roads in such a state, my word! And as she was poor herself, one could not expect more than two silver rubles, and even that problematic; and perhaps it might only be a matter of a roll of linen and a sack of oatmeal in payment. However, duty, you know, before everything: a fellow-creature may be dying. I hand over my cards at once to Kalliopin, the member of the provincial commission, and return home. I look; a wretched little trap was standing at the steps, with peasant's horses, fat—too fat—and their coat as shaggy as felt; and the coachman sitting with his cap off out of respect. Well, I think to myself, 'It's clear, my friend, these patients aren't rolling in riches.' . . . You smile; but I tell you, a poor man like me has to take everything into consideration. . . . If the coachman sits like a prince, and doesn't touch his cap, and even sneers at you behind his beard, and flicks his whip—then you may bet on six rubles. But this case, I saw, had a very different air. However, I think there's no help for it; duty before everything. I snatch up the most necessary drugs, and set off. Will you believe it? I only just managed to get there at all. The road was infernal: streams, snow, watercourses, and the dyke had suddenly burst there—that was the worst of it! However, I arrived at last. It was a little thatched house. There was a light in the windows; that meant they expected me. I was met by an old lady, very venerable, in a cap. 'Save her!' she says; 'she is dying.' I say, 'Pray don't distress yourself—Where is the invalid?' 'Come this way.' I see a clean little room, a lamp in the corner; on the bed a girl of twenty, unconscious. She was in a burning heat, and breathing heavily—it was fever. There were two other girls, her sisters, scared and in tears. 'Yesterday,' they tell me, 'she was perfectly well and had a good appetite; this morning she complained of her head, and this evening, suddenly, you see, like this.' I say again: 'Pray don't be uneasy.' It's a doctor's duty, you know—and I went up to her and bled her, told them to put on a mustard-plaster, and prescribed a mixture. Meantime I looked at her; I looked at her, you know—there, by God! I had never seen such a face!—she was a beauty, in a word! I felt quite shaken with pity. Such lovely features; such eyes! . . . But, thank God! she became easier; she fell into a perspiration, seemed to come to her senses, looked round, smiled, and passed her hand over her face. . . . Her sisters bent over her. They ask, 'How are you?' 'All right,' she says, and turns away. I looked at her; she had fallen asleep. 'Well,' I say, 'now the patient should be left alone.' So we all went out on tiptoe; only a maid remained, in case she was wanted. In the parlor there was a samovar standing on the table, and a bottle of rum; in our profession one can't get on without it. They gave me tea; asked me to stop the night. . . . I consented: where could I go, indeed, at that time of night? The old lady kept groaning. 'What is it?' I say; 'she will live; don't worry yourself; you had better take a little rest yourself; it is about two o'clock.' 'But will you send to wake me if anything happens?' 'Yes, yes.' The old lady went away, and the girls too went to their own room; they made up a bed for me in the parlor. Well, I went to bed—but I could not get to sleep, for a wonder! for in reality I was very tired. I could not get my patient out of my head. At last I could not put up with it any longer; I got up suddenly; I think to myself, 'I will go and see how the patient is getting on.' Her bedroom was next to the parlor. Well, I got up, and gently opened the door—how my heart beat! I looked in: the servant was asleep, her mouth wide open, and even snoring, the wretch! but the patient lay with her face towards me, and her arms flung wide apart, poor girl! I went up to her . . . when suddenly she opened her eyes and stared at me! 'Who is it? who is it?' I was in confusion. 'Don't be alarmed, madam,' I say; 'I am the doctor; I have come to see how you feel.' 'You the doctor?' 'Yes, the doctor; your mother sent for me from the town; we have bled you, madam; now pray go to sleep, and in a day or two, please God! we will set you on your feet again.' 'Ah, yes, yes, doctor, don't let me die. . . . please, please.' 'Why do you talk like that? God bless you!' She is in a fever again, I think to myself; I felt her pulse; yes, she was feverish. She looked at me, and then took me by the hand. 'I will tell you why I don't want to die; I will tell you. . . . Now we are alone; and only, please don't you . . . not to any one . . . Listen. . . .' I bent down; she moved her lips quite to my ear; she touched my cheek with her hair—I confess my head went round—and began to whisper. . . . I could make out nothing of it. . . . Ah, she was delirious! . . . She whispered and whispered, but so quickly, and as if it were not in Russian; at last she finished, and shivering dropped her head on the pillow, and threatened me with her finger: 'Remember, doctor, to no one.' I calmed her somehow, gave her something to drink, waked the servant, and went away."

At this point the doctor again took snuff with exasperated energy, and for a moment seemed stupefied by its effects.

"However," he continued, "the next day, contrary to my expectations, the patient was no better. I thought and thought, and suddenly decided to remain there, even though my other patients were expecting me. . . . And you know one can't afford to disregard that; one's practice suffers if one does. But, in the first place, the patient was really in danger; and secondly, to tell the truth, I felt strongly drawn to her. Besides, I liked the whole family. Though they were really badly off, they were singularly, I may say, cultivated people. . . . Their father had been a learned man, an author; he died, of course, in poverty, but he had managed before he died to give his children an excellent education; he left a lot of books too. Either because I looked after the invalid very carefully, or for some other reason; anyway, I can venture to say all the household loved me as if I were one of the family. . . . Meantime the roads were in a worse state than ever; all communications, so to say, were cut off completely; even medicine could with difficulty be got from the town. . . . The sick girl was not getting better. . . . Day after day, and day after day . . . but . . . here. . . ." (The doctor made a brief pause.) "I declare I don't know how to tell you." . . . (He again took snuff, coughed, and swallowed a little tea.) "I will tell you without beating about the bush. My patient . . . how should I say? . . . Well she had fallen in love with me . . . or, no, it was not that she was in love . . . however . . . really, how should one say?" (The doctor looked down and grew red.) "No," he went on quickly, "in love, indeed! A man should not over-estimate himself. She was an educated girl, clever and well-read, and I had even forgotten my Latin, one may say, completely. As to appearance" (the doctor looked himself over with a smile) "I am nothing to boast of there either. But God Almighty did not make me a fool; I don't take black for white; I know a thing or two; I could see very clearly, for instance that Aleksandra Andreyevna— that was her name—did not feel love for me, but had a friendly, so to say, inclination—a respect or something for me. Though she herself perhaps mistook this sentiment, anyway this was her attitude; you may form your own judgment of it. But," added the doctor, who had brought out all these disconnected sentences without taking breath, and with obvious embarrassment, "I seem to be wandering rather—you won't understand anything like this . . . There, with your leave, I will relate it all in order."

He drank off a glass of tea, and began in a calmer voice.

"Well, then. My patient kept getting worse and worse. You are not a doctor, my good sir; you cannot understand what passes in a poor fellow's heart, especially at first, when he begins to suspect that the disease is getting the upper hand of him. What becomes of his belief in himself? You suddenly grow so timid; it's indescribable. You fancy then that you have forgotten everything you knew, and that the patient has no faith in you, and that other people begin to notice how distracted you are, and tell you the symptoms with reluctance; that they are looking at you suspiciously, whispering . . . Ah! it's horrid! There must be a remedy, you think, for this disease, if one could find it. Isn't this it? You try—no, that's not it! You don't allow the medicine the necessary time to do good . . . You clutch at one thing, then at another. Sometimes you take up a book of medical prescriptions—here it is, you think! Sometimes, by Jove, you pick one out by chance, thinking to leave it to fate. . . . But meantime a fellow-creature's dying, and another doctor would have saved him. 'We must have a consultation,' you say; 'I will not take the responsibility on myself.' And what a fool you look at such times! Well, in time you learn to bear it; it's nothing to you. A man has died—but it's not your fault; you treated him by the rules. But what's still more torture to you is to see blind faith in you, and to feel yourself that you are not able to be of use. Well, it was just this blind faith that the whole of Aleksandra Andreyevna's family had in me; they had forgotten to think that their daughter was in danger. I, too, on my side assure them that it's nothing, but meantime my heart sinks into my boots. To add to our troubles, the roads were in such a state that the coachman was gone for whole days together to get medicine. And I never left the patient's room; I could not tear myself away; I tell her amusing stories, you know, and play cards with her. I watch by her side at night. The old mother thanks me with tears in her eyes; but I think to myself, 'I don't deserve your gratitude.' I frankly confess to you— there is no object in concealing it now—I was in love with my patient. And Aleksandra Andreyevna had grown fond of me; she would not sometimes let any one be in her room but me. She began to talk to me, to ask me questions; where I had studied, how I lived, who are my people, whom I go to see. I feel that she ought not to talk; but to forbid her to—to forbid her resolutely, you know—I could not. Sometimes I held my head in my hands, and asked myself, 'What are you doing, villain?' . . . And she would take my hand and hold it, give me a long, long look, and turn away, sigh, and say, 'How good you are!' Her hands were so feverish, her eyes so large and languid. . . . 'Yes,' she says, 'you are a good, kind man; you are not like our neighbors. . . . No, you are not like that. . . . Why did I not know you till now!' 'Aleksandra Andreyevna, calm yourself,' I say. . . . 'I feel, believe me, I don't know how I have gained . . . but there, calm yourself. . . . All will be right; you will be well again.' And meanwhile I must tell you," continued the doctor, bending forward and raising his eyebrows, "that they associated very little with the neighbors, because the smaller people were not on their level, and pride hindered them from being friendly with the rich. I tell you, they were an exceptionally cultivated family so you know it was gratifying for me. She would only take her medicine from my hands . . . she would lift herself up, poor girl, with my aid, take it, and gaze at me. . . . My heart felt as if it were bursting. And meanwhile she was growing worse and worse, worse and worse, all the time; she will die, I think to myself; she must die. Believe me, I would sooner have gone to the grave myself; and here were her mother and sisters watching me, looking into my eyes . . . and their faith in me was wearing away. 'Well? how is she?' 'Oh, all right, all right!' All right, indeed! My mind was failing me. Well, I was sitting one night alone again by my patient. The maid was sitting there too, and snoring away in full swing; I can't find fault with the poor girl, though! she was worn out too. Aleksandra Andreyevna had felt very unwell all the evening; she was very feverish. Until midnight she kept tossing about; at last she seemed to fall asleep; at least, she lay still without stirring. The lamp was burning in the corner before the holy image. I sat there you know, with my head bent; I even dozed a little. Suddenly it seemed as though some one touched me in the side; I turned round. . . . Good God! Aleksandra Andreyevna was gazing with intent eyes at me . . . her lips parted, her cheeks seemed burning. 'What is it?' 'Doctor, shall I die?' 'Merciful Heavens!' 'No, doctor, no; please don't tell me I shall live . . . don't say so. . . . If you knew. . . . Listen! for God's sake don't conceal my real position,' and her breath came so fast. 'If I can know for certain that I must die . . . then I will tell you all—all!' 'Aleksandra Andreyevna, I beg!' 'Listen; I have not been asleep at all . . . I have been looking at you a long while. . . . For God's sake! . . . I believe in you; you are a good man, an honest man; I entreat you by all that is sacred in the world—tell me the truth! If you knew how important it is for me. . . . Doctor, for God's sake tell me. . . . Am I in danger?' 'What can I tell you, Aleksandra Andreyevna pray?' 'For God's sake, I beseech you!' 'I can't disguise from you,' I say, 'Aleksandra Andreyevna; you are certainly in danger; but God is merciful.' 'I shall die, I shall die.' And it seemed as though she were pleased; her face grew so bright; I was alarmed. 'Don't be afraid, don't be afraid! I am not frightened of death at all.' She suddenly sat up and leaned on her elbow. 'Now . . . yes, now I can tell you that I thank you with my whole heart . . . that you are kind and good—that I love you!' I stare at her, like one possessed; it was terrible for me, you know. 'Do you hear, I love you!' 'Aleksandra Andreyevna, how have I deserved——' 'No, no, you don't—you don't understand me.' . . . And suddenly she stretched out her arms, and taking my head in her hands, she kissed it. . . . Believe me, I almost screamed aloud. . . . I threw myself on my knees, and buried my head in the pillow. She did not speak; her fingers trembled in my hair; I listen; she is weeping. I began to soothe her, to assure her. . . . I really don't know what I did say to her. 'You will wake up the girl,' I say to her; 'Aleksandra Andreyevna, I thank you . . . believe me . . . calm yourself.' 'Enough, enough!' she persisted; 'never mind all of them; let them wake, then; let them come in—it does not matter; I am dying, you see. . . . And what do you fear? why are you afraid? Lift up your head. . . . Or, perhaps, you don't love me; perhaps I am wrong. . . . In that case, forgive me.' 'Aleksandra Andreyevna, what are you saying! . . . I love you, Aleksandra Andreyevna.' She looked straight into my eyes, and opened her arms wide. 'Then take me in your arms.' I tell you frankly, I don't know how it was I did not go mad that night. I feel that my patient is killing herself; I see that she is not fully herself; I understand, too, that if she did not consider herself on the point of death, she would never have thought of me; and, indeed, say what you will, it's hard to die at twenty without having known love; this was what was torturing her; this was why, in despair, she caught at me—do you understand now? But she held me in her arms, and would not let me go. 'Have pity on me, Aleksandra Andreyevna, and have pity on yourself,' I say. 'Why,' she says; 'what is there to think of? You know I must die.' . . . This she repeated incessantly. . . . 'If I knew that I should return to life, and be a proper young lady again, I should be ashamed . . . of course, ashamed . . . but why now?' 'But who has said you will die?' 'Oh, no, leave off! you will not deceive me; you don't know how to lie—look at your face.' . . . 'You shall live, Aleksandra Andreyevna; I will cure you; we will ask your mother's blessing . . . we will be united—we will be happy.' 'No, no, I have your word; I must die . . . you have promised me . . . you have told me.' . . . It was cruel for me—cruel for many reasons. And see what trifling things can do sometimes; it seems nothing at all, but it's painful. It occurred to her to ask me, what is my name; not my surname, but my first name. I must needs be so unlucky as to be called Trifon. Yes, indeed; Trifon Ivanich. Every one in the house called me doctor. However, there's no help for it. I say, 'Trifon, madam.' She frowned, shook her head, and muttered something in French—ah, something unpleasant, of course!—and then she laughed—disagreeably too. Well, I spent the whole night with her in this way. Before morning I went away, feeling as though I were mad. When I went again into her room it was daytime, after morning tea. Good God! I could scarcely recognize her; people are laid in their grave looking better than that. I swear to you, on my honor, I don't understand—I absolutely don't understand—now, how I lived through that experience. Three days and nights my patient still lingered on. And what nights! What things she said to me! And on the last night—only imagine to yourself—I was sitting near her, and kept praying to God for one thing only: 'Take her,' I said, 'quickly, and me with her.'

Suddenly the old mother comes unexpectedly into the room. I had already the evening before told her—the mother—there was little hope, and it would be well to send for a priest. When the sick girl saw her mother she said: 'It's very well you have come; look at us, we love one another—we have given each other our word.' 'What does she say, doctor? what does she say?' I turned livid. 'She is wandering,' I say; 'the fever.' But she: 'Hush, hush; you told me something quite different just now, and have taken my ring. Why do you pretend? My mother is good—she will forgive—she will understand—and I am dying. . . . I have no need to tell lies; give me your hand.' I jumped up and ran out of the room. The old lady, of course, guessed how it was.

"I will not, however, weary you any longer, and to me too, of course, it's painful to recall all this. My patient passed away the next day. God rest her soul!" the doctor added, speaking quickly and with a sigh. "Before her death she asked her family to go out and leave me alone with her."

"'Forgive me,' she said; 'I am perhaps to blame towards you . . . my illness . . . but believe me, I have loved no one more than you . . . do not forget me . . . keep my ring.'"

The doctor turned away; I took his hand.

"Ah!" he said, "let us talk of something else, or would you care to play preference for a small stake? It is not for people like me to give way to exalted emotions. There's only one thing for me to think of; how to keep the children from crying and the wife from scolding. Since then, you know, I have had time to enter into lawful wedlock, as they say. . . . Oh . . . I took a merchant's daughter—seven thousand for her dowry. Her name's Akulina; it goes well with Trifon. She is an ill-tempered woman, I must tell you, but luckily she's asleep all day. . . . Well, shall it be preference?"

We sat down to preference for halfpenny points. Trifon Ivanich won two rubles and a half from me, and went home late, well pleased with his success.

WHITE NIGHTS

A SENTIMENTAL STORY FROM
THE DIARY OF A DREAMER

Fyodor Dostoyevsky

First Night

IT WAS a wonderful night, such a night as is only possible when we are
young, dear reader. The sky was so starry, so bright that, looking at it,
one could not help asking oneself whether ill-humored and capricious
people could live under such a sky. That is a youthful question too,
dear reader, very youthful, but may the Lord put it more frequently into
your heart! . . . Speaking of capricious and ill-humored people, I cannot help recalling my moral condition all that day. From early morning I had been oppressed by a strange despondency. It suddenly
seemed to me that I was lonely, that every one was forsaking me and
going away from me. Of course, any one is entitled to ask who "every
one" was. For though I had been living almost eight years in Petersburg
I had hardly an acquaintance. But what did I want with acquaintances?
I was acquainted with all Petersburg as it was; that was why I felt as
though they were all deserting me when all Petersburg packed up and
went to its summer villa. I felt afraid of being left alone, and for three
whole days I wandered about the town in profound dejection, not
knowing what to do with myself. Whether I walked in the Nevsky, went
to the Gardens or sauntered on the embankment, there was not one

face of those I had been accustomed to meet at the same time and place all the year. They, of course, do not know me, but I know them. I know them intimately, I have almost made a study of their faces, and am delighted when they are gay, and downcast when they are under a cloud. I have almost struck up a friendship with one old man whom I meet every blessed day, at the same hour in Fontanka. Such a grave, pensive countenance; he is always whispering to himself and brandishing his left arm, while in his right hand he holds a long gnarled stick with a gold knob. He even notices me and takes a warm interest in me. If I happen not to be at a certain time in the same spot in Fontanka, I am certain he feels disappointed. That is how it is that we almost bow to each other, especially when we are both in good humor. The other day, when we had not seen each other for two days and met on the third, we were actually touching our hats, but, realizing in time, dropped our hands and passed each other with a look of interest.

I know the houses too. As I walk along they seem to run forward in the streets to look out at me from every window, and almost to say: "Good-morning! How do you do? I am quite well, thank God, and I am to have a new story in May," or, "How are you? I am being redecorated to-morrow"; or, "I was almost burnt down and had such a fright," and so on. I have my favorites among them, some are dear friends; one of them intends to be treated by the architect this summer. I shall go every day on purpose to see that the operation is not a failure. God forbid! But I shall never forget an incident with a very pretty little house of a light pink color. It was such a charming little brick house, it looked so hospitably at me, and so proudly at its ungainly neighbors, that my heart rejoiced whenever I happened to pass it. Suddenly last week I walked along the street, and when I looked at my friend I heard a plaintive, "They are painting me yellow!" The villains! The barbarians! They had spared nothing, neither columns, nor cornices, and my poor little friend was as yellow as a canary. It almost made me bilious. And to this day I have not had the courage to visit my poor disfigured friend, painted the color of the Celestial Empire.

So now you understand, reader, in what sense I am acquainted with all Petersburg.

I have mentioned already that I had felt worried for three whole days before I guessed the cause of my uneasiness. And I felt ill at ease in the street—this one had gone and that one had gone, and what had become of the other?—and at home I did not feel like myself either. For two evenings I was puzzling my brains to think what was amiss in my corner; why I felt so uncomfortable in it. And in perplexity I scanned my grimy green walls, my ceiling covered with a spider's web, the growth of which Matrona has so successfully encouraged. I looked

over all my furniture, examined every chair, wondering whether the
trouble lay there (for if one chair is not standing in the same position
as it stood the day before, I am not myself). I looked at the window, but
it was all in vain . . . I was not a bit the better for it! I even bethought
me to send for Matrona, and was giving her some fatherly admonitions
in regard to the spider's web and sluttishness in general; but she simply
stared at me in amazement and went away without saying a word, so
that the spider's web is comfortably hanging in its place to this day. I
only at last this morning realized what was wrong. Aie! Why, they are
giving me the slip and making off to their summer villas! Forgive the
triviality of the expression, but I am in no mood for fine language . . .
for everything that had been in Petersburg had gone or was going away
for the holidays; for every respectable gentleman of dignified appearance who took a cab was at once transformed, in my eyes, into a
respectable head of a household who after his daily duties were over,
was making his way to the bosom of his family, to the summer villa; for
all the passers-by had now quite a peculiar air which seemed to say to
every one they met: "We are only here for the moment, gentlemen, and
in another two hours we shall be going off to the summer villa." If a
window opened after delicate fingers, white as snow, had tapped upon
the pane, and the head of a pretty girl was thrust out, calling to a street-
seller with pots of flowers—at once on the spot I fancied that those flowers were being bought not simply in order to enjoy the flowers and the
spring in stuffy town lodgings, but because they would all be very soon
moving into the country and could take the flowers with them. What is
more, I made such progress in my new peculiar sort of investigation
that I could distinguish correctly from the mere air of each in what
summer villa he was living. The inhabitants of Kamenny and
Aptekarsky Islands or of the Peterhof Road were marked by the studied
elegance of their manner, their fashionable summer suits, and the fine
carriages in which they drove to town. Visitors to Pargolovo and places
further away impressed one at first sight by their reasonable and dignified air; the tripper to Krestovsky Island could be recognized by his look
of irrepressible gaiety. If I chanced to meet a long procession of wagoners walking lazily with the reins in their hands beside wagons loaded
with regular mountains of furniture, tables, chairs, ottomans and sofas
and domestic utensils of all sorts, frequently with a decrepit cook sitting
on the top of it all, guarding her master's property as though it were the
apple of her eye; or if I saw boats heavily loaded with household goods
crawling along the Neva or Fontanka to the Black River or the
Islands—the wagons and the boats were multiplied tenfold, a hun-
dredfold, in my eyes. I fancied that everything was astir and moving,
everything was going in regular caravans to the summer villas. It

seemed as though Petersburg threatened to become a wilderness, so that at last I felt ashamed, mortified and sad that I had nowhere to go for the holidays and no reason to go away. I was ready to go away with every wagon, to drive off with every gentleman of respectable appearance who took a cab; but no one—absolutely no one—invited me; it seemed they had forgotten me, as though really I were a stranger to them!

I took long walks, succeeding, as I usually did, in quite forgetting where I was, when I suddenly found myself at the city gates. Instantly I felt lighthearted, and I passed the barrier and walked between cultivated fields and meadows, unconscious of fatigue, and feeling only all over as though a burden were falling off my soul. All the passers-by gave me such friendly looks that they seemed almost greeting me, they all seemed so pleased at something. They were all smoking cigars, every one of them. And I felt pleased as I never had before. It was as though I had suddenly found myself in Italy—so strong was the effect of nature upon a half-sick townsman like me, almost stifling between city walls.

There is something inexpressibly touching in nature round Petersburg, when at the approach of spring she puts forth all her might, all the powers bestowed on her by Heaven, when she breaks into leaf, decks herself out and spangles herself with flowers. . . . Somehow I cannot help being reminded of a frail, consumptive girl, at whom one sometimes looks with compassion, sometimes with sympathetic love, whom sometimes one simply does not notice; though suddenly in one instant she becomes, as though by chance, inexplicably lovely and exquisite, and, impressed and intoxicated, one cannot help asking oneself what power made those sad, pensive eyes flash with such fire? What summoned the blood to those pale, wan cheeks? What bathed with passion those soft features? What set that bosom heaving? What so suddenly called strength, life and beauty into the poor girl's face, making it gleam with such a smile, kindle with such bright, sparkling laughter? You look round, you seek for some one, you conjecture. . . . But the moment passes, and next day you meet, maybe, the same pensive and preoccupied look as before, the same pale face, the same meek and timid movements, and even signs of remorse, traces of a mortal anguish and regret for the fleeting distraction. . . . And you grieve that the momentary beauty has faded so soon never to return, that it flashed upon you so treacherously, so vainly, grieve because you had not even time to love her. . . .

And yet my night was better than my day! This was how it happened. I came back to the town very late, and it had struck ten as I was going towards my lodgings. My way lay along the canal embankment, where at that hour you never meet a soul. It is true that I live in a very remote part of the town. I walked along singing, for when I am happy I am always humming to myself like every happy man who has no friend or acquaintance with whom to share his joy. Suddenly I had a most unexpected adventure.

Leaning on the canal railing stood a woman with her elbows on the rail, she was apparently looking with great attention at the muddy water of the canal. She was wearing a very charming yellow hat and a jaunty little black mantle. "She's a girl, and I am sure she is dark," I thought. She did not seem to hear my footsteps, and did not even stir when I passed by with bated breath and loudly throbbing heart.

"Strange," I thought; "she must be deeply absorbed in something," and all at once I stopped as though petrified. I heard a muffled sob. Yes! I was not mistaken, the girl was crying, and a minute later I heard sob after sob. Good Heavens! My heart sank. And timid as I was with women, yet this was such a moment! . . . I turned, took a step towards her, and should certainly have pronounced the word "Madam!" if I had not known that that exclamation has been uttered a thousand times in every Russian society novel. It was only that reflection stopped me. But while I was seeking for a word, the girl came to herself, looked round, started, cast down her eyes and slipped by me along the embankment. I at once followed her; but she, divining this, left the embankment, crossed the road and walked along the pavement. I dared not cross the street after her. My heart was fluttering like a captured bird. All at once a chance came to my aid.

Along the same side of the pavement there suddenly came into sight, not far from the girl, a gentleman in evening dress, of dignified years, though by no means of dignified carriage; he was staggering and cautiously leaning against the wall. The girl flew straight as an arrow, with the timid haste one sees in all girls who do not want any one to volunteer to accompany them home at night, and no doubt the staggering gentleman would not have pursued her, if my good luck had not prompted him.

Suddenly, without a word to any one, the gentleman set off and flew full speed in pursuit of my unknown lady. She was racing like the wind, but the staggering gentleman was overtaking—overtook her. The girl uttered a shriek, and . . . I bless my luck for the excellent knotted stick, which happened on that occasion to be in my right hand. In a flash I was on the other side of the street; in a flash the obtrusive gentleman had taken in the position, had grasped the irresistible argument, fallen back without a word, and only when we were very far away protested against my action in rather vigorous language. But his words hardly reached us.

"Give me your arm," I said to the girl. "And he won't dare to annoy us further."

She took my arm without a word, still trembling with excitement and terror. Oh, obtrusive gentleman! How I blessed you at that moment! I stole a glance at her, she was very charming and dark—I had guessed right.

On her black eyelashes there still glistened a tear—from her recent terror or her former grief—I don't know. But there was already a gleam of a smile on her lips. She too stole a glance at me, faintly blushed and looked down.

"There, you see; why did you drive me away? If I had been here, nothing would have happened . . ."

"But I did not know you; I thought that you too . . ."

"Why, do you know me now?"

"A little! Here, for instance, why are you trembling?"

"Oh, you are right at the first guess!" I answered, delighted that my girl had intelligence; that is never out of place in company with beauty. "Yes, from the first glance you have guessed the sort of man you have to do with. Precisely; I am shy with women, I am agitated, I don't deny it, as much so as you were a minute ago when that gentleman alarmed you. I am in some alarm now. It's like a dream, and I never guessed even in my sleep that I should ever talk with any woman."

"What? Really? . . ."

"Yes; if my arm trembles, it is because it has never been held by a pretty little hand like yours. I am a complete stranger to women; that is, I have never been used to them. You see, I am alone . . . I don't even know how to talk to them. Here, I don't know now whether I have not said something silly to you! Tell me frankly; I assure you beforehand that I am not quick to take offense? . . ."

"No, nothing, nothing, quite the contrary. And if you insist on my speaking frankly, I will tell you that women like such timidity; and if you want to know more, I like it too, and I won't drive you away till I get home."

"You will make me," I said, breathless with delight, "lose my timidity, and then farewell to all my chances. . . ."

"Chances! What chances—of what? That's not so nice."

"I beg your pardon, I am sorry, it was a slip of the tongue; but how can you expect one at such a moment to have no desire. . . ."

"To be liked, eh?"

"Well, yes; but do, for goodness' sake, be kind. Think what I am! Here, I am twenty-six and I have never seen any one. How can I speak well, tactfully, and to the point? It will seem better to you when I have told you everything openly. . . . I don't know how to be silent when my heart is speaking. Well, never mind. . . . Believe me, not one woman, never, never! No acquaintance of any sort! And I do nothing but dream every day that at last I shall meet some one. Oh, if only you knew how often I have been in love in that way . . ."

"How? With whom? . . ."

"Why, with no one, with an ideal, with the one I dream of in my sleep. I make regular romances in my dreams. Ah, you don't know me! It's true, of course, I have met two or three women, but what sort of women were they? They were all landladies, that . . . But I shall make you laugh if I tell you that I have several times thought of speaking, just simply speaking, to some aristocratic lady in the street, when she is alone, I need hardly say; speaking to her, of course, timidly, respect- fully, passionately; telling her that I am perishing in solitude, begging her not to send me away; saying that I have no chance of making the acquaintance of any woman; impressing upon her that it is a positive duty for a woman not to repulse so timid a prayer from such a luckless man as me. That, in fact, all I ask is, that she should say two or three sisterly words with sympathy, should not repulse me at first sight; should take me on trust and listen to what I say; should laugh at me if she likes, encourage me, say two words to me, only two words, even though we never meet again afterwards! . . . But you are laughing; how- ever, that is why I am telling you. . . ."

"Don't be vexed; I am only laughing at your being your own enemy, and if you had tried you would have succeeded, perhaps, even though it had been in the street; the simpler the better. . . . No kind-hearted woman, unless she were stupid or, still more, vexed about something at the moment, could bring herself to send you away without those two words which you ask for so timidly. . . . But what am I saying? Of course she would take you for a madman. I was judging by myself; I know a good deal about other people's lives."

"Oh, thank you," I cried; "you don't know what you have done for me now!"

"I am glad! I am glad! But tell me how did you find out that I was the sort of woman with whom . . . well, whom you think worthy . . . of attention and friendship . . . in fact, not a landlady as you say? What made you decide to come up to me?"

"What made me? . . . But you were alone; that gentleman was too insolent; it's night. You must admit that it was a duty. . . ."

"No, no; I mean before, on the other side—you know you meant to come up to me."

"On the other side? Really I don't know how to answer; I am afraid to. . . . Do you know I have been happy to-day? I walked along singing; I went out into the country; I have never had such happy moments.

You . . . perhaps it was my fancy. . . . Forgive me for referring to it; I fancied you were crying, and I . . . could not bear to hear it . . . it made my heart ache. . . . Oh, my goodness! Surely I might be troubled about you? Surely there was no harm in feeling brotherly compassion for you. . . . I beg your pardon, I said compassion. . . . Well, in short, surely you would not be offended at my involuntary impulse to go up to you? . . ."

"Stop, that's enough, don't talk of it," said the girl, looking down, and pressing my hand. "It's my fault for having spoken of it; but I am glad I was not mistaken in you. . . . But here I am home; I must go down this turning, it's two steps from here. . . . Good-bye, thank you! . . ."

"Surely . . . surely you don't mean . . . that we shall never see each other again? . . . Surely this is not to be the end?"

"You see," said the girl, laughing, "at first you only wanted two words, and now . . . However, I won't say anything . . . perhaps we shall meet. . . ."

"I shall come here to-morrow," I said. "Oh, forgive me, I am already making demands. . . ."

"Yes, you are not very patient . . . you are almost insisting."

"Listen, listen!" I interrupted her. "Forgive me if I tell you something else. . . . I tell you what, I can't help coming here to-morrow, I am a dreamer; I have so little real life that I look upon such moments as this now, as so rare, that I cannot help going over such moments again in my dreams. I shall be dreaming of you all night, a whole week, a whole year. I shall certainly come here to-morrow, just here to this place, just at the same hour, and I shall be happy remembering to-day. This place is dear to me already. I have already two or three such places in Petersburg. I once shed tears over memories . . . like you. . . : Who knows, perhaps you were weeping ten minutes ago over some memory. . . . But, forgive me, I have forgotten myself again; perhaps you have once been particularly happy here. . . ."

"Very good," said the girl, "perhaps I will come here to-morrow, too, at ten o'clock. I see that I can't forbid you. . . . The fact is, I have to be here; don't imagine that I am making an appointment with you; I tell you beforehand that I have to be here on my own account. But . . . well, I will tell you straight out, I don't mind if you do come. To begin with, something unpleasant might happen as it did to-day, but never mind that. . . . In short, I should simply like to see you . . . to say two words to you. Only, mind, you must not think the worse of me now! Don't think I make appointments so lightly. . . . I shouldn't make it except that . . . But let that be my secret! Only a compact beforehand . . ."

"A compact! Speak, tell me, tell me all beforehand; I agree to anything, I am ready for anything," I cried delighted. "I answer for myself, I will be obedient, respectful . . . you know me. . . ."

"It's just because I do know you that I ask you to come to-morrow," said the girl, laughing. "I know you perfectly. But mind you will come on the condition, in the first place (only be good, do what I ask—you see, I speak frankly), you won't fall in love with me. . . . That's impossible, I assure you. I am ready for friendship; here's my hand. . . . But you mustn't fall in love with me, I beg you!"

"I swear," I cried, gripping her hand. . . .

"Hush, don't swear, I know you are ready to flare up like gunpowder. Don't think ill of me for saying so. If only you knew. . . . I, too, have no one to whom I can say a word, whose advice I can ask. Of course, one does not look for an adviser in the street; but you are an exception. I know you as though we had been friends for twenty years. . . . You won't deceive me, will you? . . ."

"You will see . . . the only thing is, I don't know how I am going to survive the next twenty-four hours."

"Sleep soundly. Good-night, and remember that I have trusted you already. But you exclaimed so nicely just now, 'Surely one can't be held responsible for every feeling, even for brotherly sympathy!' Do you know, that was so nicely said, that the idea struck me at once, that I might confide in you?"

"For God's sake do; but about what? What is it?"

"Wait till to-morrow. Meanwhile, let that be a secret. So much the better for you; it will give it a faint flavor of romance. Perhaps I will tell you to-morrow, and perhaps not. . . . I will talk to you a little more beforehand; we will get to know each other better. . . ."

"Oh yes, I will tell you all about myself to-morrow! But what has happened? It is as though a miracle had befallen me. . . . My God, where am I? Come, tell me aren't you glad that you were not angry and did not drive me away at the first moment, as any other woman would have done? In two minutes you have made me happy for ever. Yes, happy; who knows, perhaps you have reconciled me with myself, solved my doubts! . . . Perhaps such moments come upon me. . . . But there I will tell you all about it to-morrow, you shall know everything, everything. . . ."

"Very well, I consent; you shall begin . . ."

"Agreed."

"Good-bye till to-morrow!"

"Till to-morrow!"

And we parted. I walked about all night; I could not make up my mind to go home. I was so happy. . . . To-morrow!

Second Night

"Well, so you have survived!" she said, pressing both my hands.

"I've been here for the last two hours; you don't know what a state I have been in all day."

"I know, I know. But to business. Do you know why I have come? Not to talk nonsense, as I did yesterday. I tell you what, we must behave more sensibly in future. I thought a great deal about it last night."

"In what way—in what must we be more sensible? I am ready for my part; but, really, nothing more sensible has happened to me in my life than this, now."

"Really? In the first place, I beg you not to squeeze my hands so; secondly, I must tell you that I spent a long time thinking about you and feeling doubtful to-day."

"And how did it end?"

"How did it end? The upshot of it is that we must begin all over again, because the conclusion I reached to-day was that I don't know you at all; that I behaved like a baby last night, like a little girl; and, of course, the fact of it is, that it's my soft heart that is to blame—that is, I sang my own praises, as one always does in the end when one analyzes one's conduct. And therefore to correct my mistake, I've made up my mind to find out all about you minutely. But as I have no one from whom I can find out anything, you must tell me everything fully yourself. Well, what sort of man are you? Come, make haste—begin—tell me your whole history."

"My history!" I cried in alarm. "My history! But who has told you I have a history? I have no history. . . ."

"Then how have you lived, if you have no history?" she interrupted, laughing.

"Absolutely without any history! I have lived, as they say, keeping myself to myself, that is, utterly alone—alone, entirely alone. Do you know what it means to be alone?"

"But how alone? Do you mean you never saw any one?"

"Oh no, I see people, of course; but still I am alone."

"Why, do you never talk to any one?"

"Strictly speaking, with no one."

"Who are you then? Explain yourself! Stay, I guess: most likely, like me you have a grandmother. She is blind and will never let me go anywhere, so that I have almost forgotten how to talk; and when I played some pranks two years ago, and she saw there was no holding me in, she called me up and pinned my dress to hers, and ever since we sit like that for days together; she knits a stocking, though she's blind, and I sit beside her, sew or read aloud to her—it's such a queer habit, here for two years I've been pinned to her. . . ."

"Good Heavens! what misery! But no, I haven't a grandmother like that."

"Well, if you haven't why do you sit at home? . . ."

"Listen, do you want to know the sort of man I am?"

"Yes, yes!"

"In the strict sense of the word?"

"In the very strictest sense of the word."

"Very well, I am a type!"

"Type, type! What sort of type?" cried the girl, laughing, as though she had not had a chance of laughing for a whole year. "Yes, it's very amusing talking to you. Look, here's a seat, let us sit down. No one is passing here, no one will hear us, and—begin your history. For it's no good your telling me, I know you have a history; only you are concealing it. To begin with, what is a type?"

"A type? A type is an original, it's an absurd person!" I said, infected by her childish laughter. "It's a character. Listen; do you know what is meant by a dreamer?"

"A dreamer! Indeed I should think I do know. I am a dreamer myself. Sometimes, as I sit by grandmother, all sorts of things come into my head. Why, when one begins dreaming one lets one's fancy run away with one—why, I marry a Chinese Prince! . . . Though sometimes it is a good thing to dream! But, goodness knows! Especially when one has something to think of apart from dreams," added the girl, this time rather seriously.

"Excellent! If you have been married to a Chinese Emperor, you will quite understand me. Come, listen. . . . But one minute, I don't know your name yet."

"At last! You have been in no hurry to think of it!"

"Oh, my goodness! It never entered my head, I felt quite happy as it was. . . ."

"My name is Nastenka."

"Nastenka! And nothing else?"

"Nothing else! Why, is not that enough for you, you insatiable person?"

"Not enough? On the contrary, it's a great deal, a very great deal, Nastenka; you kind girl, if you are Nastenka for me from the first."

"Quite so! Well?"

"Well, listen, Nastenka, now for this absurd history."

I sat down beside her, assumed a pedantically serious attitude, and began as though reading from a manuscript:—

"There are, Nastenka, though you may not know it, strange nooks in Petersburg. It seems as though the same sun as shines for all Petersburg people does not peep into those spots, but some other different new one,

bespoken expressly for those nooks, and it throws a different light on everything. In these corners, dear Nastenka, quite a different life is lived, quite
unlike the life that is surging round us, but such as perhaps exists in
some unknown realm, not among us in our serious, over-serious, time.
Well, that life is a mixture of something purely fantastic, fervently ideal,
with something (alas! Nastenka) dingily prosaic and ordinary, not to say
incredibly vulgar."

"Foo! Good Heavens! What a preface! What do I hear?"

"Listen, Nastenka. (It seems to me I shall never be tired of calling you
Nastenka.) Let me tell you that in these corners live strange people—
dreamers. The dreamer—if you want an exact definition—is not a
human being, but a creature of an intermediate sort. For the most part
he settles in some inaccessible corner, as though hiding from the light
of day; once he slips into his corner, he grows to it like a snail, or, anyway, he is in that respect very much like that remarkable creature,
which is an animal and a house both at once, and is called a tortoise.
Why do you suppose he is so fond of his four walls, which are invariably painted green, grimy, dismal and reeking unpardonably of tobacco
smoke? Why is it that when this absurd gentleman is visited by one of
his few acquaintances (and he ends by getting rid of all his friends),
why does this absurd person meet him with such embarrassment,
changing countenance and overcome with confusion, as though he had
only just committed some crime within his four walls; as though he had
been forging counterfeit notes, or as though he were writing verses to be
sent to a journal with an anonymous letter, in which he states that the
real poet is dead, and that his friend thinks it his sacred duty to publish
his things? Why, tell me, Nastenka, why is it conversation is not easy
between the two friends? Why is there no laughter? Why does no lively
word fly from the tongue of the perplexed newcomer, who at other
times may be very fond of laughter, lively words, conversation about the
fair sex, and other cheerful subjects? And why does this friend, probably
a new friend and on his first visit—for there will hardly be a second, and
the friend will never come again—why is the friend himself so confused, so tongue-tied, in spite of his wit (if he has any), as he looks at the
downcast face of his host, who in his turn becomes utterly helpless and
at his wits' end after gigantic but fruitless efforts to smooth things over
and enliven the conversation, to show his knowledge of polite society, to
talk, too, of the fair sex, and by such humble endeavor, to please the
poor man, who like a fish out of water has mistakenly come to visit him?
Why does the gentleman, all at once remembering some very necessary
business which never existed, suddenly seize his hat and hurriedly make
off, snatching away his hand from the warm grip of his host, who was trying his utmost to show his regret and retrieve the lost position? Why
does the friend chuckle as he goes out of the door, and swear never to

come and see this queer creature again, though the queer creature is really a very good fellow, and at the same time he cannot refuse his imagination the little diversion of comparing the queer fellow's countenance during their conversation with the expression of an unhappy kitten treacherously captured, roughly handled, frightened and subjected to all sorts of indignities by children, till, utterly crestfallen, it hides away from them under a chair in the dark, and there must needs at its leisure bristle up, spit, and wash its insulted face with both paws, and long afterwards look angrily at life and nature, and even at the bits saved from the master's dinner for it by the sympathetic housekeeper?"

"Listen," interrupted Nastenka, who had listened to me all the time in amazement, opening her eyes and her little mouth. "Listen; I don't know in the least why it happened and why you ask me such absurd questions; all I know is, that this adventure must have happened word for word to you."

"Doubtless," I answered, with the gravest face.

"Well, since there is no doubt about it, go on," said Nastenka, "because I want very much to know how it will end."

"You want to know, Nastenka, what our hero, that is I—for the hero of the whole business was my humble self—did in his corner? You want to know why I lost my head and was upset for the whole day by the unexpected visit of a friend? You want to know why I was so startled, why I blushed when the door of my room was opened, why I was not able to entertain my visitor, and why I was crushed under the weight of my own hospitality?"

"Why, yes, yes," answered Nastenka, "that's the point. Listen. You describe it all splendidly, but couldn't you perhaps describe it a little less splendidly? You talk as though you were reading it out of a book."

"Nastenka," I answered in a stern and dignified voice, hardly able to keep from laughing, "dear Nastenka, I know I describe splendidly, but, excuse me, I don't know how else to do it. At this moment, dear Nastenka, at this moment I am like the spirit of King Solomon when, after lying a thousand years under seven seals in his urn, those seven seals were at last taken off. At this moment, Nastenka, when we have met at last after such a long separation—for I have known you for ages, Nastenka, because I have been looking for some one for ages, and that is a sign that it was you I was looking for, and it was ordained that we should meet now—at this moment a thousand valves have opened in my head, and I must let myself flow in a river of words, or I shall choke. And so I beg you not to interrupt me, Nastenka, but listen humbly and obediently, or I will be silent."

"No, no, no! Not at all. Go on! I won't say a word!"

"I will continue. There is, my friend Nastenka, one hour in my day which I like extremely. That is the hour when almost all business, work and duties are over, and every one is hurrying home to dinner, to lie down, to rest, and on the way all are cogitating on other more cheerful subjects relating to their evenings, their nights, and all the rest of their free time. At that hour our hero—for allow me, Nastenka, to tell my story in the third person, for one feels awfully ashamed to tell it in the first person—and so at that hour our hero, who had his work too, was pacing along after the others. But a strange feeling of pleasure set his pale, rather crumpled-looking face working. He looked not with indifference on the evening glow which was slowly fading on the cold Petersburg sky. When I say he looked, I am lying: he did not look at it, but saw it as it were without realizing, as though tired or preoccupied with some other more interesting subject, so that he could scarcely spare a glance for anything about him. He was pleased because till next day he was released from business irksome to him, and happy as a schoolboy let out from the class-room to his games and mischief. Take a look at him, Nastenka; you will see at once that joyful emotion has already had an effect on his weak nerves and morbidly excited fancy. You see he is thinking of something. . . . Of dinner, do you imagine? Of the evening? What is he looking at like that? Is it at that gentleman of dignified appearance who is bowing so picturesquely to the lady who rolls by in a carriage drawn by prancing horses? No, Nastenka; what are all those trivialities to him now! He is rich now with his *own individual* life; he has suddenly become rich, and it is not for nothing that the fading sunset sheds its farewell gleams so gaily before him, and calls forth a swarm of impressions from his warmed heart. Now he hardly notices the road, on which the tiniest details at other times would strike him. Now 'the Goddess of Fancy' (if you have read Zhukovsky, dear Nastenka) has already with fantastic hand spun her golden warp and begun weaving upon it patterns of marvellous magic life—and who knows, maybe, her fantastic hand has borne him to the seventh crystal heaven far from the excellent granite pavement on which he was walking his way? Try stopping him now, ask him suddenly where he is standing now, through what streets he is going—he will, probably remember nothing, neither where he is going nor where he is standing now, and flushing with vexation he will certainly tell some lie to save appearances. That is why he starts, almost cries out, and looks round with horror when a respectable old lady stops him politely in the middle of the pavement and asks her way. Frowning with vexation he strides on, scarcely noticing that more than one passer-by smiles and turns round to look after him, and that a little girl, moving out of his way in alarm, laughs aloud, gazing open-eyed at his broad meditative smile and gesticulations. But fancy catches up in its playful flight the old woman, the curious passers-by, and the laughing child, and the peasants spending their nights in their barges

on Fontanka (our hero, let us suppose, is walking along the canal-side
at that moment), and capriciously weaves every one and everything
into the canvas like a fly in a spider's web. And it is only after the queer
fellow has returned to his comfortable den with fresh stores for his
mind to work on, has sat down and finished his dinner, that he comes
to himself, when Matrona who waits upon him—always thoughtful
and depressed—clears the table and gives him his pipe; he comes to
himself then and recalls with surprise that he has dined, though he has
absolutely no notion how it has happened. It has grown dark in the
room; his soul is sad and empty; the whole kingdom of fancies drops to
pieces about him, drops to pieces without a trace, without a sound,
floats away like a dream, and he cannot himself remember what he was
dreaming. But a vague sensation faintly stirs his heart and sets it aching,
some new desire temptingly tickles and excites his fancy, and imperceptibly evokes a swarm of fresh phantoms. Stillness reigns in the little
room; imagination is fostered by solitude and idleness; it is faintly smol-
dering, faintly simmering, like the water with which old Matrona is
making her coffee as she moves quietly about in the kitchen close by.
Now it breaks out spasmodically; and the book, picked up aimlessly
and at random, drops from my dreamer's hand before he has reached
the third page. His imagination is again stirred and at work, and again
a new world, a new fascinating life opens vistas before him. A fresh
dream—fresh happiness! A fresh rush of delicate, voluptuous poison!
What is real life to him! To his corrupted eyes we live, you and I,
Nastenka, so torpidly, slowly, insipidly; in his eyes we are all so dissatisfied with our fate, so exhausted by our life! And, truly, see how at first
sight everything is cold, morose, as though ill-humored among us. . . .
Poor things! thinks our dreamer. And it is no wonder that he thinks it!
Look at these magic phantasms, which so enchantingly, so whimsi-
cally, so carelessly and freely group before him in such a magic, animated picture, in which the most prominent figure in the foreground
is of course himself, our dreamer, in his precious person. See what varied adventures, what an endless swarm of ecstatic dreams. You ask,
perhaps, what he is dreaming of. Why ask that?—why, of everything . . .
of the lot of the poet, first unrecognized, then crowned with laurels; of
friendship with Hoffmann, St. Bartholomew's Night, of Diana Vernon,
of playing the hero at the taking of Kazan by Ivan Vassilyevitch, of
Clara Mowbray, of Effie Deans, of the council of the prelates and Huss
before them, of the rising of the dead in 'Robert the Devil' (do you
remember the music, it smells of the churchyard!), of Minna and
Brenda, of the battle of Berezina, of the reading of a poem at Countess
V. D.'s, of Danton, of Cleopatra *ei suoi amanti*, of a little house in
Kolomna, of a little home of one's own and beside one a dear creature

who listens to one on a winter's evening, opening her little mouth and eyes as you are listening to me now, my angel. . . . No, Nastenka, what is there, what is there for him, voluptuous sluggard, in this life, for which you and I have such a longing? He thinks that this is a poor pitiful life, not foreseeing that for him too, maybe, sometime the mournful hour may strike, when for one day of that pitiful life he would give all his years of fantasy, and would give them not only for joy and for happiness, but without caring to make distinctions in that hour of sadness, remorse and unchecked grief. But so far that threatening time has not arrived—he desires nothing, because he is superior to all desire, because he has everything, because he is satiated, because he is the artist of his own life, and creates it for himself every hour to suit his latest whim. And you know this fantastic world of fairyland is so easily, so naturally created! As though it were not a delusion! Indeed, he is ready to believe at some moments that all this life is not suggested by feeling, is not mirage, not a delusion of the imagination, but that it is concrete, real, substantial! Why is it, Nastenka, why is it at such moments one holds one's breath? Why, by what sorcery, through what incomprehensible caprice, is the pulse quickened, does a tear start from the dreamer's eye, while his pale moist cheeks glow, while his whole being is suffused with an inexpressible sense of consolation? Why is it that whole sleepless nights pass like a flash in inexhaustible gladness and happiness, and when the dawn gleams rosy at the window and daybreak floods the gloomy room with uncertain, fantastic light, as in Petersburg, our dreamer, worn out and exhausted, flings himself on his bed and drops asleep with thrills of delight in his morbidly overwrought spirit, and with a weary sweet ache in his heart? Yes, Nastenka, one deceives oneself and unconsciously believes that real true passion is stirring one's soul; one unconsciously believes that there is something living, tangible in one's immaterial dreams! And is it delusion? Here love, for instance, is bound up with all its fathomless joy, all its torturing agonies in his bosom. . . . Only look at him, and you will be convinced! Would you believe, looking at him, dear Nastenka, that he has never known her whom he loves in his ecstatic dreams? Can it be that he has only seen her in seductive visions, and that this passion has been nothing but a dream? Surely they must have spent years hand in hand together—alone the two of them, casting off all the world and each uniting his or her life with the other's? Surely when the hour of parting came she must have lain sobbing and grieving on his bosom, heedless of the tempest raging under the sullen sky, heedless of the wind which snatches and bears away the tears from her black eyelashes? Can all of that have been a dream—and that garden, dejected, forsaken, run wild, with its little moss-grown paths, solitary, gloomy, where they used to walk so happily together, where they hoped, grieved, loved, loved each other so long, "so long and so fondly?" And that queer ancestral house where she spent so many years lonely and sad with her morose old husband, always silent and splenetic, who frightened them, while timid as children they hid their love from each other? What torments they suffered, what agonies of terror, how innocent, how pure was their love, and how (I need hardly say, Nastenka) malicious people were! And, good Heavens! surely he met her afterwards, far from their native shores, under alien skies, in the hot south in the divinely eternal city, in the dazzling splendor of the ball to the crash of music, in a *palazzo* (it must be in a *palazzo*), drowned in a sea of lights, on the balcony, wreathed in myrtle and roses, where, recognizing him, she hurriedly removes her mask and whispering, 'I am free,' flings herself trembling into his arms, and with a cry of rapture, clinging to one another, in one instant they forget their sorrow and their parting and all their agonies, and the gloomy house and the old man and the dismal garden in that distant land, and the seat on which with a last passionate kiss she tore herself away from his arms numb with anguish and despair. . . . Oh, Nastenka, you must admit that one would start, betray confusion, and blush like a schoolboy who has just stuffed in his pocket an apple stolen from a neighbor's garden, when your uninvited visitor, some stalwart, lanky fellow, a festive soul fond of a joke, opens your door and shouts out as though nothing were happening; 'My dear boy, I have this minute come from Pavlovsk.' My goodness! the old count is dead, unutterable happiness is close at hand—and people arrive from Pavlovsk!"

Finishing my pathetic appeal, I paused pathetically. I remembered that I had an intense desire to force myself to laugh, for I was already feeling that a malignant demon was stirring within me, that there was a lump in my throat, that my chin was beginning to twitch, and that my eyes were growing more and more moist.

I expected Nastenka, who listened to me opening her clever eyes, would break into her childish, irrepressible laugh; and I was already regretting that I had gone so far, that I had unnecessarily described what had long been simmering in my heart, about which I could speak as though from a written account of it, because I had long ago passed judgment on myself and now could not resist reading it, making my confession, without expecting to be understood; but to my surprise she was silent, waiting a little, then she faintly pressed my hand and with timid sympathy asked—

"Surely you haven't lived like that all your life?"

"All my life, Nastenka," I answered; "all my life, and it seems to me I shall go on so to the end."

"No, that won't do," she said uneasily, "that must not be; and so, maybe, I shall spend all my life beside grandmother. Do you know, it is not at all good to live like that?"

"I know, Nastenka, I know!" I cried, unable to restrain my feelings longer. "And I realize now, more than ever, that I have lost all my best years! And now I know it and feel it more painfully from recognizing that God has sent me you, my good angel, to tell me that and show it. Now that I sit beside you and talk to you it is strange for me to think of the future, for in the future—there is loneliness again, again this musty, useless life; and what shall I have to dream of when I have been so happy in reality beside you! Oh, may you be blessed, dear girl, for not having repulsed me at first, for enabling me to say that for two evenings, at least, I have lived."

"Oh, no, no!" cried Nastenka and tears glistened in her eyes. "No, it mustn't be so any more; we must not part like that! what are two evenings?"

"Oh, Nastenka, Nastenka! Do you know how far you have reconciled me to myself? Do you know now that I shall not think so ill of myself, as I have at some moments? Do you know that, maybe, I shall leave off grieving over the crime and sin of my life? for such a life is a crime and a sin. And do not imagine that I have been exaggerating anything—for goodness' sake don't think that, Nastenka: for at times such misery comes over me, such misery. . . . Because it begins to seem to me at such times that I am incapable of beginning a life in real life, because it has seemed to me that I have lost all touch, all instinct for the actual, the real; because at last I have cursed myself; because after my fantastic nights I have moments of returning sobriety, which are awful! Meanwhile, you hear the whirl and roar of the crowd in the vortex of life around you; you hear, you see, men living in reality; you see that life for them is not forbidden, that their life does not float away like a dream, like a vision; that their life is being eternally renewed, eternally youthful, and not one hour of it is the same as another; while fancy is so spiritless, monotonous to vulgarity and easily scared, the slave of shadows, of the idea, the slave of the first cloud that shrouds the sun, and overcasts with depression the true Petersburg heart so devoted to the sun—and what is fancy in depression! One feels that this *inexhaustible* fancy is weary at last and worn out with continual exercise, because one is growing into manhood, outgrowing one's old ideals: they are being shattered into fragments, into dust; if there is no other life one must build one up from the fragments. And meanwhile the soul longs and craves for something else! And in vain the dreamer rakes over his old dreams, as though seeking a spark among the embers, to fan them into flame, to warm his chilled heart by the rekindled fire, and to rouse up in it again all that was so sweet, that touched his heart, that set his blood boiling, drew tears from his eyes, and so luxuriously deceived him! Do you know, Nastenka, the point I have reached? Do you know that I am forced now to celebrate the anniversary of my own sensations, the anniversary of that which was once so sweet, which never existed in reality—for this anniversary is kept in memory of those same foolish, shadowy dreams—and to do this because those foolish dreams are no more, because I have nothing to earn them with; you know even dreams do not come for nothing! Do you know that I love now to recall and visit at certain dates the places where I was once happy in my own way? I love to build up my present in harmony with the irrevocable past, and I often wander like a shadow, aimless, sad and dejected, about the streets and crooked lanes of Petersburg. What memories they are! To remember, for instance, that here just a year ago, just at this time, at this hour, on this pavement, I wandered just as lonely, just as dejected as today. And one remembers that then one's dreams were sad, and though the past was no better one feels as though it had somehow been better, and that life was more peaceful, that one was free from the black thoughts that haunt one now; that one was free from the gnawing of conscience—the gloomy, sullen gnawing which now gives me no rest by day or by night. And one asks oneself where are one's dreams. And one shakes one's head and says how rapidly the years fly by! And again one asks oneself what has one done with one's years. Where have you buried your best days? Have you lived or not? Look, one says to oneself, look how cold the world is growing. Some more years will pass, and after them will come gloomy solitude; then will come old age trembling on its crutch, and after it misery and desolation. Your fantastic world will grow pale, your dreams will fade and die and will fall like the yellow leaves from the trees. . . . Oh, Nastenka! you know it will be sad to be left alone, utterly alone, and to have not even anything to regret—nothing, absolutely nothing . . . for all that you have lost, all that, all was nothing, stupid, simple nullity, there has been nothing but dreams!"

"Come, don't work on my feelings any more," said Nastenka, wiping away a tear which was trickling down her cheek. "Now it's over! Now we shall be two together. Now, whatever happens to me, we will never part. Listen; I am a simple girl, I have not had much education, though grandmother did get a teacher for me, but truly I understand you, for all that you have described I have been through myself, when grandmother pinned me to her dress. Of course, I should not have described it so well as you have; I am not educated," she added timidly, for she was still feeling a sort of respect for my pathetic eloquence and lofty style; "but I am very glad that you have been quite open with me. Now I know you thoroughly, all of you. And do you know what? I want to tell you my history too, all without concealment, and after that you must give me advice. You are a very clever man; will you promise to give me advice?"

"Ah, Nastenka," I cried, "though I have never given advice, still less sensible advice, yet I see now that if we always go on like this that it will be very sensible, and that each of us will give the other a great deal of sensible advice! Well, my pretty Nastenka, what sort of advice do you want? Tell me frankly; at this moment I am so gay and happy, so bold and sensible, that it won't be difficult for me to find words."

"No, no!" Nastenka interrupted, laughing. "I don't only want sensible advice, I want warm brotherly advice, as though you had been fond of me all your life!"

"Agreed, Nastenka, agreed!" I cried delighted; "and if I had been fond of you for twenty years, I couldn't have been fonder of you than I am now."

"Your hand," said Nastenka.

"Here it is," said I, giving her my hand.

"And so let us begin my history!"

Nastenka's History

"Half my story you know already—that is, you know that I have an old grandmother. . . ."

"If the other half is as brief as that . . ." I interrupted laughing.

"Be quiet and listen. First of all you must agree not to interrupt me, or else, perhaps I shall get in a muddle! Come, listen quietly.

"I have an old grandmother. I came into her hands when I was quite a little girl, for my father and mother are dead. It must be supposed that grandmother was once richer, for now she recalls better days. She taught me French, and then got a teacher for me. When I was fifteen (and now I am seventeen) we gave up having lessons. It was at that time that I got into mischief; what I did I won't tell you; it's enough to say that it wasn't very important. But grandmother called me to her one morning and said that as she was blind she could not look after me; she took a pin and pinned my dress to hers, and said that we should sit like that for the rest of our lives if, of course, I did not become a better girl. In fact, at first it was impossible to get away from her: I had to work, to read and to study all beside grandmother. I tried to deceive her once, and persuaded Fekla to sit in my place. Fekla is our charwoman, she is deaf. Fekla sat there instead of me; grandmother was asleep in her armchair at the time, and I went off to see a friend close by. Well, it ended in trouble. Grandmother woke up while I was out, and asked some questions; she thought I was still sitting quietly in my place. Fekla saw that grandmother was asking her something, but could not tell what it was; she wondered what to do, undid the pin and ran away. . . ."

At this point Nastenka stopped and began laughing. I laughed with her. She left off at once.

"I tell you what, don't you laugh at grandmother. I laugh because it's funny. . . . What can I do, since grandmother is like that; but yet I am fond of her in a way. Oh, well, I did catch it that time. I had to sit down in my place at once, and after that I was not allowed to stir.

"Oh, I forgot to tell you that our house belongs to us, that is to grandmother; it is a little wooden house with three windows as old as grandmother herself, with a little upper story; well, there moved into our upper story a new lodger."

"Then you had an old lodger," I observed casually.

"Yes, of course," answered Nastenka, "and one who knew how to hold his tongue better than you do. In fact, he hardly ever used his tongue at all. He was a dumb, blind, lame, dried-up little old man, so that at last he could not go on living, he died; so then we had to find a new lodger, for we could not live without a lodger—the rent, together with grandmother's pension, is almost all we have. But the new lodger, as luck would have it, was a young man, a stranger not of these parts. As he did not haggle over the rent, grandmother accepted him, and only afterwards she asked me: 'Tell me, Nastenka, what is our lodger like—is he young or old?' I did not want to lie, so I told grandmother that he wasn't exactly young and that he wasn't old.

"'And is he pleasant looking?' asked grandmother.

"Again I did not want to tell a lie: 'Yes, he is pleasant looking, grandmother,' I said. And grandmother said: 'Oh, what a nuisance, what a nuisance! I tell you this, grandchild, that you may not be looking after him. What times these are! Why a paltry lodger like this, and he must be pleasant looking too; it was very different in the old days!'

"Grandmother was always regretting the old days—she was younger in old days, and the sun was warmer in old days, and cream did not turn so sour in old days—it was always the old days! I would sit still and hold my tongue and think to myself: why did grandmother suggest it to me? Why did she ask whether the lodger was young and good-looking? But that was all, I just thought it, began counting my stitches again, went on knitting my stocking, and forgot all about it.

"Well, one morning the lodger came in to see us; he asked about a promise to paper his rooms. One thing led to another. Grandmother was talkative, and she said: 'Go, Nastenka, into my bedroom and bring me my reckoner.' I jumped up at once; I blushed all over, I don't know why, and forgot I was sitting pinned to grandmother; instead of quietly undoing the pin, so that the lodger should not see—I jumped so that grandmother's chair moved. When I saw that the lodger knew all about me now, I blushed, stood still as though I had been shot, and suddenly began to cry—I felt so ashamed and miserable at that minute, that I didn't know where to look! Grandmother called out, 'What are you waiting for?' and I went on worse than ever. When the lodger saw, saw that I was ashamed on his account, he bowed and went away at once!

"After that I felt ready to die at the least sound in the passage. 'It's the lodger,' I kept thinking; I stealthily undid the pin in case. But it always turned out not to be, he never came. A fortnight passed; the lodger sent word through Fekla that he had a great number of French books, and that they were all good books that I might read, so would not grandmother like me to read them that I might not be dull? Grandmother agreed with gratitude, but kept asking if they were moral books, for if the books were immoral it would be out of the question, one would learn evil from them.

"'And what should I learn, grandmother? What is there written in them?'

"'Ah,' she said, 'what's described in them, is how young men seduce virtuous girls; how, on the excuse that they want to marry them, they carry them off from their parents' houses; how afterwards they leave these unhappy girls to their fate, and they perish in the most pitiful way. I read a great many books,' said grandmother, 'and it is all so well described that one sits up all night and reads them on the sly. So mind you don't read them, Nastenka,' said she. 'What books has he sent?'

"'They are all Walter Scott's novels, grandmother.'

"'Walter Scott's novels! But stay, isn't there some trick about it? Look, hasn't he stuck a love-letter among them?'

"'No, grandmother,' I said, 'there isn't a love-letter.'

"'But look under the binding; they sometimes stuff it under the bindings, the rascals!'

"'No, grandmother, there is nothing under the binding.'

"'Well, that's all right.'

"So we began reading Walter Scott, and in a month or so we had read almost half. Then he sent us more and more. He sent us Pushkin, too; so that at last I could not get on without a book, and left off dreaming of how fine it would be to marry a Chinese Prince.

"That's how things were when I chanced one day to meet our lodger on the stairs. Grandmother had sent me to fetch something. He stopped, I blushed and he blushed; he laughed, though, said good-morning to me, asked after grandmother, and said, 'Well, have you read the books?' I answered that I had. 'Which did you like best?' he asked. I said, 'Ivanhoe, and Pushkin best of all,' and so our talk ended for that time.

"A week later I met him again on the stairs. That time grandmother had not sent me, I wanted to get something for myself. It was past two, and the lodger used to come home at that time. 'Good-afternoon,' said he. I said good-afternoon, too.

"'Aren't you dull,' he said, 'sitting all day with your grandmother?'

"When he asked that, I blushed, I don't know why; I felt ashamed, and again I felt offended—I suppose because other people had begun to ask me about that. I wanted to go away without answering, but I hadn't the strength.

"'Listen,' he said, 'you are a good girl. Excuse my speaking to you like that, but I assure you that I wish for your welfare quite as much as your grandmother. Have you no friends that you could go and visit?'

"I told him I hadn't any, that I had had no friend but Mashenka, and she had gone away to Pskov.

"'Listen,' he said, 'would you like to go to the theater with me?'

"'To the theater. What about grandmother?'

"'But you must go without your grandmother's knowing it,' he said.

"'No,' I said, 'I don't want to deceive my grandmother. Good-bye.'

"'Well, good-bye,' he answered, and said nothing more.

"Only after dinner he came to see us; sat a long time talking to grandmother; asked her whether she ever went out anywhere, whether she had acquaintances, and suddenly said: 'I have taken a box at the opera for this evening; they are giving *The Barber of Seville*. My friends meant to go, but afterwards refused, so the ticket is left on my hands.'

"'The Barber of Seville,' cried grandmother; 'why, the same they used to act in old days?'

"'Yes, it's the same barber,' he said, and glanced at me. I saw what it meant and turned crimson, and my heart began throbbing with suspense.

"'To be sure, I know it,' said grandmother; 'why, I took the part of Rosina myself in old days, at a private performance!'

"'So wouldn't you like to go to-day?' said the lodger. 'Or my ticket will be wasted.'

"'By all means let us go,' said grandmother; 'why shouldn't we? And my Nastenka here has never been to the theater.'

"My goodness, what joy! We got ready at once, put on our best clothes, and set off. Though grandmother was blind, still she wanted to hear the music; besides, she is a kind old soul, what she cared most for was to amuse me, we should never have gone of ourselves.

"What my impressions of *The Barber of Seville* were I won't tell you; but all that evening our lodger looked at me so nicely, talked so nicely, that I saw at once that he had meant to test me in the morning when he proposed that I should go with him alone. Well, it was joy! I went to bed so proud, so gay, my heart beat so that I was a little feverish, and all night I was raving about *The Barber of Seville*.

"I expected that he would come and see us more and more often after that, but it wasn't so at all. He almost entirely gave up coming. He would just come in about once a month, and then only to invite us to the theater. We went twice again. Only I wasn't at all pleased with that; I saw that he was simply sorry for me because I was so hardly treated by grandmother, and that was all. As time went on, I grew more and more restless, I couldn't sit still, I couldn't read, I couldn't work; sometimes I laughed and did something to annoy grandmother, at another time I would cry. At last I grew thin and was very nearly ill. The opera season was over, and our lodger had quite given up coming to see us; whenever we met—always on the same staircase, of course—he would bow so silently, so gravely, as though he did not want to speak, and go down to the front door, while I went on standing in the middle of the stairs, as red as a cherry, for all the blood rushed to my head at the sight of him.

"Now the end is near. Just a year ago, in May, the lodger came to us and said to grandmother that he had finished his business here, and that he must go back to Moscow for a year. When I heard that, I sank into a chair half dead; grandmother did not notice anything; and having informed us that he should be leaving us, he bowed and went away.

"What was I to do? I thought and thought and fretted and fretted, and at last I made up my mind. Next day he was to go away, and I made up my mind to end it all that evening when grandmother went to bed. And so it happened. I made up all my clothes in a parcel—all the linen I needed—and with the parcel in my hand, more dead than alive, went upstairs to our lodger. I believe I must have stayed an hour on the staircase. When I opened his door he cried out as he looked at me. He thought I was a ghost, and rushed to give me some water, for I could hardly stand up. My heart beat so violently that my head ached, and I did not know what I was doing. When I recovered I began by laying my parcel on his bed, sat down beside it, hid my face in my hands and went into floods of tears. I think he understood it all at once, and looked at me so sadly that my heart was torn.

"'Listen,' he began, 'listen, Nastenka, I can't do anything; I am a poor man, for I have nothing, not even a decent berth. How could we live, if I were to marry you?'

"We talked a long time; but at last I got quite frantic, I said I could not go on living with grandmother, that I should run away from her, that I did not want to be pinned to her, and that I would go to Moscow if he liked, because I could not live without him. Shame and pride and love were all clamoring in me at once, and I fell on the bed almost in convulsions, I was so afraid of a refusal.

"He sat for some minutes in silence, then got up, came up to me and took me by the hand.

"'Listen, my dear good Nastenka, listen; I swear to you that if I am ever in a position to marry, you shall make my happiness. I assure you that now you are the only one who could make me happy. Listen, I am going to Moscow and shall be there just a year; I hope to establish my position. When I come back, if you still love me, I swear that we will be happy. Now it is impossible, I am not able, I have not the right to promise anything. Well, I repeat, if it is not within a year it will certainly be some time; that is, of course, if you do not prefer any one else, for I cannot and dare not bind you by any sort of promise.'

"That was what he said to me, and next day he went away. We agreed together not to say a word to grandmother: that was his wish. Well, my history is nearly finished now. Just a year has past. He has arrived; he has been here three days, and—and——"

"And what?" I cried, impatient to hear the end.

"And up to now has not shown himself!" answered Nastenka, as though screwing up all her courage. "There's no sign or sound of him."

Here she stopped, paused for a minute, bent her head, and covering her face with her hands broke into such sobs that it sent a pang to my heart to hear them. I had not in the least expected such a *dénouement*.

"Nastenka," I began timidly in an ingratiating voice, "Nastenka! For goodness' sake don't cry! How do you know? Perhaps he is not here yet . . . ."

"He is, he is," Nastenka repeated. "He is here, and I know it. We *made an agreement* at the time, that evening, before he went away: when we said all that I have told you, and had come to an understanding, then we came out here for a walk on this embankment. It was ten o'clock; we sat on this seat. I was not crying then; it was sweet to me to hear what he said. . . . And he said that he would come to us directly he arrived, and if I did not refuse him, then we would tell grandmother about it all. Now he is here, I know it, and yet he does not come!"

And again she burst into tears.

"Good God, can I do nothing to help you in your sorrow?" I cried, jumping up from the seat in utter despair. "Tell me, Nastenka, wouldn't it be possible for me to go to him?"

"Would that be possible?" she asked suddenly, raising her head.

"No, of course not," I said pulling myself up; "but I tell you what, write a letter."

"No, that's impossible, I can't do that," she answered with decision, bending her head and not looking at me.

"How impossible—why is it impossible?" I went on, clinging to my idea. "But, Nastenka, it depends what sort of letter; there are letters and letters and. . . . Ah, Nastenka, I am right; trust to me, trust to me, I will not give you bad advice. It can all be arranged! You took the first step— why not now?"

"I can't. I can't! It would seem as though I were forcing myself on him. . . ."

"Ah, my good little Nastenka," I said, hardly able to conceal a smile; "no, no, you have a right to, in fact, because he made you a promise. Besides, I can see from everything that he is a man of delicate feeling; that he behaved very well," I went on, more and more carried away by the logic of my own arguments and convictions. "How did he behave? He bound himself by a promise: he said that if he married at all he would marry no one but you; he gave you full liberty to refuse him at once. . . . Under such circumstances you may take the first step; you have the right; you are in the privileged position—if, for instance, you wanted to free him from his promise. . . ."

"Listen; how would you write?"

"Write what?"

"This letter."

"I tell you how I would write: 'Dear Sir' . . ."

"Must I really begin like that, 'Dear Sir'?"

"You certainly must! Though, after all, I don't know, I imagine. . . ."

"Well, well, what next?"

"'Dear Sir,—I must apologize for——' But, no, there's no need to apologize; the fact itself justifies everything. Write simply:—

"'I am writing to you. Forgive me my impatience; but I have been happy for a whole year in hope; am I to blame for being unable to endure a day of doubt now? Now that you have come, perhaps you have changed your mind. If so, this letter is to tell you that I do not repine, nor blame you. I do not blame you because I have no power over your heart, such is my fate!

"'You are an honorable man. You will not smile or be vexed at these impatient lines. Remember they are written by a poor girl; that she is alone; that she has no one to direct her, no one to advise her, and that she herself could never control her heart. But forgive me that a doubt has stolen—if only for one instant—into my heart. You are not capable of insulting, even in thought, her who so loved and so loves you.'"

"Yes, yes; that's exactly what I was thinking!" cried Nastenka, and her eyes beamed with delight. "Oh, you have solved my difficulties: God has sent you to me! Thank you, thank you!"

"What for? What for? For God's sending me?" I answered, looking delighted at her joyful little face.

"Why, yes; for that too."

"Ah, Nastenka! Why, one thanks some people for being alive at the same time with one; I thank you for having met me, for my being able to remember you all my life!"

"Well, enough, enough! But now I tell you what, listen: we made an agreement then that as soon as he arrived he would let me know, by leaving a letter with some good simple people of my acquaintance who know nothing about it; or, if it were impossible to write a letter to me, for a letter does not always tell everything, he would be here at ten o'clock on the day he arrived, where we had arranged to meet. I know he has arrived already; but now it's the third day, and there's no sign of him and no letter. It's impossible for me to get away from grandmother in the morning. Give my letter to-morrow to those kind people I spoke to you about: they will send it on to him, and if there is an answer you bring it to-morrow at ten o'clock."

"But the letter, the letter! You see, you must write the letter first! So perhaps it must all be the day after to-morrow."

"The letter . . ." said Nastenka, a little confused, "the letter . . . but . . ."

But she did not finish. At first she turned her little face away from me, flushed like a rose, and suddenly I felt in my hand a letter which had evidently been written long before, all ready and sealed up. A familiar sweet and charming reminiscence floated through my mind.

"R, o—Ro; s, i—si; n, a—na," I began.

"Rosina!" we both hummed together; I almost embracing her with delight, while she blushed as only she could blush, and laughed through the tears which gleamed like pearls on her black eyelashes.

"Come, enough, enough! Good-bye now," she said, speaking rapidly. "Here is the letter, here is the address to which you are to take it. Good-bye, till we meet again! Till to-morrow!"

She pressed both my hands warmly, nodded her head, and flew like an arrow down her side street. I stood still for a long time following her with my eyes.

"Till to-morrow! till to-morrow!" was ringing in my ears as she vanished from my sight.

Third Night

To-day was a gloomy, rainy day without a glimmer of sunlight, like the old age before me. I am oppressed by such strange thoughts, such gloomy sensations; questions still so obscure to me are crowding into my brain—and I seem to have neither power nor will to settle them. It's not for me to settle all this!

To-day we shall not meet. Yesterday, when we said good-bye, the clouds began gathering over the sky and a mist rose. I said that to-morrow it would be a bad day; she made no answer, she did not want to speak against her wishes; for her that day was bright and clear, not one cloud should obscure her happiness.

"If it rains we shall not see each other," she said, "I shall not come."

I thought that she would not notice to-day's rain, and yet she has not come.

Yesterday was our third interview, our third white night. . . .

But how fine joy and happiness makes any one! How brimming over with love the heart is! One seems longing to pour out one's whole heart; one wants everything to be gay, everything to be laughing. And how infectious that joy is! There was such a softness in her words, such a kindly feeling in her heart towards me yesterday. . . . How solicitous and friendly she was; how tenderly she tried to give me courage! Oh, the coquetry of happiness! While I . . . I took it all for the genuine thing, I thought that she. . . .

But, my God, how could I have thought it? How could I have been so blind, when everything had been taken by another already, when nothing was mine; when, in fact, her very tenderness to me, her anxiety, her love . . . yes, love for me, was nothing else but joy at the thought of seeing another man so soon, desire to include me, too, in her happiness? . . . When he did not come, when we waited in vain, she frowned, she grew timid and discouraged. Her movements, her words, were no longer so light, so playful, so gay; and, strange to say, she redoubled her attentiveness to me, as though instinctively desiring to lavish on me what she desired for herself so anxiously, if her wishes were not accomplished. My Nastenka was so downcast, so dismayed, that I think she realized at last that I loved her, and was sorry for my poor love. So when we are unhappy we feel the unhappiness of others more; feeling is not destroyed but concentrated . . .

I went to meet her with a full heart, and was all impatience. I had no presentiment that I should feel as I do now, that it would not all end happily. She was beaming with pleasure; she was expecting an answer. The answer was himself. He was to come, to run at her call. She arrived a whole hour before I did. At first she giggled at everything, laughed at every word I said. I began talking, but relapsed into silence.

"Do you know why I am so glad," she said, "so glad to look at you? — why I like you so much to-day?"

"Well?" I asked, and my heart began throbbing.

"I like you because you have not fallen in love with me. You know that some men in your place would have been pestering and worrying me, would have been sighing and miserable, while you are so nice!"

Then she wrung my hand so hard that I almost cried out. She laughed.

"Goodness, what a friend you are!" she began gravely a minute later. "God sent you to me. What would have happened to me if you had not been with me now? How disinterested you are! How truly you care for

me! When I am married we will be great friends, more than brother
and sister; I shall care almost as I do for him. . . ."

I felt horribly sad at that moment, yet something like laughter was
stirring in my soul.

"You are very much upset," I said; "you are frightened; you think he
won't come."

"Oh dear!" she answered; "if I were less happy, I believe I should cry
at your lack of faith, at your reproaches. However, you have made me
think and have given me a lot to think about; but I shall think later, and
now I will own that you are right. Yes, I am somehow not myself; I am
all suspense, and feel everything as it were too lightly. But hush! that's
enough about feelings. . . ."

At that moment we heard footsteps, and in the darkness we saw a figure coming towards us. We both started; she almost cried out; I
dropped her hand and made a movement as though to walk away. But
we were mistaken, it was not he.

"What are you afraid of! Why did you let go of my hand?" she said,
giving it to me again. "Come, what is it! We will meet him together; I
want him to see how fond we are of each other."

"How fond we are of each other!" I cried. ("Oh, Nastenka,
Nastenka," I thought, "how much you have told me in that saying!
Such fondness at *certain* moments makes the heart cold and the soul
heavy. Your hand is cold, mine burns like fire. How blind you are,
Nastenka! . . . Oh, how unbearable a happy person is sometimes! But I
could not be angry with you!")

At last my heart was too full.

"Listen, Nastenka!" I cried. "Do you know how it has been with me
all day?"

"Why, how, how? Tell me quickly! Why have you said nothing all
this time?"

"To begin with, Nastenka, when I had carried out all your commis-
sions, given the letter, gone to see your good friends, then . . . then I
went home and went to bed."

"Is that all?" she interrupted, laughing.

"Yes, almost all," I answered restraining myself, for foolish tears were
already starting into my eyes. "I woke an hour before our appointment,
and yet, as it were, I had not been asleep. I don't know what happened
to me. I came to tell you all about it, feeling as though time were standing still, feeling as though one sensation, one feeling must remain with
me from that time for ever; feeling as though one minute must go on
for all eternity, and as though all life had come to a standstill for me. . . .
When I woke up it seemed as though some musical motive long familiar, heard somewhere in the past, forgotten and voluptuously sweet,

had come back to me now. It seemed to me that it had been clamoring at my heart all my life, and only now. . . ."

"Oh my goodness, my goodness," Nastenka interrupted, "what does all that mean? I don't understand a word."

"Ah, Nastenka, I wanted somehow to convey to you that strange impression. . . ." I began in a plaintive voice, in which there still lay hid a hope, though a very faint one.

"Leave off. Hush!" she said, and in one instant the sly puss had guessed.

Suddenly she became extraordinarily talkative, gay, mischievous; she took my arm, laughed, wanted me to laugh too, and every confused word I uttered evoked from her prolonged ringing laughter. . . . I began to feel angry, she had suddenly begun flirting.

"Do you know," she began, "I feel a little vexed that you are not in love with me? There's no understanding human nature! But all the same, Mr. Unapproachable, you cannot blame me for being so simple; I tell you everything, everything, whatever foolish thought comes into my head."

"Listen! That's eleven, I believe," I said as the slow chime of a bell rang out from a distant tower. She suddenly stopped, left off laughing and began to count.

"Yes, it's eleven," she said at last in a timid, uncertain voice.

I regretted at once that I had frightened her, making her count the strokes, and I cursed myself for my spiteful impulse; I felt sorry for her, and did not know how to atone for what I had done.

I began comforting her, seeking for reasons for his not coming, advancing various arguments, proofs. No one could have been easier to deceive than she was at that moment; and, indeed, any one at such a moment listens gladly to any consolation, whatever it may be, and is overjoyed if a shadow of excuse can be found.

"And indeed it's an absurd thing," I began, warming to my task and admiring the extraordinary clearness of my argument, "why, he could not have come; you have muddled and confused me, Nastenka, so that I too, have lost count of the time. . . . Only think: he can scarcely have received the letter; suppose he is not able to come, suppose he is going to answer the letter, could not come before to-morrow. I will go for it as soon as it's light to-morrow and let you know at once. Consider, there are thousands of possibilities; perhaps he was not at home when the letter came, and may not have read it even now! Anything may happen, you know."

"Yes, yes!" said Nastenka. "I did not think of that. Of course anything may happen?" she went on in a tone that offered no opposition, though some other far-away thought could be heard like a vexatious discord in it. "I tell you what you must do," she said, "you go as early as possible to-morrow morning, and if you get anything let me know at once. You know where I live, don't you?"

And she began repeating her address to me.

Then she suddenly became so tender, so solicitous with me. She seemed to listen attentively to what I told her; but when I asked her some question she was silent, was confused, and turned her head away. I looked into her eyes—yes, she was crying.

"How can you? How can you? Oh, what a baby you are! what childishness! . . . Come, come!"

She tried to smile, to calm herself, but her chin was quivering and her bosom was still heaving.

"I was thinking about you," she said after a minute's silence. "You are so kind that I should be a stone if I did not feel it. Do you know what has occurred to me now? I was comparing you two. Why isn't he you? Why isn't he like you? He is not as good as you, though I love him more than you."

I made no answer. She seemed to expect me to say something.

"Of course, it may be that I don't understand him fully yet. You know I was always as it were afraid of him; he was always so grave, as it were so proud. Of course I know it's only that he seems like that, I know there is more tenderness in his heart than in mine. . . . I remember how he looked at me when I went in to him—do you remember?—with my bundle; but yet I respect him too much, and doesn't that show that we are not equals?"

"No, Nastenka, no," I answered, "it shows that you love him more than anything in the world, and far more than yourself."

"Yes, supposing that is so," answered Nastenka naïvely. "But do you know what strikes me now? Only I am not talking about him now, but speaking generally; all this came into my mind some time ago. Tell me, how is it that we can't all be like brothers together? Why is it that even the best of men always seem to hide something from other people and to keep something back? Why not say straight out what is in one's heart, when one knows that one is not speaking idly? As it is every one seems harsher than he really is, as though all were afraid of doing injustice to their feelings, by being too quick to express them."

"Oh, Nastenka, what you say is true; but there are many reasons for that," I broke in suppressing my own feelings at that moment more than ever.

"No, no!" she answered with deep feeling. "Here you, for instance, are not like other people! I really don't know how to tell you what I feel; but it seems to me that you, for instance . . . at the present moment . . . it seems to me that you are sacrificing something for me," she added timidly, with a fleeting glance at me. "Forgive me for saying so, I am a simple girl you know. I have seen very little of life, and I really sometimes don't know how to say things," she added in a voice that quivered with some hidden feeling, while she tried to smile; "but I only wanted to tell you that I am grateful, that I feel it all too . . . Oh, may God give you happiness for it! What you told me about your dreamer is quite untrue now—that is, I mean, it's not true of you. You are recovering, you are quite a different man from what you described. If you ever fall in love with some one, God give you happiness with her! I won't wish anything for her, for she will be happy with you. I know, I am a woman myself, so you must believe me when I tell you so."

She ceased speaking, and pressed my hand warmly. I too could not speak without emotion. Some minutes passed.

"Yes, it's clear he won't come to-night," she said at last raising her head. "It's late."

"He will come to-morrow," I said in the most firm and convincing tone.

"Yes," she added with no sign of her former depression. "I see for myself now that he could not come till to-morrow. Well, good-bye, till to-morrow. If it rains perhaps I shall not come. But the day after to-morrow, I shall come. I shall come for certain, whatever happens; be sure to be here, I want to see you, I will tell you everything."

And then when we parted she gave me her hand and said, looking at me candidly: "We shall always be together, shan't we?"

Oh, Nastenka, Nastenka! If only you knew how lonely I am now!

As soon as it struck nine o'clock I could not stay indoors, but put on my things, and went out in spite of the weather. I was there, sitting on our seat. I went to her street, but I felt ashamed, and turned back without looking at their windows, when I was two steps from her door. I went home more depressed than I had ever been before. What a damp, dreary day! If it had been fine I should have walked about all night. . . .

But to-morrow, to-morrow! To-morrow she will tell me everything. The letter has not come to-day, however. But that was to be expected. They are together by now. . . .

Fourth Night

My God, how it has all ended! What it has all ended in! I arrived at nine o'clock. She was already there. I noticed her a good way off; she was standing as she had been that first time, with her elbows on the railing, and she did not hear me coming up to her.

"Nastenka!" I called to her, suppressing my agitation with an effort.

She turned to me quickly.

"Well?" she said. "Well? Make haste!"

I looked at her in perplexity.

"Well, where is the letter? Have you brought the letter?" she repeated clutching at the railing.

"No, there is no letter," I said at last. "Hasn't he been to you yet?" She turned fearfully pale and looked at me for a long time without moving. I had shattered her last hope.

"Well, God be with him," she said at last in a breaking voice; "God be with him if he leaves me like that."

She dropped her eyes, then tried to look at me and could not. For several minutes she was struggling with her emotion. All at once she turned away, leaning her elbows against the railing and burst into tears.

"Oh don't, don't!" I began; but looking at her I had not the heart to go on, and what was I to say to her?

"Don't try and comfort me," she said; "don't talk about him; don't tell me that he will come, that he has not cast me off so cruelly and so inhumanly as he has. What for—what for? Can there have been something in my letter, that unlucky letter?"

At that point sobs stifled her voice; my heart was torn as I looked at her.

"Oh, how inhumanly cruel it is!" she began again. "And not a line, not a line! He might at least have written that he does not want me, that he rejects me—but not a line for three days! How easy it is for him to wound, to insult a poor, defenseless girl, whose only fault is that she loves him! Oh, what I've suffered during these three days! Oh, dear! When I think that I was the first to go to him, that I humbled myself before him, cried, that I begged of him a little love! . . . and after that! Listen," she said, turning to me, and her black eyes flashed, "it isn't so! It can't be so; it isn't natural. Either you are mistaken or I; perhaps he has not received the letter? Perhaps he still knows nothing about it? How could any one—judge for yourself, tell me, for goodness' sake explain it to me, I can't understand it—how could any one behave with such barbarous coarseness as he has behaved to me? Not one word! Why, the lowest creature on earth is treated more compassionately. Perhaps he has heard something, perhaps some one has told him something about me," she cried, turning to me inquiringly: "What do you think?"

"Listen, Nastenka, I shall go to him to-morrow in your name."

"Yes?"

"I will question him about everything; I will tell him everything."

"Yes, yes?"

"You write a letter. Don't say no, Nastenka, don't say no! I will make him respect your action, he shall hear all about it, and if——"

"No, my friend, no," she interrupted. "Enough! Not another word, not another line from me—enough! I don't know him; I don't love him any more. I will . . . forget him."

She could not go on.

"Calm yourself, calm yourself! Sit here, Nastenka," I said, making her sit down on the seat.

"I am calm. Don't trouble. It's nothing! It's only tears, they will soon dry. Why, do you imagine I shall do away with myself, that I shall throw myself into the river?"

My heart was full: I tried to speak, but I could not.

"Listen," she said taking my hand. "Tell me: you wouldn't have behaved like this, would you? You would not have abandoned a girl who had come to you of herself, you would not have thrown into her face a shameless taunt at her weak foolish heart? You would have taken care of her? You would have realized that she was alone, that she did not know how to look after herself, that she could not guard herself from loving you, that it was not her fault, not her fault—that she had done nothing. . . . Oh dear, oh dear!"

"Nastenka!" I cried at last, unable to control my emotion. "Nastenka, you torture me! You wound my heart, you are killing me, Nastenka! I cannot be silent! I must speak at last, give utterance to what is surging in my heart!"

As I said this I got up from the seat. She took my hand and looked at me in surprise.

"What is the matter with you?" she said at last.

"Listen," I said resolutely. "Listen to me, Nastenka! What I am going to say to you now is all nonsense, all impossible, all stupid! I know that this can never be, but I cannot be silent. For the sake of what you are suffering now, I beg you beforehand to forgive me!"

"What is it? What is it?" she said, drying her tears and looking at me intently, while a strange curiosity gleamed in her astonished eyes. "What is the matter?"

"It's impossible, but I love you, Nastenka! There it is! Now everything is told," I said with a wave of my hand. "Now you will see whether you can go on talking to me as you did just now, whether you can listen to what I am going to say to you." . . .

"Well, what then?" Nastenka interrupted me. "What of it? I knew you loved me long ago, only I always thought that you simply liked me very much. . . . Oh dear, oh dear!"

"At first it was simply liking, Nastenka, but now, now! I am just in the same position as you were when you went to him with your bundle. In a worse position than you, Nastenka, because he cared for no one else as you do."

"What are you saying to me! I don't understand you in the least. But

tell me, what's this for; I don't mean what for, but why are you . . . so
suddenly. . . . Oh dear, I am talking nonsense! But you . . ."

And Nastenka broke off in confusion. Her cheeks flamed; she
dropped her eyes.

"What's to be done, Nastenka, what am I to do? I am to blame. I
have abused your . . . But no, no, I am not to blame, Nastenka; I feel
that, I know that, because my heart tells me I am right, for I cannot hurt
you in any way, I cannot wound you! I was your friend, but I am still
your friend, I have betrayed no trust. Here my tears are falling,
Nastenka. Let them flow, let them flow—they don't hurt anybody.
They will dry, Nastenka."

"Sit down, sit down," she said, making me sit down on the seat. "Oh,
my God!"

"No, Nastenka, I won't sit down; I cannot stay here any longer, you cannot see me again; I will tell you everything and go away. I only want to say
that you would never have found out that I loved you. I should have kept
my secret. I would not have worried you at such a moment with my ego-
ism. No! But I could not resist it now; you spoke of it yourself, it is your
fault, your fault and not mine. You cannot drive me away from you. . . ."

"No, no, I don't drive you away, no!" said Nastenka, concealing her
confusion as best she could, poor child.

"You don't drive me away? No! But I meant to run from you myself.
I will go away, but first I will tell you all, for when you were crying here
I could not sit unmoved, when you wept, when you were in torture at
being—at being—I will speak of it, Nastenka—at being forsaken, at
your love being repulsed, I felt that in my heart there was so much love
for you, Nastenka, so much love! And it seemed so bitter that I could
not help you with my love, that my heart was breaking and I . . . I could
not be silent, I had to speak, Nastenka, I had to speak!"

"Yes, yes! tell me, talk to me," said Nastenka with an indescribable
gesture. "Perhaps you think it strange that I talk to you like this, but . . .
speak! I will tell you afterwards! I will tell you everything."

"You are sorry for me, Nastenka, you are simply sorry for me, my dear
little friend! What's done can't be mended. What is said cannot be taken
back. Isn't that so? Well, now you know. That's the starting-point. Very
well. Now it's all right, only listen. When you were sitting crying I thought
to myself (oh, let me tell you what I was thinking!), I thought, that (of
course it cannot be, Nastenka), I thought that you . . . I thought that you
somehow . . . quite apart from me, had ceased to love him. Then—I
thought that yesterday and the day before yesterday, Nastenka—then I
would—I certainly would—have succeeded in making you love me; you
know, you said yourself, Nastenka, that you almost loved me. Well, what
next? Well, that's nearly all I wanted to tell you; all that is left to say is how

it would be if you loved me, only that, nothing more! Listen, my friend—for any way you are my friend—I am, of course, a poor, humble man, of no great consequence; but that's not the point (I don't seem to be able to say what I mean, Nastenka, I am so confused), only I would love you, I would love you so, that even if you still loved him, even if you went on loving the man I don't know, you would never feel that my love was a burden to you. You would only feel every minute that at your side was beating a grateful, grateful heart, a warm heart ready for your sake. . . . Oh Nastenka, Nastenka! What have you done to me?"

"Don't cry; I don't want you to cry," said Nastenka, getting up quickly from the seat. "Come along, get up, come with me, don't cry, don't cry," she said, drying her tears with her handkerchief; "let us go now; maybe I will tell you something. . . . If he has forsaken me now, if he has forgotten me, though I still love him (I do not want to deceive you) . . . but listen, answer me. If I were to love you, for instance, that is, if I only. . . . Oh my friend, my friend! To think, to think how I wounded you, when I laughed at your love, when I praised you for not falling in love with me. Oh dear! How was it I did not foresee this, how was it I did not foresee this, how could I have been so stupid? But . . . Well, I have made up my mind, I will tell you."

"Look here, Nastenka, do you know what? I'll go away, that's what I'll do. I am simply tormenting you. Here you are remorseful for having laughed at me, and I won't have you . . . in addition to your sorrow. . . . Of course it is my fault, Nastenka, but good-bye!"

"Stay, listen to me: can you wait?"

"What for? How?"

"I love him; but I shall get over it, I must get over it, I cannot fail to get over it; I am getting over it, I feel that. . . . Who knows? Perhaps it will all end to-day, for I hate him, for he has been laughing at me, while you have been weeping here with me, for you have not repulsed me as he has, for you love me while he has never loved me, for in fact, I love you myself. . . . Yes, I love you! I love you as you love me; I have told you so before, you heard it yourself—I love you because you are better than he is, because you are nobler than he is, because, because he——"

The poor girl's emotion was so violent that she could not say more; she laid her head upon my shoulder, then upon my bosom, and wept bitterly. I comforted her, I persuaded her, but she could not stop crying; she kept pressing my hand, and saying between her sobs: "Wait, wait, it will be over in a minute! I want to tell you . . . you mustn't think that these tears—it's nothing, it's weakness, wait till it's over." . . . At last she left off crying, dried her eyes and we walked on again. I wanted to speak, but she still begged me to wait. We were silent. . . . At last she plucked up courage and began to speak.

"It's like this," she began in a weak and quivering voice, in which, however, there was a note that pierced my heart with a sweet pang; "don't think that I am so light and inconstant, don't think that I can forget and change so quickly. I have loved him for a whole year, and I swear by God that I have never, never, even in thought, been unfaithful to him. . . . He has despised me, he has been laughing at me—God forgive him! But he has insulted me and wounded my heart. I . . . I do not love him, for I can only love what is magnanimous, what understands me, what is generous; for I am like that myself and he is not worthy of me—well, that's enough of him. He has done better than if he had deceived my expectations later, and shown me later what he was. . . . Well, it's over! But who knows, my dear friend," she went on pressing my hand, "who knows, perhaps my whole love was a mistaken feeling, a delusion—perhaps it began in mischief, in nonsense, because I was kept so strictly by grandmother? Perhaps I ought to love another man, not him, a different man, who would have pity on me and . . . and . . . But don't let us say any more about that," Nastenka broke off, breathless with emotion, "I only wanted to tell you . . . I wanted to tell you that if, although I love him (no, did love him), if, in spite of this you still say. . . . If you feel that your love is so great that it may at last drive from my heart my old feeling—if you will have pity on me—if you do not want to leave me alone to my fate, without hope, without consolation—if you are ready to love me always as you do now—I swear to you that gratitude . . . that my love will be at last worthy of your love. . . . Will you take my hand?"

"Nastenka!" I cried breathless with sobs. "Nastenka, oh, Nastenka!"

"Enough, enough! Well, now it's quite enough," she said, hardly able to control herself. "Well, now all has been said, hasn't it? Hasn't it? You are happy—I am happy too. Not another word about it, wait; spare me. . . . talk of something else, for God's sake."

"Yes, Nastenka, yes! Enough about that, now I am happy. I—— Yes, Nastenka, yes, let us talk of other things, let us make haste and talk. Yes! I am ready."

And we did not know what to say: we laughed, we wept, we said thousands of things meaningless and incoherent; at one moment we walked along the pavement, then suddenly turned back and crossed the road; then we stopped and went back again to the embankment; we were like children.

"I am living alone now, Nastenka," I began, "but to-morrow! Of course you know, Nastenka, I am poor, I have only got twelve hundred rubles, but that doesn't matter."

"Of course not, and granny has her pension, so she will be no burden. We must take granny."

"Of course we must take granny. But there's Matrona."

"Yes, and we've got Fekla too!"

"Matrona is a good woman, but she has one fault: she has no imagination, Nastenka, absolutely none; but that doesn't matter."

"That's all right—they can live together; only you must move to us to-morrow."

"To you? How so? All right, I am ready."

"Yes, hire a room from us. We have a top floor, it's empty. We had an old lady lodging there, but she has gone away; and I know granny would like to have a young man. I said to her, 'Why a young man?' And she said, 'Oh, because I am old; only don't you fancy, Nastenka, that I want him as a husband for you.' So I guessed it was with that idea."

"Oh, Nastenka!"

And we both laughed.

"Come, that's enough, that's enough. But where do you live? I've forgotten."

"Over that way, near X bridge, Barannikov's Buildings."

"It's that big house?"

"Yes, that big house."

"Oh, I know, a nice house; only you know you had better give it up and come to us as soon as possible."

"To-morrow, Nastenka, to-morrow; I owe a little for my rent there, but that doesn't matter. I shall soon get my salary."

"And do you know I will perhaps give lessons; I will learn something myself and then give lessons."

"Capital! And I shall soon get a bonus."

"So by to-morrow you will be my lodger."

"And we will go to *The Barber of Seville*, for they are soon going to give it again."

"Yes, we'll go," said Nastenka, "but better see something else and not *The Barber of Seville*."

"Very well, something else. Of course that will be better, I did not think——"

As we talked like this we walked along in a sort of delirium, a sort of intoxication, as though we did not know what was happening to us. At one moment we stopped and talked for a long time at the same place; then we went on again, and goodness knows where we went; and again tears and again laughter. All of a sudden Nastenka would want to go home, and I would not dare to detain her but would want to see her to the house; we set off, and in a quarter of an hour found ourselves at the embankment by our seat. Then she would sigh, and tears would come into her eyes again; I would turn chill with dismay. . . . But she would press my hand and force me to walk, to talk, to chatter as before.

"It's time I was home at last; I think it must be very late," Nastenka said at last. "We must give over being childish."

"Yes, Nastenka, only I shan't sleep to-night; I am not going home."

"I don't think I shall sleep either; only see me home."

"I should think so!"

"Only this time we really must get to the house."

"We must, we must."

"Honor bright? For you know one must go home some time!"

"Honor bright," I answered laughing.

"Well, come along!"

"Come along! Look at the sky, Nastenka. Look! To-morrow it will be a lovely day; what a blue sky, what a moon! Look; that yellow cloud is covering it now, look, look! No, it has passed by. Look, look!"

But Nastenka did not look at the cloud; she stood mute as though turned to stone; a minute later she huddled timidly close up to me. Her hand trembled in my hand; I looked at her. She pressed still more closely to me.

At that moment a young man passed by us. He suddenly stopped, looked at us intently, and then again took a few steps on. My heart began throbbing.

"Who is it, Nastenka?" I said in an undertone.

"It's he," she answered in a whisper, huddling up to me, still more closely, still more tremulously. . . . I could hardly stand on my feet.

"Nastenka, Nastenka! It's you!" I heard a voice behind us and at the same moment the young man took several steps towards us.

My God, how she cried out! How she started! How she tore herself out of my arms and rushed to meet him! I stood and looked at them, utterly crushed. But she had hardly given him her hand, had hardly flung herself into his arms, when she turned to me again, was beside me in a flash, and before I knew where I was she threw both arms round my neck and gave me a warm, tender kiss. Then, without saying a word to me, she rushed back to him again, took his hand, and drew him after her.

I stood a long time looking after them. At last the two vanished from my sight.

Morning

My night ended with the morning. It was a wet day. The rain was falling and beating disconsolately upon my window pane; it was dark in the room and grey outside. My head ached and I was giddy; fever was stealing over my limbs.

"There's a letter for you, sir; the postman brought it," Matrona said stooping over me.

"A letter? From whom?" I cried, jumping up from my chair.

"I don't know, sir, better look—maybe it is written there whom it is from."

I broke the seal. It was from her!

> "Oh, forgive me, forgive me! I beg you on my knees to forgive me! I deceived you and myself. It was a dream, a mirage. . . . My heart aches for you to-day; forgive me, forgive me!
>
> "Don't blame me, for I have not changed to you in the least. I told you that I would love you, I love you now, I more than love you. Oh, my God! If only I could love you both at once! Oh, if only you were he!"

["Oh, if only he were you," echoed in my mind. I remembered your words, Nastenka!]

> "God knows what I would do for you now! I know that you are sad and dreary. I have wounded you, but you know when one loves a wrong is soon forgotten. And you love me.
>
> "Thank you, yes, thank you for that love! For it will live in my memory like a sweet dream which lingers long after awakening; for I shall remember for ever that instant when you opened your heart to me like a brother and so generously accepted the gift of my shattered heart to care for it, nurse it, and heal it . . . If you forgive me, the memory of you will be exalted by a feeling of everlasting gratitude which will never be effaced from my soul. . . . I will treasure that memory: I will be true to it, I will not betray it, I will not betray my heart: it is too constant. It returned so quickly yesterday to him to whom it has always belonged.
>
> "We shall meet, you will come to us, you will not leave us, you will be for ever a friend, a brother to me. And when you see me you will give me your hand. . . . yes? You will give it to me, you have forgiven me, haven't you? You love me *as before?*
>
> "Oh, love me, do not forsake me, because I love you so at this moment, because I am worthy of your love, because I will deserve it . . . my dear! Next week I am to be married to him. He has come back in love, he has never forgotten me. You will not be angry at my writing about him. But I want to come and see you with him; you will like him, won't you?
>
> "Forgive me, remember and love your
> "NASTENKA."

I read that letter over and over again for a long time; tears gushed to my eyes. At last it fell from my hands and I hid my face.

"Dearie! I say dearie——" Matrona began.

"What is it, Matrona?"

"I have taken all the cobwebs off the ceiling; you can have a wedding or give a party."

I looked at Matrona. She was still a hearty, *youngish* old woman, but I don't know why all at once I suddenly pictured her with lusterless eyes, a wrinkled face, bent, decrepit. . . . I don't know why I suddenly pictured my room grown old like Matrona. The walls and the floors looked discolored, everything seemed dingy; the spiders' webs were thicker than ever. I don't know why, but when I looked out of the window it seemed to me that the house opposite had grown old and dingy too, that the stucco on the columns was peeling off and crumbling, that the cornices were cracked and blackened, and that the walls, of a vivid deep yellow, were patchy.

Either the sunbeams suddenly peeping out from the clouds for a moment were hidden again behind a veil of rain, and everything had grown dingy again before my eyes; or perhaps the whole vista of my future flashed before me so sad and forbidding, and I saw myself just as I was now, fifteen years hence, older, in the same room, just as solitary, with the same Matrona grown no cleverer for those fifteen years.

But to imagine that I should bear you a grudge, Nastenka! That I should cast a dark cloud over your serene, untroubled happiness; that by my bitter reproaches I should cause distress to your heart, should poison it with secret remorse and should force it to throb with anguish at the moment of bliss; that I should crush a single one of those tender blossoms which you have twined in your dark tresses when you go with him to the altar . . . Oh never, never! May your sky be clear, may your sweet smile be bright and untroubled, and may you be blessed for that moment of blissful happiness which you gave to another, lonely and grateful heart!

My God, a whole moment of happiness! Is that too little for the whole of a man's life?

HOW MUCH LAND DOES A MAN NEED?

Leo Tolstoy

I

AN ELDER sister came to visit her younger sister in the country. The elder was married to a tradesman in town, the younger to a peasant in the village. As the sisters sat over their tea talking, the elder began to boast of the advantages of town life: saying how comfortably they lived there, how well they dressed, what fine clothes her children wore, what good things they ate and drank, and how she went to the theater, promenades, and entertainments.

The younger sister was piqued, and in turn disparaged the life of a tradesman, and stood up for that of a peasant.

"I would not change my way of life for yours," said she. "We may live roughly, but at least we are free from anxiety. You live in better style than we do, but though you often earn more than you need, you are very likely to lose all you have. You know the proverb, 'Loss and gain are brothers twain.' It often happens that people who are wealthy one day are begging their bread the next. Our way is safer. Though a peasant's life is not a fat one, it is a long one. We shall never grow rich, but we shall always have enough to eat."

The elder sister said sneeringly:

"Enough? Yes, if you like to share with the pigs and the calves! What do you know of elegance or manners! However much your goodman may slave, you will die as you are living—on a dung heap—and your children the same."

"Well, what of that?" replied the younger. "Of course our work is rough and coarse. But, on the other hand, it is sure, and we need not bow to anyone. But you, in your towns, are surrounded by temptations; to-day all may be right, but to-morrow the Evil One may tempt your husband with cards, wine, or women, and all will go to ruin. Don't such things happen often enough?"

Pahóm, the master of the house, was lying on the top of the stove and he listened to the women's chatter.

"It is perfectly true," thought he. "Busy as we are from childhood tilling mother earth, we peasants have no time to let any nonsense settle in our heads. Our only trouble is that we haven't land enough. If I had plenty of land, I shouldn't fear the Devil himself!"

The women finished their tea, chatted a while about dress, and then cleared away the tea-things and lay down to sleep.

But the Devil had been sitting behind the stove, and had heard all that was said. He was pleased that the peasant's wife had led her husband into boasting, and that he had said that if he had plenty of land he would not fear the Devil himself.

"All right," thought the Devil. "We will have a tussle. I'll give you land enough; and by means of that land I will get you into my power."

II

Close to the village there lived a lady, a small landowner who had an estate of about three hundred acres.[1] She had always lived on good terms with the peasants until she engaged as her steward an old soldier, who took to burdening the people with fines. However careful Pahom tried to be, it happened again and again that now a horse of his got among the lady's oats, now a cow strayed into her garden, now his calves found their way into her meadows—and he always had to pay a fine.

Pahom paid up, but grumbled and, going home in a temper, was rough with his family. All through that summer, Pahom had much trouble because of this steward, and he was even glad when winter came and the cattle had to be stabled. Though he grudged the fodder when they could no longer graze on the pasture-land, at least he was free from anxiety about them.

In the winter the news got about that the lady was going to sell her

---

[1] 120 desyatins. The desyatina is properly 2.7 acres; but in this story round numbers are used.

land and that the keeper of the inn on the high road was bargaining for it. When the peasants heard this they were very much alarmed.

"Well," thought they, "if the innkeeper gets the land, he will worry us with fines worse than the lady's steward. We all depend on that estate."

So the peasants went on behalf of their Commune, and asked the lady not to sell the land to the innkeeper, offering her a better price for it themselves. The lady agreed to let them have it. Then the peasants tried to arrange for the Commune to buy the whole estate, so that it might be held by them all in common. They met twice to discuss it, but could not settle the matter; the Evil One sowed discord among them and they could not agree. So they decided to buy the land individually, each according to his means; and the lady agreed to this plan as she had to the other.

Presently Pahom heard that a neighbor of his was buying fifty acres, and that the lady had consented to accept one half in cash and to wait a year for the other half. Pahom felt envious.

"Look at that," thought he, "the land is all being sold, and I shall get none of it." So he spoke to his wife.

"Other people are buying," said he, "and we must also buy twenty acres or so. Life is becoming impossible. That steward is simply crushing us with his fines."

So they put their heads together and considered how they could manage to buy it. They had one hundred rubles laid by. They sold a colt and one half of their bees, hired out one of their sons as a laborer and took his wages in advance; borrowed the rest from a brother-in-law, and so scraped together half the purchase money.

Having done this, Pahom chose out a farm of forty acres, some of it wooded, and went to the lady to bargain for it. They came to an agreement, and he shook hands with her upon it and paid her a deposit in advance. Then they went to town and signed the deeds; he paying half the price down, and undertaking to pay the remainder within two years.

So now Pahom had land of his own. He borrowed seed, and sowed it on the land he had bought. The harvest was a good one, and within a year he had managed to pay off his debts both to the lady and to his brother-in-law. So he became a landowner, ploughing and sowing his own land, making hay on his own land, cutting his own trees, and feeding his cattle on his own pasture. When he went out to plough his fields, or to look at his growing corn, or at his grass-meadows, his heart would fill with joy. The grass that grew and the flowers that bloomed there seemed to him unlike any that grew elsewhere. Formerly, when he had passed by that land, it had appeared the same as any other land, but now it seemed quite different.

III

So Pahom was well-contented, and everything would have been right if the neighboring peasants would only not have trespassed on his cornfields and meadows. He appealed to them most civilly, but they still went on: now the Communal herdsmen would let the village cows stray into his meadows, then horses from the night pasture would get among his corn. Pahom turned them out again and again, and forgave their owners, and for a long time he forbore to prosecute any one. But at last he lost patience and complained to the District Court. He knew it was the peasants' want of land, and no evil intent on their part, that caused the trouble, but he thought:

"I cannot go on overlooking it or they will destroy all I have. They must be taught a lesson."

So he had them up, gave them one lesson, and then another, and two or three of the peasants were fined. After a time Pahom's neighbors began to bear him a grudge for this, and would now and then let their cattle on to his land on purpose. One peasant even got into Pahom's wood at night and cut down five young lime trees for their bark. Pahom passing through the wood one day noticed something white. He came nearer and saw the stripped trunks lying on the ground, and close by stood the stumps where the trees had been. Pahom was furious.

"If he had only cut one here and there it would have been bad enough," thought Pahom, "but the rascal has actually cut down a whole clump. If I could only find out who did this, I would pay him out."

He racked his brain as to who it could be. Finally he decided: "It must be Simon—no one else could have done it." So he went to Simon's homestead to have a look round, but he found nothing, and only had an angry scene. However, he now felt more certain than ever that Simon had done it, and he lodged a complaint. Simon was summoned. The case was tried, and retried, and at the end of it all Simon was acquitted, there being no evidence against him. Pahom felt still more aggrieved, and let his anger loose upon the Elder and the Judges.

"You let thieves grease your palms," said he. "If you were honest folk yourselves you would not let a thief go free."

So Pahom quarreled with the Judges and with his neighbors. Threats to burn his building began to be uttered. So though Pahom had more land, his place in the Commune was much worse than before.

About this time a rumor got about that many people were moving to new parts.

"There's no need for me to leave my land," thought Pahom. "But some of the others might leave our village and then there would be more room for us. I would take over their land myself and make my estate a bit bigger. I could then live more at ease. As it is, I am still too cramped to be comfortable."

One day Pahom was sitting at home when a peasant, passing through the village, happened to call in. He was allowed to stay the night, and supper was given him. Pahom had a talk with this peasant and asked him where he came from. The stranger answered that he came from beyond the Volga, where he had been working. One word led to another, and the man went on to say that many people were settling in those parts. He told how some people from his village had settled there. They had joined the Commune, and had had twenty-five acres per man granted them. The land was so good, he said, that the rye sown on it grew as high as a horse, and so thick that five cuts of a sickle made a sheaf. One peasant, he said, had brought nothing with him but his bare hands, and now he had six horses and two cows of his own.

Pahom's heart kindled with desire. He thought:

"Why should I suffer in this narrow hole, if one can live so well elsewhere? I will sell my land and my homestead here, and with the money I will start afresh over there and get everything new. In this crowded place one is always having trouble. But I must first go and find out all about it myself."

Towards summer he got ready and started. He went down the Volga on a steamer to Samara, then walked another three hundred miles on foot, and at last reached the place. It was just as the stranger had said. The peasants had plenty of land: every man had twenty-five acres of Communal land given him for his use, and any one who had money could buy, besides, at a ruble an acre as much good freehold land as he wanted.

Having found out all he wished to know, Pahom returned home as autumn came on, and began selling off his belongings. He sold his land at a profit, sold his homestead and all his cattle, and withdrew from membership in the Commune. He only waited till the spring, and then started with his family for the new settlement.

IV

As soon as Pahom and his family reached their new abode, he applied for admission into the Commune of a large village. He stood treat to the Elders and obtained the necessary documents. Five shares of Communal land were given him for his own and his sons' use: that is to say—125 acres (not all together, but in different fields) besides the use of the Communal pasture. Pahom put up the buildings he needed, and bought cattle. Of the Communal land alone he had three times as much as at his former home, and the land was good corn-land. He was ten times better off than he had been. He had plenty of arable land and pasturage, and could keep as many head of cattle as he liked.

At first, in the bustle of building and settling down, Pahom was pleased with it all, but when he got used to it he began to think that even here he had not enough land. The first year, he sowed wheat on his share of the Communal land and had a good crop. He wanted to go on sowing wheat, but had not enough Communal land for the purpose, and what he had already used was not available; for in those parts wheat is only sown on virgin soil or on fallow land. It is sown for one or two years, and then the land lies fallow till it is again overgrown with prairie grass. There were many who wanted such land and there was not enough for all; so that people quarreled about it. Those who were better off wanted it for growing wheat, and those who were poor wanted it to let to dealers, so that they might raise money to pay their taxes. Pahom wanted to sow more wheat, so he rented land from a dealer for a year. He sowed much wheat and had a fine crop, but the land was too far from the village—the wheat had to be carted more than ten miles. After a time Pahom noticed that some peasant-dealers were living on separate farms and were growing wealthy; and he thought:

"If I were to buy some freehold land and have a homestead on it, it would be a different thing altogether. Then it would all be nice and compact."

The question of buying freehold land recurred to him again and again.

He went on in the same way for three years, renting land and sowing wheat. The seasons turned out well and the crops were good, so that he began to lay money by. He might have gone on living contentedly, but he grew tired of having to rent other people's land every year, and having to scramble for it. Wherever there was good land to be had, the peasants would rush for it and it was taken up at once, so that unless you were sharp about it you got none. It happened in the third year that he and a dealer together rented a piece of pasture-land from some peasants; and they had already ploughed it up, when there was some dispute and the peasants went to law about it, and things fell out so that the labor was all lost.

"If it were my own land," thought Pahom, "I should be independent, and there would not be all this unpleasantness."

So Pahom began looking out for land which he could buy; and he came across a peasant who had bought thirteen hundred acres, but having got into difficulties was willing to sell again cheap. Pahom bargained and haggled with him, and at last they settled the price at 1,500 rubles, part in cash and part to be paid later. They had all but clinched the matter when a passing dealer happened to stop at Pahom's one day to get a feed for his horses. He drank tea with Pahom and they had a talk. The dealer said that he was just returning from the land of the Bashkirs,[2] far away, where he had bought thirteen thousand acres of land, all for 1,000 rubles. Pahom questioned him further, and the tradesman said:

"All one need do is to make friends with the chiefs. I gave away about one hundred rubles' worth of silk robes and carpets, besides a case of tea, and I gave wine to those who would drink it; and I got the land for less than a penny an acre."[3] And he showed Pahom the title-deeds, saying:

"The land lies near a river, and the whole prairie is virgin soil."

Pahom plied him with questions, and the tradesman said:

"There is more land there than you could cover if you walked a year, and it all belongs to the Bashkirs. They are as simple as sheep, and land can be got almost for nothing."

"There now," thought Pahom, "with my one thousand rubles, why should I get only thirteen hundred acres, and saddle myself with a debt besides? If I take it out there, I can get more than ten times as much for the money."

V

Pahom inquired how to get to the place, and as soon as the tradesman had left him, he prepared to go there himself. He left his wife to look after the homestead, and started on his journey taking his man with him. They stopped at a town on their way and bought a case of tea, some wine, and other presents, as the tradesman had advised. On and on they went until they had gone more than three hundred miles, and on the seventh day they came to a place where the Bashkirs had pitched their tents. It was all just as the tradesman had said. The people lived on the steppes, by a river, in felt-covered tents.[4] They neither tilled the ground, nor ate bread. Their cattle and horses grazed in herds

---

[2] [Turkic people dwelling on both sides of the Urals.]
[3] Five kopeks for a desyatina.
[4] A kibitka is a movable dwelling, made up of detachable wooden frames, forming a round, and covered over with felt.

on the steppe. The colts were tethered behind the tents, and the mares were driven to them twice a day. The mares were milked, and from the milk kumiss[5] was made. It was the women who prepared kumiss, and they also made cheese. As far as the men were concerned, drinking kumiss and tea, eating mutton, and playing on their pipes, was all they cared about. They were all stout and merry, and all the summer long they never thought of doing any work. They were quite ignorant, and knew no Russian, but were good-natured enough.

As soon as they saw Pahom, they came out of their tents and gathered round their visitor. An interpreter was found, and Pahom told them he had come about some land. The Bashkirs seemed very glad; they took Pahom and led him into one of the best tents, where they made him sit on some down cushions placed on a carpet, while they sat round him. They gave him some tea and kumiss, and had a sheep killed, and gave him mutton to eat. Pahom took presents out of his cart and distributed them among the Bashkirs, and divided the tea amongst them. The Bashkirs were delighted. They talked a great deal among themselves, and then told the interpreter to translate.

"They wish to tell you," said the interpreter, "that they like you, and that it is our custom to do all we can to please a guest and to repay him for his gifts. You have given us presents, now tell us which of the things we possess please you best, that we may present them to you."

"What pleases me best here," answered Pahom, "is your land. Our land is crowded and the soil is exhausted; but you have plenty of land and it is good land. I never saw the like of it."

The interpreter translated. The Bashkirs talked among themselves for a while. Pahom could not understand what they were saying, but saw that they were much amused and that they shouted and laughed. Then they were silent and looked at Pahom while the interpreter said:

"They wish me to tell you that in return for your presents they will gladly give you as much land as you want. You have only to point it out with your hand and it is yours."

The Bashkirs talked again for a while and began to dispute. Pahom asked what they were disputing about, and the interpreter told him that some of them thought they ought to ask their Chief about the land and not act in his absence, while others thought there was no need to wait for his return.

---

[5] [A fermented drink.]

VI

While the Bashkirs were disputing, a man in a large fox-fur cap appeared on the scene. They all became silent and rose to their feet. The interpreter said, "This is our Chief himself."

Pahom immediately fetched the best dressing-gown and five pounds of tea, and offered these to the Chief. The Chief accepted them, and seated himself in the place of honor. The Bashkirs at once began telling him something. The Chief listened for a while, then made a sign with his head for them to be silent, and addressing himself to Pahom, said in Russian:

"Well, let it be so. Choose whatever piece of land you like; we have plenty of it."

"How can I take as much as I like?" thought Pahom. "I must get a deed to make it secure, or else they may say, 'It is yours,' and afterwards may take it away again."

"Thank you for your kind words," he said aloud. "You have much land, and I only want a little. But I should like to be sure which bit is mine. Could it not be measured and made over to me? Life and death are in God's hands. You good people give it to me, but your children might wish to take it away again."

"You are quite right," said the Chief. "We will make it over to you."

"I heard that a dealer had been here," continued Pahom, "and that you gave him a little land, too, and signed title-deeds to that effect. I should like to have it done in the same way."

The Chief understood.

"Yes," replied he, "that can be done quite easily. We have a scribe, and we will go to town with you and have the deed properly sealed."

"And what will be the price?" asked Pahom.

"Our price is always the same: one thousand rubles a day."

Pahom did not understand.

"A day? What measure is that? How many acres would that be?"

"We do not know how to reckon it out," said the Chief. "We sell it by the day. As much as you can go round on your feet in a day is yours, and the price is one thousand rubles a day."

Pahom was surprised.

"But in a day you can get round a large tract of land," he said.

The Chief laughed.

"It will all be yours!" said he. "But there is one condition: If you don't return on the same day to the spot whence you started, your money is lost."

"But how am I to mark the way that I have gone?"

"Why, we shall go to any spot you like, and stay there. You must start from that spot and make your round, taking a spade with you. Wherever you think necessary, make a mark. At every turning, dig a hole and pile up the turf; then afterwards we will go round with a plough from hole to hole. You may make as large a circuit as you please, but before the sun sets you must return to the place you started from. All the land you cover will be yours."

Pahom was delighted. It was decided to start early next morning. They talked a while, and after drinking some more kumiss and eating some more mutton, they had tea again, and then the night came on. They gave Pahom a feather-bed to sleep on, and the Bashkirs dispersed for the night, promising to assemble the next morning at daybreak and ride out before sunrise to the appointed spot.

VII

Pahom lay on the feather-bed, but could not sleep. He kept thinking about the land.

"What a large tract I will mark off!" thought he. "I can easily do thirty-five miles in a day. The days are long now, and within a circuit of thirty-five miles what a lot of land there will be! I will sell the poorer land, or let it to peasants, but I'll pick out the best and farm it. I will buy two oxteams, and hire two more laborers. About a hundred and fifty acres shall be plough-land, and I will pasture cattle on the rest."

Pahom lay awake all night, and dozed off only just before dawn. Hardly were his eyes closed when he had a dream. He thought he was lying in that same tent and heard somebody chuckling outside. He wondered who it could be, and rose and went out, and he saw the Bashkir Chief sitting in front of the tent holding his sides and rolling about with laughter. Going nearer to the Chief, Pahom asked: "What are you laughing at?" But he saw that it was no longer the Chief, but the dealer who had recently stopped at his house and had told him about the land. Just as Pahom was going to ask, "Have you been here long?" he saw that it was not the dealer, but the peasant who had come up from the Volga, long ago, to Pahom's old home. Then he saw that it was not the peasant either, but the Devil himself with hoofs and horns, sitting there and chuckling, and before him lay a man barefoot, prostrate on the ground, with only trousers and a shirt on. And Pahom dreamt that he looked more attentively to see what sort of a man it was that was lying there, and he saw that the man was dead, and that it was himself! He awoke horror-struck.

"What things one does dream," thought he.

Looking round he saw through the open door that the dawn was breaking.

"It's time to wake them up," thought he. "We ought to be starting."

He got up, roused his man (who was sleeping in his cart), bade him harness; and went to call the Bashkirs.

"It's time to go to the steppe to measure the land," he said.

The Bashkirs rose and assembled, and the Chief came too. Then they began drinking kumiss again, and offered Pahom some tea, but he would not wait.

"If we are to go, let us go. It is high time," said he.

VIII

The Bashkirs got ready and they all started: some mounted on horses, and some in carts. Pahom drove in his own small cart with his servant and took a spade with him. When they reached the steppe, the morning red was beginning to kindle. They ascended a hillock (called by the Bashkirs a *shikhan*) and dismounting from their carts and their horses, gathered in one spot. The Chief came up to Pahom and stretching out his arm towards the plain:

"See," said he, "all this, as far as your eye can reach, is ours. You may have any part of it you like."

Pahom's eyes glistened: it was all virgin soil, as flat as the palm of your hand, as black as the seed of a poppy, and in the hollows different kinds of grasses grew breast high.

The Chief took off his fox-fur cap, placed it on the ground and said:

"This will be the mark. Start from here, and return here again. All the land you go round shall be yours."

Pahom took out his money and put it on the cap. Then he took off his outer coat, remaining in his sleeveless under-coat. He unfastened his girdle and tied it tight below his stomach, put a little bag of bread into the breast of his coat, and tying a flask of water to his girdle, he drew up the tops of his boots, took the spade from his man, and stood ready to start. He considered for some moments which way he had better go—it was tempting everywhere.

"No matter," he concluded, "I will go towards the rising sun."

He turned his face to the east, stretched himself, and waited for the sun to appear above the rim.

"I must lose no time," he thought, "and it is easier walking while it is still cool."

The sun's rays had hardly flashed above the horizon, before Pahom, carrying the spade over his shoulder, went down into the steppe.

Pahom started walking neither slowly nor quickly. After having gone a thousand yards he stopped, dug a hole, and placed pieces of turf one on another to make it more visible. Then he went on; and now that he had walked off his stiffness he quickened his pace. After a while he dug another hole.

Pahom looked back. The hillock could be distinctly seen in the sunlight, with the people on it, and the glittering tires of the cart-wheels. At a rough guess Pahom concluded that he had walked three miles. It was growing warmer; he took off his under-coat, flung it across his shoulder, and went on again. It had grown quite warm now; he looked at the sun, it was time to think of breakfast.

"The first shift is done, but there are four in a day, and it is too soon yet to turn. But I will just take off my boots," said he to himself.

He sat down, took off his boots, stuck them into his girdle, and went on. It was easy walking now.

"I will go on for another three miles," thought he, "and then turn to the left. This spot is so fine, that it would be a pity to lose it. The further one goes, the better the land seems."

He went straight on for a while, and when he looked round, the hillock was scarcely visible and the people on it looked like black ants, and he could just see something glistening there in the sun.

"Ah," thought Pahom, "I have gone far enough in this direction, it is time to turn. Besides I am in a regular sweat, and very thirsty."

He stopped, dug a large hole, and heaped up pieces of turf. Next he untied his flask, had a drink, and then turned sharply to the left. He went on and on; the grass was high, and it was very hot.

Pahom began to grow tired: he looked at the sun and saw that it was noon.

"Well," he thought, "I must have a rest."

He sat down, and ate some bread and drank some water; but he did not lie down, thinking that if he did he might fall asleep. After sitting a little while, he went on again. At first he walked easily: the food had strengthened him; but it had become terribly hot and he felt sleepy, still he went on, thinking: "An hour to suffer, a life-time to live."

He went a long way in this direction also, and was about to turn to the left again, when he perceived a damp hollow: "It would be a pity to leave that out," he thought. "Flax would do well there." So he went on past the hollow, and dug a hole on the other side of it before he turned the corner. Pahom looked towards the hillock. The heat made the air hazy: it seemed to be quivering, and through the haze the people on the hillock could scarcely be seen.

"Ah!" thought Pahom, "I have made the sides too long; I must make this one shorter." And he went along the third side, stepping faster. He looked at the sun: it was nearly half-way to the horizon, and he had not yet done two miles of the third side of the square. He was still ten miles from the goal.

"No," he thought, "though it will make my land lop-sided, I must hurry back in a straight line now. I might go too far, and as it is I have a great deal of land."

So Pahom hurriedly dug a hole, and turned straight towards the hillock.

IX

Pahom went straight towards the hillock, but he now walked with difficulty. He was done up with the heat, his bare feet were cut and bruised, and his legs began to fail. He longed to rest, but it was impossible if he meant to get back before sunset. The sun waits for no man, and it was sinking lower and lower.

"Oh dear," he thought, "if only I have not blundered trying for too much! What if I am too late?"

He looked towards the hillock and at the sun. He was still far from his goal, and the sun was already near the rim.

Pahom walked on and on; it was very hard walking but he went quicker and quicker. He pressed on, but was still far from the place. He began running, threw away his coat, his boots, his flask, and his cap, and kept only the spade which he used as a support.

"What shall I do," he thought again, "I have grasped too much and ruined the whole affair. I can't get there before the sun sets."

And this fear made him still more breathless. Pahom went on running, his soaking shirt and trousers stuck to him and his mouth was parched. His breast was working like a blacksmith's bellows, his heart was beating like a hammer, and his legs were giving way as if they did not belong to him. Pahom was seized with terror lest he should die of the strain.

Though afraid of death, he could not stop. "After having run all that way they will call me a fool if I stop now," thought he. And he ran on and on, and drew near and heard the Bashkirs yelling and shouting to him, and their cries inflamed his heart still more. He gathered his last strength and ran on.

The sun was close to the rim, and cloaked in mist looked large, and red as blood. Now, yes now, it was about to set! The sun was quite low, but he was also quite near his aim. Pahom could already see the people on the hillock waving their arms to hurry him up. He could see the fox-fur cap on the ground and the money on it, and the Chief sitting on the ground holding his sides. And Pahom remembered his dream.

"There is plenty of land," thought he, "but will God let me live on it? I have lost my life, I have lost my life! I shall never reach that spot!"

Pahom looked at the sun, which had reached the earth: one side of it had already disappeared. With all his remaining strength he rushed on, bending his body forward so that his legs could hardly follow fast enough to keep him from falling. Just as he reached the hillock it suddenly grew dark. He looked up—the sun had already set! He gave a cry: "All my labor has been in vain," thought he, and was about to stop, but he heard the Bashkirs still shouting, and remembered that though to him, from below, the sun seemed to have set, they on the hillock could still see it. He took a long breath and ran up the hillock. It was still light there. He reached the top and saw the cap. Before it sat the Chief laughing and holding his sides. Again Pahom remembered his dream, and he uttered a cry: his legs gave way beneath him, he fell forward and reached the cap with his hands.

"Ah, that's a fine fellow!" exclaimed the Chief. "He has gained much land!"

Pahom's servant came running up and tried to raise him, but he saw that blood was flowing from his nostril. Pahom was dead!

The Bashkirs clicked their tongues to show their pity.

His servant picked up the spade and dug a grave long enough for Pahom to lie in, and buried him in it. Six feet from his head to his heels was all he needed.

THE CLOTHESMENDER

Nicholay Leskov

I

WHAT A silly custom it is to wish everyone new happiness in the new year, yet sometimes something of the sort does come true. On this subject allow me to tell you of a little episode having a perfectly Yuletide character.

During one of my stays in Moscow in times long gone by, I was held up longer than I had expected and got fed up with living in a hotel. The psalmodist of one of the Court churches heard me complain to a friend of mine, a priest of that church, about the discomforts I had to put up with and said:

"Why shouldn't the gentleman stay with my gossip, father? Just now he has a room free, facing the street."

"What gossip?" asks the priest.

"Vasily Konych."

"Ah, that's the *maître tailleur* Lepoutant!"

"Just so."

"Well, that is really a very good idea."

And the priest explained to me that he knew those people and that the room was excellent, while the psalmodist mentioned one additional advantage:

"If," he says, "something gets torn, or the bottoms of your trousers get frayed, everything will be put right, and invisible to the eye."

I thought all further inquiries superfluous and did not even go to see the room, but gave the psalmodist the key to my hotel room with a note of authorization on my card, and entrusted him with the settling of my hotel bill, collecting my things from there and taking them all to his gossip. Then I asked him to call for me where I was and conduct me to my new quarters.

II

The psalmodist managed to carry out my commission very quickly, and within a little more than an hour called for me at the priest's.

"Let's go," says he, "all your possessions are already unpacked and set out there, and we've unshuttered the windows for you and opened the door on the little balcony to the garden, and my gossip and I even had some tea on that same balcony. It's nice there," he goes on, "flowers all around, birds nesting in the gooseberries and a nightingale trilling away in a cage under the window. Better than in the country, because it's green, and yet all household affairs are in order, and if some button of yours gets loose or your trouser bottoms get frayed, it'll be fixed up in no time."

The psalmodist was a tidy fellow and a great dandy and therefore kept stressing this particular advantage of my new quarters.

The priest supported him, too.

"Yes," says he, "*tailleur* Lepoutant is an artist in that line the like of whom you won't find, whether in Moscow or in Petersburg."

"An expert," gravely chimed in the psalmodist as he helped me into my coat.

Who was this *Lepoutant*—I couldn't make out; moreover, it didn't concern me.

III

We set off on foot.

The psalmodist assured me that it wasn't worth taking a cab since it was supposedly just "two steps of *promenage*."

In actual fact, however, it turned out to be about half an hour's walk, but the psalmodist seemed to want a "promenage," perhaps not without an intention of displaying the cane with a purple silk tassel which he had in his hand.

The district where Lepoutant's house was located was beyond the Moscow river, toward the Yauza, somewhere on its banks. I no longer remember in what parish it was nor what the street was called. Strictly speaking, it wasn't a street but rather a sort of dead-end alley, something like an old churchyard. A little church stood there, and at a right angle to it, there was a close and in it six or seven little cottages, all very small, grey, wooden, one of them on a stone semi-basement. This one was more showy and bigger than all the others, and along the whole length of its façade was fixed a large iron signboard on which, in big and clear letters of gold on a black background, was inscribed:

> "*Maitr taileur Lepoutant.*"

Apparently, my new quarters were here, but it appeared strange to me: why did my landlord, whose name was Vasily Konych, call himself '*maitr taileur Lepoutant*'? When the priest called him that, I thought it was no more than a joke and did not attach any importance to it, but now, seeing the sign, I had to change my mind. Apparently this was in all earnest, and I therefore asked my guide:

"Is Vasily Konych a Russian or a Frenchman?"

The psalmodist even looked surprised and seemed not to have understood my question at once. But then he answered:

"What are you saying? Why should he be a Frenchman? He's as Russian as they come. Even the clothes he makes for sale are all Russian: *poddyovkas* and suchlike. But he is most famous all over Moscow for his mending: ever so much old clothing that passes through his hands is sold for new."

"But all the same," I persisted in my curiosity, "he must be of French descent?"

Again the psalmodist was surprised.

"No," said he, "why French? He is of the regular local breed, Russian that is, and godfather to my children, and after all we of the clerical calling, we all belong to the Orthodox Church. And why should you really imagine that he has any connection with the French nation?"

"The name on his signboard is French."

"Oh, that," says he, "that's nothing at all, that's sheer formality. And anyhow, the main sign is in French, but right here, by the gate, you see, there is another sign, in Russian, that's the correct one."

I look and indeed by the gate there is another sign on which are painted an *armyak* and a *poddyovka* and two black waistcoats with silver buttons shining like stars in darkness, and, underneath, the inscription:

> "Garments of Russian and Clerical Dress Made. Specializing in Nap, Turning Out and Repairs."

Under this second sign the name of the maker of "garments, turning out and repairs" was not indicated; there were only the two initials "V. L."

IV

Accommodation and landlord turned out indeed to be above all praise and description bestowed upon them, so that I immediately felt at home there and soon grew fond of my good host, Vasily Konych. Before long we took to joining one another for tea and conversing peaceably on diverse subjects. Thus, one day, sitting at tea on the little balcony, we began discoursing on the royal themes of the Koheleth about the vanity of all things under the sun and about our inherent propensity to succumb to all vanity. That is how we came upon the subject of Lepoutant.

I do not remember how it actually happened but it so came about that Vasily Konych signified his desire to tell me the odd story of how and why he had assumed a "French title."

This has some relation to social mores and to literature, even though it is written on a sign.

Konych began in a simple but very interesting fashion:

"My family name, sir," said he, "is not Lepoutant at all but something else, and it is *fate* itself which endowed me with a French title.

V

I am a native, true-blue Muscovite, of the poorest class. Our grandfather used to sell insoles outside the Rogozhsky Gate to venerable Old Believers. An excellent old man he was, saintlike—all greyish, like a faded little rabbit; but until his very death he lived by his own labor. He would buy a bit of felt, cut it into pieces for soles, tack them into pairs with a bit of thread and go "among the Christians," chanting affectionately: "Little insoles, little insoles, who needs little insoles?" Thus he would make the round of Moscow, and though he had but a pennysworth of merchandise, he made a living. My father was a tailor in the old style. He made old-fashioned coats with three pleats for the most faithful Old Believers, and he taught me his craft. But from childhood on I had a special gift for darning. My cutting is not stylish, but darning is my first love. I've got such a knack for it that I could darn over the most conspicuous place and it would be very hard to notice.

The old men said to my father:

"This youngster has a Godsent talent, and where there is talent there will be good fortune."

And so it came about; but to attain good fortune, you know, you have to show humble patience, and I was also sent two major trials: first, my parents died, leaving me when I was still young in years, and secondly, the place where I lived burned down the night before Christmas while

I was in church at matins, and with it all my equipment was burnt—
my iron, and my tailor's dummy, and the customers' clothes I had
taken in to darn. I found myself at the time in great distress, but it was
from that that I took my first step toward my good fortune.

VI

One customer whose fur-lined coat burned in my disaster came to me
and said: "My loss is great, and it's awkward to be left without a coat just
before the holidays, yet I can see that there's no claim to make against
you but rather you must be helped. If you're a sensible lad, I'll put you
on the right path provided you will eventually repay me."

I answered:

"If only God pleases, with the greatest of pleasure. I'll deem it my
first duty to repay my debt."

He told me to dress and took me to the hotel opposite the Governor-
General's house, to the assistant barman, and said to him in my presence: "Here," he says, "is that same apprentice who, I told you, could
be very useful in your line of trade."

Their trade consisted in pressing all kinds of clothing as it would
come wrinkled from the suitcases, and doing all kinds of necessary
repairs for the newly arrived guests.

The assistant barman gave me one piece to do by way of trial, saw
that I could do a good job, and told me to stay.

"Now," he says, "it is Christ's feast, and a great many gentlemen have
come and are drinking and making merry, and there are still the New
Year and the Twelfth Night to come, there will be still more goings-on,
so you stay here. . . ."

I answer:

"I am willing."

And the one who brought me says: "Well, mind you, get going—here
one can make a good pile. But just listen to him (that is, the assistant barman) as to a shepherd. God will provide a shelter and give you a shepherd."

I was given a little corner by the window in the back passage and I
got going. A great many were the gentlemen—I daresay I couldn't even
count them—whom I fixed up, but it would be a sin to complain, I got
myself pretty well fixed up, too, for there was an awful lot of work to do
and the pay was good. Ordinary men did not stop there, only the big
shots who liked the idea of staying in the same location as the
Governor-General, window to window with him.

The pay for patching and darning was particularly good when the
damage was unexpectedly discovered in clothes which had to be worn

right away. Sometimes I felt even ashamed—the hole was the size of a dime, but mend it invisibly—you get a gold piece.

Less than ten rubles was never paid for darning a tiny hole. But naturally real skill was demanded, so that the piece would be pieced in as two drops of water run together and you can't tell them apart.

Of the money that was paid each time, I was given one third; one third was taken by the assistant barman, and the other by the room servants who unpack the gentlemen's suitcases and brush their clothes. It is they really who matter most because it is they who crumple the things and scuff them, and pick a little hole, and that's why they got two parts and the rest went to me. But even so my share was more than enough, so that I moved from my corner in the passage and rented a quieter room in the same yard, and a year later the sister of the assistant barman came from her village and I married her. My present spouse, as you see her—that's her, she has reached old age with honor, and it was for her sake perhaps that God gave us all this. And as for marrying, it was simply like this: the assistant barman said: "She's an orphan and you must make her happy, and then through her you will have good luck." And she also said: "I bring luck," says she, "God will reward you on my behalf," and suddenly, as if because of this, an astonishing surprise really happened.

VII

Christmas came again, and again New Year's Eve. I am sitting in the evening in my room, darning something or other, and already thinking of stopping work and going to bed when one of the room servants runs in and said:

"Run quickly, a terrible Big Shot is staying in Room One. I reckon he's beaten everybody and whomever he strikes he tips ten rubles. Now he's demanding you."

"What does he want from me?" I ask.

"He started dressing to go to a ball," says he, "and at the very last moment noticed a hole burnt in his tailcoat in a conspicuous place. He gave a thrashing and three gold pieces to the man who had brushed it. Run as quickly as you can, he's so furious he looks like all the wild beasts put together."

I just shook my head, for I knew how they purposely ruined the clothes of their hotel guests, to derive profit from the mending; nevertheless I dressed and went to see the Big Shot who resembled all the wild beasts put together.

The pay certainly would be high because Room One in any hotel is considered to be a room for Big Shots, and none but luxury trade stops there; and in our hotel the price for Room One per day was what is now fifteen rubles and in those days was figured in paper money, amounting to fifty-two fifty, and whoever stopped there was known as the Big Shot.

The one to whom I was brought now was really fearful to look upon—of enormous stature, swarthy-faced and wild, and truly looking like all the wild beasts.

"You," he asks me in a fierce voice, "can you mend a hole so well that it can't be noticed?"

I answer:

"Depends on what kind of thing it is. If the stuff is napped then it can be done very well, but if it's shiny satin or silky *mauvais*-stuff, then I won't undertake it."

"*Mauvais* yourself," says he, "but some bastard, who was probably sitting behind me yesterday, burnt a hole in my tailcoat with his cigarette: Here, look it over and tell me."

I looked it over and said:

"This can be done well."

"And how long will it take?"

"Well, in an hour's time," I answer, "it will be ready."

"Do it," says he, "and if you do it well, you'll get a pot of money, and if you don't you'll get a knock on the head. Go and ask the lads here how I thrashed them, and you can be sure that I'll thrash you a hundred times worse."

VIII

I went off to do the repair; none too pleased about it, however, because you can't always be sure of how it will come off: a more loosely woven bit of cloth will blend in better, but the one with the harder finish, it is difficult to work in the nap inconspicuously.

I did a good job, however, but I didn't take it back myself, for I didn't at all like the way he treated me. It's tricky work, and no matter how well you may do it, if the customer is set on finding fault, it can easily lead to unpleasantness.

I sent my wife with the tailcoat to her brother and told her to hand it over to him and hurry home, and as soon as she came running back we put the door on the hook and went to bed.

In the morning I got up and began the day in my usual way. There I sit at my work waiting to see what sort of reward from the Big Shot gentleman they will come to announce to me—a pot of money or a knock on the head.

And suddenly, soon after one o'clock or so, the room servant comes and says:

"The gentleman from Room One demands you."

I say: "I won't go for anything."

"Why so?"

"Just so; I won't go, and that's flat. Rather let my work be wasted, but I have no wish to see him."

But the servant began to insist:

"You've no call to be scared: he is very pleased and saw the New Year in at the ball in your tailcoat and nobody noticed the hole in it. And now he has guests for lunch who have come to wish him a Happy New Year. They've had a few drinks under their belt, and, getting to talk of your work, they had a wager—which of them will find the hole, but not one of them did. Now, for sheer joy, using this as an excuse, they are toasting your Russian skill and wish to see you in person. Go quickly, this will bring you new luck in the new year."

My wife also insisted. "Do go," she said, "my heart tells me that this will be the beginning of our new fortune."

I obeyed them and went.

IX

I found about ten gentlemen in Room One and all of them had had a lot in the way of drinks, and as soon as I came in they handed me right off a glass of wine, and said: "Drink with us to your Russian skill through which you can bring glory to our nation."

And in their cups they said all sorts of things like that which the whole business was not worth at all.

Naturally, I thank them and bow, and drank two glasses of wine to Russia and to their health, but I could not, I said, drink any more of sweet wine, not being used to it, and, besides, unworthy of such company.

To which the terrible gentleman from Room One replies:

"You, my friend, are an ass and a fool and a brute—you don't know your own worth nor how much you deserve through your talent. You helped me on New Year's Eve to set straight the whole course of my life, because yesterday at the ball I disclosed my love to my beloved betrothed of high birth and received her consent, and when the fast is over I'll have a wedding."

"I wish you and your future spouse," I say, "to enter into wedlock with full happiness."

"Have a drink to it then."

I could not refuse and drank, but asked to be excused from any more.

"All right," says he, "only tell me where you live and what is your name, patronymic, and surname. I want to be your benefactor."

I reply: "My name is Vasily, son of Konon, and by surname Laputin. And my workshop is right here, next door, there is a small sign there, too, saying 'Laputin'."

There I stood telling all this and not noticing that at my words all the guests snorted and burst into gales of laughter, and the gentleman whose tailcoat I had repaired up and landed me one on the ear, and then one on the other ear, so that I could not keep on my feet. Then he shooed me to the door and threw me out over the threshold.

I couldn't understand a thing and made off as fast as my legs would carry me.

I come home and my wife asks me:

"Tell me quickly, Vasenka, how has my luck served you?"

I say: "Don't you, Mashenka, ask me for all particulars, but if this is only the first taste and there is more of the same to come, then I'd rather not live by your luck. He beat me up, my angel, he did, this gentleman."

My wife was worried. What, how and what for? But I naturally could not tell her because I didn't know myself.

But while we were having this conversation, suddenly there was clatter, noise, crashing, and in comes my benefactor from Room One.

We both got up from our places and stared at him while he, flushed with innermost feelings or from having had more wine, was holding in one hand the janitor's long-handled ax and in the other, chopped up into splinters, the little board on which I had my wretched little sign, indicating my poor craft and surname: OLD CLOTHES MENDED AND TURNED OUT. LAPUTIN.

X

In walked the gentleman with those splintered little boards and flung them straight away into the stove, and said to me: "Get dressed, you're coming with me in my carriage, I'll make your life's fortune. Or else I'll chop up you and your wife and everything you have, just as I did those boards."

I thought that rather than argue with such a rowdy I'd better get him out of the house as soon as possible lest he do some harm to my wife.

I dressed hastily, said to my wife, "Make the sign of the cross over me, Mashenka," and off we went. We drove to Bronnaya where the well-known real estate agent Prokhor Ivanych lived, and the gentleman asked him straight away:

"What houses are there for sale and in what location, priced from twenty-five to thirty thousand or a little more?" Naturally in paper money as was used then. "But I need such a house," he explains, "that can be taken over and moved into this very moment."

The agent took a ledger out of his cupboard, put on his spectacles, looked at one page and at another, and said:

"There is a house suitable to you in every way but you'll have to add a bit."

"I can do it."

"You will have to go up to thirty-five thousand."

"I am willing."

"Then," says he, "we'll complete the deal in an hour and it will be possible to move in tomorrow because in this house a deacon choked on a chicken bone at a christening and died, and that's why nobody lives there now."

And that's this very same little house where you and I are sitting now. There was some talk about the late deacon walking about at night and choking, but all this is absolute nonsense and nobody has seen him here in our time. My wife and I moved in here the very next day because the gentleman transferred the title-deed to this house to us as a gift; and the day after that he comes with some workmen, more than six or seven of them, and with them a ladder and this very signboard that makes me out a French tailor.

They came and nailed it on and went away, and the gentleman instructed me:

"I have just one order for you," he says, "don't you ever dare change this signboard, and always answer to this name." And all of a sudden he exclaimed:

"Lepoutant!"

I respond: "Yes, sir."

"Good lad," says he, "here is another 1000 rubles for spoons and saucers, but mind you, Lepoutant, follow my commandments with care and you'll be taken care of, but if anything . . . and if, God forbid, you start asserting your former name and I find out . . . then, to begin with, I'll give you a sound hiding, and secondly, according to the law 'the gift reverts to the giver.' But if you are loyal to my wish, then just say what else you want and you'll get everything from me."

I thank him and say that I have no wishes and can think of nothing except for one thing—if he can be so good to tell me what is the meaning of all this and why did I receive the house.

But that he wouldn't tell me.

"That," says he, "you don't need to know at all; just remember that from now on you are called Lepoutant and are thus named in my gift deed. Keep this name; you will gain thereby."

XI

We set up housekeeping in our own home, and everything went very well, and we believed that all this was due to my wife's good luck, because for a long time we could not come upon the true explanation from anybody; but one day two gentlemen hurried past our house, and suddenly stopped and came in.

The wife asks them:

"Can I help you?"

They replied:

"We need Monsieur Lepoutant himself."

I come out, and they exchanged glances, both of them laughed at the same time and began talking to me in French.

I apologize, saying I do not understand French.

"Have you hung out this sign for a long time?"

I told them how many years it was.

"Well, that's it. We remember you," they say, "and saw how you did a marvelous job mending a gentleman's tailcoat for a ball on New Year's Eve, and later suffered unpleasantness at his hands in our presence in the hotel."

"That's quite right," I say, "there was such an occasion, but I am grateful to that gentleman, and it is through him that my life began; but I don't know his name or surname, for all this has been kept from me."

They told me his name, and his surname, they added, was Laputin.

"What do you mean, Laputin?"

"Yes, of course," they say, "Laputin. Didn't you really know why he showered on you all those benefactions? So that his name should not appear on your signboard."

"Fancy that," I say, "and we couldn't understand it at all to this very day; we enjoyed the benefaction but in the dark as it were."

"However," continue my visitors, "it didn't do him any good. Yesterday he got involved in a new mixup."

And they told me a bit of news that made me feel very sorry for my erstwhile namesake.

XII

Laputin's wife, to whom he proposed in his darned tail-coat, was even more snobbish than her husband, and adored pomp. Neither of them was particularly high-born, it was just that their fathers had grown rich through government contracts; but they sought the acquaintance of the nobility only. And at that time our governor-general in Moscow was

Count Zakrevsky, who himself, they say, was also from the Polish gentry, and real gentlemen like Prince Sergey Mikhailovich Golitsyn did not rate him high, but all the rest were flattered to be received in his house. The spouse of the man who used to have the same name as mine also thirsted for this honor. Yet, goodness knows why, this eluded them for a long time, but at last Mr. Laputin found the opportunity of pleasing the Count, and the latter said to him:

"Come and see me, my dear fellow, I'll leave orders to have you admitted. Tell me, lest I forget, what is your name?"

The other answered that his name was Laputin.

"Laputin?" asked the Count. "Laputin . . . Wait a moment, wait a moment, if you please. Laputin . . . I seem to remember something. This is someone's name."

"That's right, your excellency," he says, "that's my name."

"Yes, yes, my dear fellow, it is indeed your name, but I remember something—there seems to have been another Laputin. Perhaps it's your father who was Laputin?"

The gentleman replied that indeed his father had been Laputin.

"That's why I remember it, I do. Laputin. It's quite possible that it was your father. I have a very good memory; come, Laputin, come tomorrow. I'll leave orders for you to be admitted, Laputin."

The latter was beside himself with joy and the very next day went there.

XIII

But Count Zakrevsky, even though he had boasted of his memory, nevertheless had slipped up on this occasion and said nothing about admitting Mr. Laputin.

The latter came flying.

"I'm So-and-So," says he, "and I wish to see the Count."

But the doorman would not let him in.

"There are no orders," he says, "to admit anyone."

The gentleman tries to argue with him this way and that. "I haven't come on my own," he says, "but at the invitation of the Count." The doorman remains adamant.

"I have no orders to admit anyone," he says. "And if you've come on business go to the office."

"I have not come on business," the gentleman says, "but through personal acquaintance. The Count must have given you my name—Laputin, and you must have mixed it up."

"The count didn't give me any name yesterday."

"That can't be. You've simply forgotten the name—Laputin."

"I never forget anything, and as for this name I am not likely to forget it because I am Laputin myself."

The gentleman simply boiled over.

"What do you mean," says he, "you're Laputin yourself! Who put you onto calling yourself that?!"

And the doorman replies:

"No one put me onto it, but that's our stock, and there is any number of Laputins in Moscow, only the others are of no account and I'm the only one who has come up in the world."

And at that moment, while they were arguing, the Count comes down the stairs and says:

"That's right, he is the one I had in mind, he is that very Laputin, and in my house he's a scoundrel, too. And you come some other time, I am busy now. Good day."

Well, naturally, how can you pay a call after this?

XIV

Maître tailleur Lepoutant told me this story with an air of compassionate modesty, adding by way of finale that the very next day, as he walked along the boulevard with his work, he happened to run into anecdotic Laputin himself, whom Vasily Konych had reason to regard as his benefactor.

"He is sitting on a bench," he said, "very sad. I wanted to slip past, but the moment he noticed me he said:

'Good morning, Monsieur Lepoutant. How's life treating you?'

'Very well, by the grace of God and with your help. And you, sir, how are you?'

'Couldn't be worse. A most wretched thing happened to me.'

'I have heard about it, sir,' I say, 'and was glad that at least you didn't lay hands on him.'

'I couldn't lay hands on him because he is not a man of free profession but the Count's knave; but what I want to know is: Who bribed him to play this filthy trick on me?'"

And Konych, in his simplicity, began to comfort the gentleman.

"Don't look, sir," he says, "for instigation. There really are many Laputins and among them some very honest folk, as for example my late grandfather; he used to sell insoles all over Moscow. . . ."

"And at those words he suddenly let me have it across the back with his stick. I ran away, and since then I haven't seen him, but have heard that he and his spouse went abroad, to France, and there he got ruined

and died, and she erected a monument to him and they say that the
inscription happened to be the same as that on my sign: *'Lepoutant.'*
Thus we became namesakes once more."

XV

Vasily Konych concluded and I asked him why he wouldn't now
change his sign and display his lawful Russian name.

"Well, sir," he says, "why should I stir up that which brought me new
fortune—this way I can harm the whole neighborhood."

"But what harm will it do the neighborhood?"

"Well, you see, my French sign, even though, I suppose, everybody
knows that it is mere formality, yet because of it our neighborhood has
got a different stamp, and the houses of all my neighbors have now a
different value from what they had before."

Thus Konych has remained a Frenchman for the good of the resi-
dents of his little side-lane beyond the Moscow River while his aristocratic namesake has rotted away at Père-Lachaise, under a pseudonym,
without doing any good.

THE SIGNAL
Vsevolod M. Garshin

SEMYON IVANOV was a track-walker. His hut was ten versts away from a railroad station in one direction and twelve versts away in the other. About four versts away there was a cotton mill that had opened the year before, and its tall chimney rose up darkly from behind the forest. The only dwellings around were the distant huts of the other track-walkers.

Semyon Ivanov's health had been completely shattered. Nine years before he had served right through the war as servant to an officer. The sun had roasted him, the cold frozen him, and hunger famished him on the forced marches of forty and fifty versts a day in the heat and the cold and the rain and the shine. The bullets had whizzed about him, but, thank God! none had struck him.

Semyon's regiment had once been on the firing line. For a whole week there had been skirmishing with the Turks, only a deep ravine separating the two hostile armies; and from morn till eve there had been a steady cross-fire. Thrice daily Semyon carried a steaming samovar and his officer's meals from the camp kitchen to the ravine. The bullets hummed about him and rattled viciously against the rocks. Semyon was terrified and cried sometimes, but still he kept right on. The officers were pleased with him, because he always had hot tea ready for them.

He returned from the campaign with limbs unbroken but crippled with rheumatism. He had experienced no little sorrow since then. He arrived home to find that his father, an old man, and his little four-year-old son had died. Semyon remained alone with his wife. They could not do much. It was difficult to plough with rheumatic arms and legs.

They could no longer stay in their village; so they started off to seek their fortune in new places. They stayed for a short time on the line, in Kherson and Donshchina, but nowhere found luck. Then the wife went out to service, and Semyon continued to travel about. Once he happened to ride on an engine, and at one of the stations the face of the station-master seemed familiar to him. Semyon looked at the station-master and the station-master looked at Semyon, and they recognized each other. He had been an officer in Semyon's regiment.

"You are Ivanov?" he said.

"Yes, your Excellency."

"How do you come to be here?"

Semyon told him all.

"Where are you off to?"

"I cannot tell you, sir."

"Idiot! What do you mean by 'cannot tell you?'"

"I mean what I say, your Excellency. There is nowhere for me to go to. I must hunt for work, sir."

The station-master looked at him, thought a bit, and said: "See here, friend, stay here a while at the station. You are married, I think. Where is your wife?"

"Yes, your Excellency, I am married. My wife is at Kursk, in service with a merchant."

"Well, write to your wife to come here. I will give you a free pass for her. There is a position as track-walker open. I will speak to the Chief on your behalf."

"I shall be very grateful to you, your Excellency," replied Semyon.

He stayed at the station, helped in the kitchen, cut firewood, kept the yard clean, and swept the platform. In a fortnight's time his wife arrived, and Semyon went on a hand-trolley to his hut. The hut was a new one and warm, with as much wood as he wanted. There was a little vegetable garden, the legacy of former track-walkers, and there was about half a desyatin of ploughed land on either side of the railway embankment. Semyon was rejoiced. He began to think of doing some farming, of purchasing a cow and a horse.

He was given all necessary stores — a green flag, a red flag, lanterns, a horn, hammer, screw-wrench for the nuts, a crow-bar, spade, broom, bolts, and nails; they gave him two books of regulations and a time-table of the trains. At first Semyon could not sleep at night, and learnt the whole time-table by heart. Two hours before a train was due he would go over his section, sit on the bench at his hut, and look and listen whether the rails were trembling or the rumble of the train could be heard. He even learned the regulations by heart, although he could only read by spelling out each word.

It was summer; the work was not heavy; there was no snow to clear away, and the trains on that line were infrequent. Semyon used to go over his verst twice a day, examine and screw up nuts here and there, keep the bed level, look at the water-pipes, and then go home to his own affairs. There was only one drawback—he always had to get the inspector's permission for the least little thing he wanted to do. Semyon and his wife were even beginning to be bored.

Two months passed, and Semyon commenced to make the acquaintance of his neighbors, the track-walkers on either side of him. One was a very old man, whom the authorities were always meaning to relieve. He scarcely moved out of his hut. His wife used to do all his work. The other track-walker, nearer the station, was a young man, thin, but muscular. He and Semyon met for the first time on the line midway between the huts. Semyon took off his hat and bowed. "Good health to you, neighbor," he said.

The neighbor glanced askance at him. "How do you do?" he replied; then turned around and made off.

Later the wives met. Semyon's wife passed the time of day with her neighbor, but neither did she say much.

On one occasion Semyon said to her: "Young woman, your husband is not very talkative."

The woman said nothing at first, then replied: "But what is there for him to talk about? Every one has his own business. Go your way, and God be with you."

However, after another month or so they became acquainted. Semyon would go with Vasily along the line, sit on the edge of a pipe, smoke, and talk of life. Vasily, for the most part, kept silent, but Semyon talked of his village, and of the campaign through which he had passed.

"I have had no little sorrow in my day," he would say; "and goodness knows I have not lived long. God has not given me happiness, but what He may give, so will it be. That's so, friend Vasily Stepanych."

Vasily Stepanych knocked the ashes out of his pipe against a rail, stood up, and said: "It is not luck which follows us in life, but human beings. There is no crueller beast on this earth than man. Wolf does not eat wolf, but man will readily devour man."

"Come, friend, don't say that; a wolf eats wolf."

"The words came into my mind and I said it. All the same, there is nothing crueller than man. If it were not for his wickedness and greed, it would be possible to live. Everybody tries to sting you to the quick, to bite and eat you up."

Semyon pondered a bit. "I don't know, brother," he said; "perhaps it is as you say, and perhaps it is God's will."

"And perhaps," said Vasily, "it is waste of time for me to talk to you. To put everything unpleasant on God, and sit and suffer, means, brother, being not a man but an animal. That's what I have to say." And he turned and went off without saying good-bye.

Semyon also got up. "Neighbor," he called, "why do you lose your temper?" But his neighbor did not look round, and kept on his way.

Semyon gazed after him until he was lost to sight in the cutting at the turn. He went home and said to his wife: "Arina, our neighbor is a wicked person, not a man."

However, they did not quarrel. They met again and discussed the same topics.

"Ah, friend, if it were not for men we should not be poking in these huts," said Vasily, on one occasion.

"And what if we are poking in these huts? It's not so bad. You can live in them."

"Live in them, indeed! Bah, you! . . . You have lived long and learned little, looked at much and seen little. What sort of life is there for a poor man in a hut here or there? The cannibals are devouring you. They are sucking up all your life-blood, and when you become old, they will throw you out just as they do husks to feed the pigs on. What pay do you get?"

"Not much, Vasily Stepanych—twelve rubles."

"And I, thirteen and a half rubles. Why? By the regulations the company should give us fifteen rubles a month with firing and lighting. Who decides that you should have twelve rubles, or I thirteen and a half? Ask yourself! And you say a man can live on that? You understand it is not a question of one and a half rubles or three rubles—even if they paid us each the whole fifteen rubles. I was at the station last month. The director passed through. I saw him. I had that honor. He had a separate coach. He came out and stood on the platform. . . . I shall not stay here long; I shall go somewhere, anywhere, follow my nose."

"But where will you go, Stepanych? Leave well enough alone. Here you have a house, warmth, a little piece of land. Your wife is a worker."

"Land! You should look at my piece of land. Not a twig on it— nothing. I planted some cabbages in the spring, just when the inspector came along. He said: 'What is this? Why have you not reported this? Why have you done this without permission? Dig them up, roots and all.' He was drunk. Another time he would not have said a word, but this time it struck him. Three rubles fine! . . ."

Vasily kept silent for a while, pulling at his pipe, then added quietly: "A little more and I should have done for him."

"You are hot-tempered."

"No, I am not hot-tempered, but I tell the truth and think. Yes, he will still get a bloody nose from me. I will complain to the Chief. We will see then!" And Vasily did complain to the Chief.

Once the Chief came to inspect the line. Three days later important personages were coming from St. Petersburg and would pass over the line. They were conducting an inquiry, so that previous to their journey it was necessary to put everything in order. Ballast was laid down, the bed was levelled, the sleepers carefully examined, spikes were driven in a bit, nuts screwed up, posts painted, and orders given for yellow sand to be sprinkled at the level crossings. The woman at the neighboring hut turned her old man out to weed. Semyon worked for a whole week. He put everything in order, mended his *caftan*, cleaned and polished his brass plate until it fairly shone. Vasily also worked hard. The Chief arrived on a trolley, four men working the handles and the levers making the six wheels hum. The trolley traveled at twenty versts an hour, but the wheels squeaked. It reached Semyon's hut, and he ran out and reported in soldierly fashion. All appeared to be in repair.

"Have you been here long?" inquired the Chief.

"Since the second of May, your Excellency."

"All right. Thank you. And who is at hut No. 164?"

The traffic inspector (he was traveling with the Chief on the trolley) replied: "Vasily Spiridov."

"Spiridov, Spiridov. . . . Ah! is he the man against whom you made a note last year?"

"He is."

"Well, we will see Vasily Spiridov. Go on!" The workmen laid to the handles, and the trolley got under way. Semyon watched it, and thought, "There will be trouble between them and my neighbor."

About two hours later he started on his round. He saw some one coming along the line from the cutting. Something white showed on his head. Semyon began to look more attentively. It was Vasily. He had a stick in his hand, a small bundle on his shoulder, and his cheek was bound up in a handkerchief.

"Where are you off to?" cried Semyon.

Vasily came quite close. He was very pale, white as chalk, and his eyes had a wild look. Almost choking, he muttered: "To town—to Moscow—to the head office."

"Head office? Ah, you are going to complain, I suppose. Give it up! Vasily Stepanych, forget it."

"No, mate, I will not forget. It is too late. See! He struck me in the face, drew blood. So long as I live I will not forget. I will not leave it like this!"

Semyon took his hand. "Give it up, Stepanych. I am giving you good advice. You will not better things. . . ."

"Better things! I know myself I shan't better things. You were right about Fate. It would be better for me not to do it, but one must stand up for the right."

"But tell me, how did it happen?"

"How? He examined everything, got down from the trolley, looked into the hut. I knew beforehand that he would be strict, and so I had put everything into proper order. He was just going when I made my complaint. He immediately cried out: 'Here is a Government inquiry coming, and you make a complaint about a vegetable garden. Here are privy councillors coming, and you annoy me with cabbages!' I lost patience and said something—not very much, but it offended him, and he struck me in the face. I stood still; I did nothing, just as if what he did was perfectly all right. They went off; I came to myself, washed my face, and left."

"And what about the hut?"

"My wife is staying there. She will look after things. Never mind about their roads."

Vasily got up and collected himself. "Good-bye, Ivanov. I do not know whether I shall get any one at the office to listen to me."

"Surely you are not going to walk?"

"At the station I will try to get on a freight train, and to-morrow I shall be in Moscow."

The neighbors bade each other farewell. Vasily was absent for some time. His wife worked for him night and day. She never slept, and wore herself out waiting for her husband. On the third day the commission arrived. An engine, luggage-van, and two first-class saloons; but Vasily was still away. Semyon saw his wife on the fourth day. Her face was swollen from crying and her eyes were red.

"Has your husband returned?" he asked. But the woman only made a gesture with her hands, and without saying a word went her way.

* * *

Semyon had learnt when still a lad to make flutes out of a kind of reed. He used to burn out the heart of the stalk, make holes where necessary, drill them, fix a mouthpiece at one end, and tune them so well that it was possible to play almost any air on them. He made a number of them in his spare time, and sent them by his friends amongst the freight brakemen to the bazaar in the town. He got two kopeks apiece for them. On the day following the visit of the commission he left his wife at home to meet the six o'clock train, and started off to the forest to cut some sticks. He went to the end of his section—at this point the line made a sharp turn—descended the embankment, and struck into the wood at the foot of the mountain. About half a verst away there was a big marsh, around which splendid reeds for his flutes grew. He cut a whole bundle of stalks and started back home. The sun was already dropping low, and in the dead stillness only the twittering of the birds was audible, and the crackle of the dead wood under his feet. As he walked along rapidly, he fancied he heard the clang of iron striking iron, and he redoubled his pace. There was no repair going on in his section. What did it mean? He emerged from the woods, the railway embankment stood high before him; on the top a man was squatting on the bed of the line busily engaged in something. Semyon commenced quietly to crawl up towards him. He thought it was some one after the nuts which secure the rails. He watched, and the man got up, holding a crow-bar in his hand. He had loosened a rail, so that it would move to one side. A mist swam before Semyon's eyes; he wanted to cry out, but could not. It was Vasily! Semyon scrambled up the bank, as Vasily with crow-bar and wrench slid headlong down the other side.

"Vasily Stepanych! My dear friend, come back! Give me the crow-bar. We will put the rail back; no one will know. Come back! Save your soul from sin!"

Vasily did not look back, but disappeared into the woods.

Semyon stood before the rail which had been torn up. He threw down his bundle of sticks. A train was due; not a freight, but a passenger-train. And he had nothing with which to stop it, no flag. He could not replace the rail and could not drive in the spikes with his bare hands. It was necessary to run, absolutely necessary to run to the hut for some tools. "God help me!" he murmured.

Semyon started running towards his hut. He was out of breath, but still ran, falling every now and then. He had cleared the forest; he was only a few hundred feet from his hut, not more, when he heard the distant hooter of the factory sound—six o'clock! In two minutes' time No. 7 train was due. "Oh, Lord! Have pity on innocent souls!" In his mind Semyon saw the engine strike against the loosened rail with its left wheel, shiver, careen, tear up and splinter the sleepers—and just there, there was a curve and the embankment seventy feet high, down which the engine would topple—and the third-class carriages would be packed . . . little children. . . . All sitting in the train now, never dreaming of danger. "Oh, Lord! Tell me what to do! . . . No, it is impossible to run to the hut and get back in time."

Semyon did not run on to the hut, but turned back and ran faster than before. He was running almost mechanically, blindly; he did not know himself what was to happen. He ran as far as the rail which had been pulled up; his sticks were lying in a heap. He bent down, seized one without knowing why, and ran on farther. It seemed to him the train was already coming. He heard the distant whistle; he heard the quiet, even tremor of the rails; but his strength was exhausted, he could run no farther, and came to a halt about six hundred feet from the awful spot. Then an idea came into his head, literally like a ray of light. Pulling off his cap, he took out of it a cotton scarf, drew his knife out of the upper part of his boot, and crossed himself, muttering, "God bless me!"

He buried the knife in his left arm above the elbow; the blood spurted out, flowing in a hot stream. In this he soaked his scarf, smoothed it out, tied it to the stick and hung out his red flag.

He stood waving his flag. The train was already in sight. The driver would not see him—would come close up, and a heavy train cannot be pulled up in six hundred feet.

And the blood kept on flowing. Semyon pressed the sides of the wound together so as to close it, but the blood did not diminish. Evidently he had cut his arm very deep. His head commenced to swim, black spots began to dance before his eyes, and then it became dark. There was a ringing in his ears. He could not see the train or hear the noise. Only one thought possessed him. "I shall not be able to keep standing up. I shall fall and drop the flag; the train will pass over me. Help me, oh Lord!"

All turned black before him, his mind became a blank, and he dropped the flag; but the blood-stained banner did not fall to the ground. A hand seized it and held it high to meet the approaching train. The engineer saw it, shut the regulator, and reversed steam. The train came to a standstill.

People jumped out of the carriages and collected in a crowd. They saw a man lying senseless on the footway, drenched in blood, and another man standing beside him with a blood-stained rag on a stick.

Vasily looked around at all. Then, lowering his head, he said: "Bind me. I tore up a rail!"

THE LADY WITH THE TOY DOG

Anton Chekhov

I

IT WAS reported that a new face had been seen on the quay; a lady with a little dog. Dimitri Dimitrich Gomov, who had been a fortnight at Yalta and had got used to it, had begun to show an interest in new faces. As he sat in the pavilion at Verné's he saw a young lady, blond and fairly tall, and wearing a broad-brimmed hat, pass along the quay. After her ran a white Pomeranian.

Later he saw her in the park and in the square several times a day. She walked by herself, always in the same broad-brimmed hat, and with this white dog. Nobody knew who she was, and she was spoken of as the lady with the toy dog.

"If," thought Gomov, "if she is here without a husband or a friend, it would be as well to make her acquaintance."

He was not yet forty, but he had a daughter of twelve and two boys at school. He had married young, in his second year at the University, and now his wife seemed half as old again as himself. She was a tall woman, with dark eyebrows, erect, grave, stolid, and she thought herself an intellectual woman. She read a great deal, called her husband not Dimitri, but Demitri, and in his private mind he thought her short-witted, narrow-minded, and ungracious. He was afraid of her and disliked being at home. He had begun to betray her with other women long ago, betrayed her frequently, and probably for that reason nearly always spoke ill of women, and when they were discussed in his presence he would maintain that they were an inferior race.

It seemed to him that his experience was bitter enough to give him the right to call them any name he liked, but he could not live a couple of days without the "inferior race." With men he was bored and ill at ease, cold and unable to talk, but when he was with women, he felt easy and knew what to talk about, and how to behave, and even when he was silent with them he felt quite comfortable. In his appearance as in his character, indeed in his whole nature, there was something attractive, indefinable, which drew women to him and charmed them; he knew it, and he, too, was drawn by some mysterious power to them.

His frequent, and, indeed, bitter experiences had taught him long ago that every affair of that kind, at first a divine diversion, a delicious smooth adventure, is in the end a source of worry for a decent man, especially for men like those at Moscow who are slow to move, irresolute, domesticated, for it becomes at last an acute and extraordinarily complicated problem and a nuisance. But whenever he met and was interested in a new woman, then his experience would slip away from his memory, and he would long to live, and everything would seem so simple and amusing.

And it so happened that one evening he dined in the gardens, and the lady in the broad-brimmed hat came up at a leisurely pace and sat at the next table. Her expression, her gait, her dress, her coiffure told him that she belonged to society, that she was married, that she was paying her first visit to Yalta, that she was alone, and that she was bored. . . . There is a great deal of untruth in the gossip about the immorality of the place. He scorned such tales, knowing that they were for the most part concocted by people who would be only too ready to sin if they had the chance, but when the lady sat down at the next table, only a yard or two away from him, his thoughts were filled with tales of easy conquests, of trips to the mountains; and he was suddenly possessed by the alluring idea of a quick transitory liaison, a moment's affair with an unknown woman whom he knew not even by name.

He beckoned to the little dog, and when it came up to him, wagged his finger at it. The dog began to growl. Gomov again wagged his finger.

The lady glanced at him and at once cast her eyes down.

"He won't bite," she said and blushed.

"May I give him a bone?"—and when she nodded emphatically, he asked affably: "Have you been in Yalta long?"

"About five days."

"And I am just dragging through my second week."

They were silent for a while.

"Time goes quickly," she said, "and it is amazingly boring here."

"It is the usual thing to say that it is boring here. People live quite happily in dull holes like Bieliev or Zhidra, but as soon as they come here they say: 'How boring it is! The very dregs of dulness!' One would think they came from Spain."

She smiled. Then both went on eating in silence as though they did not know each other; but after dinner they went off together—and then began an easy, playful conversation as though they were perfectly happy, and it was all one to them where they went or what they talked of. They walked and talked of how the sea was strangely luminous; the water lilac, so soft and warm, and athwart it the moon cast a golden streak. They said how stifling it was after the hot day. Gomov told her how he came from Moscow and was a philologist by education, but in a bank by profession; and how he had once wanted to sing in opera, but gave it up; and how he had two houses in Moscow. . . . And from her he learned that she came from Petersburg, was born there, but married at S. where she had been living for the last two years; that she would stay another month at Yalta, and perhaps her husband would come for her, because, he too, needed a rest. She could not tell him what her husband was—Provincial Administration or Zemstvo Council—and she seemed to think it funny. And Gomov found out that her name was Anna Sergueyevna.

In his room at night, he thought of her and how they would meet next day. They must do so. As he was going to sleep, it struck him that she could only lately have left school, and had been at her lessons even as his daughter was then; he remembered how bashful and gauche she was when she laughed and talked with a stranger—it must be, he thought, the first time she had been alone, and in such a place with men walking after her and looking at her and talking to her, all with the same secret purpose which she could not but guess. He thought of her slender white neck and her pretty, grey eyes.

"There is something touching about her," he thought as he began to fall asleep.

II

A week passed. It was a blazing day. Indoors it was stifling, and in the streets the dust whirled along. All day long he was plagued with thirst and he came into the pavilion every few minutes and offered Anna Sergueyevna an iced drink or an ice. It was impossibly hot.

In the evening, when the air was fresher, they walked to the jetty to see the steamer come in. There was quite a crowd all gathered to meet somebody, for they carried bouquets. And among them were clearly marked the peculiarities of Yalta: the elderly ladies were youngly dressed and there were many generals.

The sea was rough and the steamer was late, and before it turned into the jetty it had to do a great deal of maneuvering. Anna Sergueyevna looked through her lorgnette at the steamer and the passengers as though she were looking for friends, and when she turned to Gomov, her eyes shone. She talked much and her questions were abrupt, and she forgot what she had said; and then she lost her lorgnette in the crowd.

The well-dressed people went away, the wind dropped, and Gomov and Anna Sergueyevna stood as though they were waiting for somebody to come from the steamer. Anna Sergueyevna was silent. She smelled her flowers and did not look at Gomov.

"The weather has got pleasanter toward evening," he said. "Where shall we go now? Shall we take a carriage?"

She did not answer.

He fixed his eyes on her and suddenly embraced her and kissed her lips, and he was kindled with the perfume and the moisture of the flowers; at once he started and looked round; had not some one seen?

"Let us go to your——" he murmured.

And they walked quickly away.

Her room was stifling, and smelled of scents which she had bought at the Japanese shop. Gomov looked at her and thought: "What strange chances there are in life!" From the past there came the memory of earlier good-natured women, gay in their love, grateful to him for their happiness, short though it might be; and of others—like his wife—who loved without sincerity, and talked overmuch and affectedly, hysterically, as though they were protesting that it was not love, nor passion, but something more important; and of the few beautiful cold women, into whose eyes there would flash suddenly a fierce expression, a stubborn desire to take, to snatch from life more than it can give; they were no longer in their first youth, they were capricious, unstable, domineering, imprudent, and when Gomov became cold toward them then their beauty roused him to hatred, and the lace on their lingerie reminded him of the scales of fish.

But here there was the shyness and awkwardness of inexperienced youth, a feeling of constraint; an impression of perplexity and wonder, as though some one had suddenly knocked at the door. Anna Sergueyevna, "the lady with the toy dog," took what had happened somehow seriously, with a particular gravity, as though thinking that this was her downfall and very strange and improper. Her features seemed to sink and wither, and on either side of her face her long hair hung mournfully down; she sat crestfallen and musing, exactly like a woman taken in sin in some old picture.

"It is not right," she said. "You are the first to lose respect for me."

There was a melon on the table. Gomov cut a slice and began to eat it slowly. At least half an hour passed in silence.

Anna Sergueyevna was very touching; she irradiated the purity of a simple, devout, inexperienced woman; the solitary candle on the table hardly lighted her face, but it showed her very wretched.

"Why should I cease to respect you?" asked Gomov. "You don't know what you are saying."

"God forgive me!" she said, and her eyes filled with tears. "It is horrible."

"You seem to want to justify yourself."

"How can I justify myself? I am a wicked, low woman and I despise myself. I have no thought of justifying myself. It is not my husband that I have deceived, but myself. And not only now but for a long time past. My husband may be a good honest man, but he is a lackey. I do not know what work he does, but I do know that he is a lackey in his soul. I was twenty when I married him. I was overcome by curiosity. I longed for something. 'Surely,' I said to myself, 'there is another kind of life.' I longed to live! To live, and to live. . . . Curiosity burned me up. . . . You do not understand it, but I swear by God, I could no longer control myself. Something strange was going on in me. I could not hold myself in. I told my husband that I was ill and came here. . . . And here I have been walking about dizzily, like a lunatic. . . . And now I have become a low, filthy woman whom everybody may despise."

Gomov was already bored; her simple words irritated him with their unexpected and inappropriate repentance; but for the tears in her eyes he might have thought her to be joking or playing a part.

"I do not understand," he said quietly. "What do you want?"

She hid her face in his bosom and pressed close to him.

"Believe, believe me, I implore you," she said. "I love a pure, honest life, and sin is revolting to me. I don't know myself what I am doing. Simple people say: 'The devil entrapped me,' and I can say of myself: 'The Evil One tempted me.'"

"Don't, don't," he murmured.

He looked into her her staring, frightened eyes, kissed her, spoke quietly and tenderly, and gradually quieted her and she was happy again, and they both began to laugh.

Later, when they went out, there was not a soul on the quay; the town with its cypresses looked like a city of the dead, but the sea still roared and broke against the shore; a boat swung on the waves; and in it sleepily twinkled the light of a lantern.

They found a cab and drove out to the Oreanda.

"Just now in the hall," said Gomov, "I discovered your name written on the board—von Didenitz. Is your husband a German?"

"No. His grandfather, I believe, was a German, but he himself is an Orthodox Russian."

At Oreanda they sat on a bench, not far from the church, looked down at the sea and were silent. Yalta was hardly visible through the morning mist. The tops of the hills were shrouded in motionless white clouds. The leaves of the trees never stirred, the cicadas trilled, and the monotonous dull sound of the sea, coming up from below, spoke of the rest, the eternal sleep awaiting us. So the sea roared when there was neither Yalta nor Oreanda, and so it roars and will roar, dully, indifferently when we shall be no more. And in this continual indifference to the life and death of each of us lives pent up the pledge of our eternal salvation, of the uninterrupted movement of life on earth and its unceasing perfection. Sitting side by side with a young woman, who in the dawn seemed so beautiful, Gomov, appeased and enchanted by the sight of the fairy scene, the sea, the mountains, the clouds, the wide sky, thought how at bottom, if it were thoroughly explored, everything on earth was beautiful, everything, except what we ourselves think and do when we forget the higher purposes of life and our own human dignity.

A man came up—a coast-guard—gave a look at them, then went away. He, too, seemed mysterious and enchanted. A steamer came over from Feodossia, by the light of the morning star, its own lights already put out.

"There is dew on the grass," said Anna Sergueyevna after a silence.

"Yes. It is time to go home."

They returned to the town.

Then every afternoon they met on the quay, and lunched together, dined, walked, enjoyed the sea. She complained that she slept badly, that her heart beat alarmingly. She would ask the same question over and over again, and was troubled now by jealousy, now by fear that he did not sufficiently respect her. And often in the square or the gardens, when there was no one near, he would draw her close and kiss her passionately. Their complete idleness, these kisses in the full daylight, given timidly and fearfully lest any one should see, the heat, the smell of the sea and the continual brilliant parade of leisured, well-dressed, well-fed people almost regenerated him. He would tell Anna Sergueyevna how delightful she was, how tempting. He was impatiently passionate, never left her side, and she would often brood, and even asked him to confess that he did not respect her, did not love her at all, and only saw in her a loose woman. Almost every evening, rather late, they would drive out of the town, to Oreanda, or to the waterfall; and these drives were always delightful, and the impressions won during them were always beautiful and sublime.

They expected her husband to come. But he sent a letter in which he said that his eyes were bad and implored his wife to come home. Anna Sergueyevna began to worry.

"It is a good thing I am going away," she would say to Gomov. "It is fate."

She went in a carriage and he accompanied her. They drove for a whole day. When she took her seat in the car of an express-train and when the second bell sounded, she said:

"Let me have another look at you. . . . Just one more look. Just as you are."

She did not cry, but was sad and low-spirited, and her lips trembled.

"I will think of you—often," she said. "Good-bye. Good-bye. Don't think ill of me. We part for ever. We must, because we ought not to have met at all. Now, good-bye."

The train moved off rapidly. Its lights disappeared, and in a minute or two the sound of it was lost, as though everything were agreed to put an end to this sweet, oblivious madness. Left alone on the platform, looking into the darkness, Gomov heard the trilling of the grasshoppers and the humming of the telegraph-wires, and felt as though he had just woke up. And he thought that it had been one more adventure, one more affair, and it also was finished and had left only a memory. He was moved, sad, and filled with a faint remorse; surely the young woman, whom he would never see again, had not been happy with him; he had been kind to her, friendly, and sincere, but still in his attitude toward her, in his tone and caresses, there had always been a thin shadow of raillery, the rather rough arrogance of the successful male aggravated by the fact that he was twice as old as she. And all the time she had called him kind, remarkable, noble, so that he was never really himself to her, and had involuntarily deceived her. . . .

Here at the station, the smell of autumn was in the air, and the evening was cool.

"It is time for me to go North," thought Gomov, as he left the platform. "It is time."

III

At home in Moscow, it was already like winter; the stoves were heated, and in the mornings, when the children were getting ready to go to school, and had their tea, it was dark and their nurse lighted the lamp for a short while. The frost had already begun. When the first snow falls, the first day of driving in sledges, it is good to see the white earth, the white roofs; one breathes easily, eagerly, and then one remembers the days of youth. The old lime-trees and birches, white with hoarfrost, have a kindly expression; they are nearer to the heart than cypresses and palm-trees, and with the dear familiar trees there is no need to think of mountains and the sea.

Gomov was a native of Moscow. He returned to Moscow on a fine frosty day, and when he donned his fur coat and warm gloves, and took a stroll through Petrovka, and when on Saturday evening he heard the church-bells ringing, then his recent travels and the places he had visited lost all their charms. Little by little he sank back into Moscow life, read eagerly three newspapers a day, and said that he did not read Moscow papers as a matter of principle. He was drawn into a round of restaurants, clubs, dinner-parties, parties, and he was flattered to have his house frequented by famous lawyers and actors, and to play cards with a professor at the University club. He could eat a whole plateful of hot *sielianka*.[1]

So a month would pass, and Anna Sergueyevna, he thought, would be lost in the mists of memory and only rarely would she visit his dreams with her touching smile, just as other women had done. But more than a month passed, full winter came, and in his memory everything was clear, as though he had parted from Anna Sergueyevna only yesterday. And his memory was lit by a light that grew ever stronger. No matter how, through the voices of his children saying their lessons, penetrating to the evening stillness of his study, through hearing a song, or the music in a restaurant, or the snow-storm howling in the chimney, suddenly the whole thing would come to life again in his memory: the meeting on the jetty, the early morning with the mists on the mountains, the steamer from Feodossia and their kisses. He would pace up and down his room and remember it all and smile, and then his memories would drift into dreams, and the past was confused in his imagination with the future. He did not dream at night of Anna Sergueyevna, but she followed him everywhere, like a shadow, watching him. As he shut his eyes, he could see her, vividly, and she seemed handsomer, tenderer, younger than in reality; and he seemed to himself better than he had been at Yalta. In the evenings she would look at him from the bookcase, from the fireplace, from the corner; he could hear her breathing and the soft rustle of her dress. In the street he would gaze at women's faces to see if there were not one like her. . . .

He was filled with a great longing to share his memories with some one. But at home it was impossible to speak of his love, and away from home—there was no one. Impossible to talk of her to the other people in the house and the men at the bank. And talk of what? Had he loved

---

[1] [Thick soup, or steamed cabbage, with meat or fish.]

then? Was there anything fine, romantic, or elevating or even interesting in his relations with Anna Sergueyevna? And he would speak vaguely of love, of women, and nobody guessed what was the matter, and only his wife would raise her dark eyebrows and say:

"Demitri, the rôle of coxcomb does not suit you at all."

One night, as he was coming out of the club with his partner, an official, he could not help saying:

"If only I could tell what a fascinating woman I met at Yalta."

The official seated himself in his sledge and drove off, but suddenly called:

"Dimitri Dimitrich!"

"Yes."

"You were right. The sturgeon was tainted."

These banal words suddenly roused Gomov's indignation. They seemed to him degrading and impure. What barbarous customs and people!

What preposterous nights, what dull, empty days! Furious card-playing, gourmandizing, drinking, endless conversations about the same things, futile activities and conversations taking up the best part of the day and all the best of man's forces, leaving only a stunted, wingless life, just rubbish; and to go away and escape was impossible—one might as well be in a lunatic asylum or in prison with hard labor.

Gomov did not sleep that night, but lay burning with indignation, and then all next day he had a headache. And the following night he slept badly, sitting up in bed and thinking, or pacing from corner to corner of his room. His children bored him, the bank bored him, and he had no desire to go out or speak to any one.

In December when the holidays came he prepared to go on a journey and told his wife he was going to Petersburg to present a petition for a young friend of his—and went to S. Why? He did not know. He wanted to see Anna Sergueyevna, to talk to her, and if possible to arrange an assignation.

He arrived at S. in the morning and occupied the best room in the hotel, where the whole floor was covered with a grey canvas, and on the table there stood an inkstand grey with dust, adorned with a horseman on a headless horse holding a net in his raised hand. The porter gave him the necessary information: von Didenitz; Old Goncharna Street, his own house—not far from the hotel; lives well, has his own horses, every one knows him.

Gomov walked slowly to Old Goncharna Street and found the house. In front of it was a long, grey fence spiked with nails.

"No getting over a fence like that," thought Gomov, glancing from the windows to the fence.

He thought: "To-day is a holiday and her husband is probably at home. Besides it would be tactless to call and upset her." If he sent a note then it might fall into her husband's hands and spoil everything. It would be better to wait for an opportunity. And he kept on walking up and down the street, and round the fence, waiting for his opportunity. He saw a beggar go in at the gate and the dogs attack him. He heard a piano and the sounds came faintly to his ears. It must be Anna Sergueyevna playing. The door suddenly opened and out of it came an old woman, and after her ran the familiar white Pomeranian. Gomov wanted to call the dog, but his heart suddenly began to thump and in his agitation he could not remember the dog's name.

He walked on, and more and more he hated the grey fence and thought with a gust of irritation that Anna Sergueyevna had already forgotten him, and was perhaps already amusing herself with some one else, as would be only natural in a young woman forced from morning to night to behold the accursed fence. He returned to his room and sat for a long time on the sofa, not knowing what to do. Then he dined and afterward slept for a long while.

"How idiotic and tiresome it all is," he thought as he awoke and saw the dark windows; for it was evening. "I've had sleep enough, and what shall I do to-night?"

He sat on his bed, which was covered with a cheap, grey blanket, exactly like those used in a hospital, and tormented himself.

"So much for the lady with the toy dog. . . . So much for the great adventure. . . . Here you sit."

However, in the morning, at the station, his eye had been caught by a poster with large letters: "First Performance of 'The Geisha.'" He remembered that and went to the theater.

"It is quite possible she will go to the first performance," he thought.

The theater was full and, as usual in all provincial theaters, there was a thick mist above the lights, the gallery was noisily restless; in the first row before the opening of the performance stood the local dandies with their hands behind their backs, and there in the governor's box, in front, sat the governor's daughter, and the governor himself sat modestly behind the curtain and only his hands were visible. The curtain quivered; the orchestra tuned up for a long time, and while the audience were coming in and taking their seats, Gomov gazed eagerly round.

At last Anna Sergueyevna came in. She took her seat in the third row, and when Gomov glanced at her his heart ached and he knew that for him there was no one in the whole world nearer, dearer, and more important than she; she was lost in this provincial rabble, the little undistinguished woman, with a common lorgnette in her hands, yet she filled his whole life; she was his grief, his joy, his only happiness, and he longed for her; and through the noise of the bad orchestra with its tenth-rate fiddles, he thought how dear she was to him. He thought and dreamed.

With Anna Sergueyevna there came in a young man with short sidewhiskers, very tall, stooping; with every movement he shook and bowed continually. Probably he was the husband whom in a bitter mood at Yalta she had called a lackey. And, indeed, in his long figure, his sidewhiskers, the little bald patch on the top of his head, there was something of the lackey; he had a modest sugary smile and in his buttonhole he wore a University badge exactly like a lackey's number.

In the first entr'acte the husband went out to smoke, and she was left alone. Gomov, who was also in the pit, came up to her and said in a trembling voice with a forced smile:

"How do you do?"

She looked up at him and went pale. Then she glanced at him again in terror, not believing her eyes, clasped her fan and lorgnette tightly together, apparently struggling to keep herself from fainting. Both were silent. She sat, he stood; frightened by her emotion, not daring to sit down beside her. The fiddles and flutes began to play and suddenly it seemed to them as though all the people in the boxes were looking at them. She got up and walked quickly to the exit; he followed, and both walked absently along the corridors, down the stairs, up the stairs, with the crowd shifting and shimmering before their eyes; all kinds of uniforms, judges, teachers, crown-estates, and all with badges; ladies shone and shimmered before them, like fur coats on moving rows of clothespegs, and there was a draft howling through the place laden with the smell of tobacco and cigar-ends. And Gomov, whose heart was thudding wildly, thought:

"Oh, Lord! Why all these men and that beastly orchestra?"

At that very moment he remembered how when he had seen Anna Sergueyevna off that evening at the station he had said to himself that everything was over between them, and they would never meet again. And now how far off they were from the end!

On a narrow, dark staircase over which was written: "This Way to the Amphitheater," she stopped:

"How you frightened me!" she said, breathing heavily, still pale and apparently stupefied. "Oh! how you frightened me! I am nearly dead. Why did you come? Why?"

"Understand me, Anna," he whispered quickly. "I implore you to understand. . . ."

She looked at him fearfully, in entreaty, with love in her eyes, gazing fixedly to gather up in her memory every one of his features.

"I suffer so!" she went on, not listening to him. "All the time, I thought only of you. I lived with thoughts of you. . . . And I wanted to forget, to forget, but why, why did you come?"

A little above them, on the landing, two schoolboys stood and smoked and looked down at them, but Gomov did not care. He drew her to him and began to kiss her cheeks, her hands.

"What are you doing? What are you doing?" she said in terror, thrusting him away. . . . "We were both mad. Go away to-night. You must go away at once. . . . I implore you, by everything you hold sacred, I implore you. . . . The people are coming——"

Some one passed them on the stairs.

"You must go away," Anna Sergueyevna went on in a whisper. "Do you hear, Dimitri Dimitrich? I'll come to you in Moscow. I never was happy. Now I am unhappy and I shall never, never be happy, never! Don't make me suffer even more! I swear, I'll come to Moscow. And now let us part. My dear, dearest darling, let us part!"

She pressed his hand and began to go quickly downstairs, all the while looking back at him, and in her eyes plainly showed that she was most unhappy. Gomov stood for a while, listened, then, when all was quiet he found his coat and left the theater.

IV

And Anna Sergueyevna began to come to him in Moscow. Once every two or three months she would leave S., telling her husband that she was going to consult a specialist in women's diseases. Her husband half believed and half disbelieved her. At Moscow she would stay at the "Slaviansky Bazaar" and send a message at once to Gomov. He would come to her, and nobody in Moscow knew.

Once as he was going to her as usual one winter morning—he had not received her message the night before—he had his daughter with him, for he was taking her to school which was on the way. Great wet flakes of snow were falling.

"Three degrees above freezing," he said, "and still the snow is falling. but the warmth is only on the surface of the earth. In the upper strata of the atmosphere there is quite a different temperature."

"Yes, papa. Why is there no thunder in winter?"

He explained this too, and as he spoke he thought of his assignation, and that not a living soul knew of it, or ever would know. He had two lives; one obvious, which every one could see and know, if they were sufficiently interested, a life full of conventional truth and conventional fraud, exactly like the lives of his friends and acquaintances; and another, which moved underground. And by a strange conspiracy of circumstances, everything that was to him important, interesting, vital, everything that enabled him to be sincere and denied self-deception and was the very core of his being, must dwell hidden away from the others, and everything that made him false, a mere shape in which he hid himself in order to conceal the truth, as for instance his work in the bank, arguments at the club, his favorite gibe about women, going to parties with his wife—all this was open. And, judging others by himself, he did not believe the things he saw, and assumed that everybody else also had his real vital life passing under a veil of mystery as under the cover of the night. Every man's intimate existence is kept mysterious, and perhaps, in part, because of that civilized people are so nervously anxious that a personal secret should be respected.

When he had left his daughter at school, Gomov went to the "Slaviansky Bazaar." He took off his fur coat downstairs, went up and knocked quietly at the door. Anna Sergueyevna, wearing his favorite grey dress, tired by the journey, had been expecting him to come all night. She was pale, and looked at him without a smile, and flung herself on his breast as soon as he entered. Their kiss was long and lingering as though they had not seen each other for a couple of years.

"Well, how are you getting on down there?" he asked. "What is your news?"

"Wait. I'll tell you presently. . . . I cannot."

She could not speak, for she was weeping. She turned her face from him and dried her eyes.

"Well, let her cry a bit. . . . I'll wait," he thought, and sat down.

Then he rang and ordered tea, and then, as he drank it, she stood and gazed out of the window. . . . She was weeping in distress, in the bitter knowledge that their life had fallen out so sadly; only seeing each other in secret, hiding themselves away like thieves! Was not their life crushed?

"Don't cry. . . . Don't cry," he said.

It was clear to him that their love was yet far from its end, which there was no seeing. Anna Sergueyevna was more and more passionately attached to him; she adored him and it was inconceivable that he should tell her that their love must some day end; she would not believe it.

He came up to her and patted her shoulder fondly and at that moment he saw himself in the mirror.

His hair was already going grey. And it seemed strange to him that in the last few years he should have got so old and ugly. Her shoulders were warm and trembled to his touch. He was suddenly filled with pity for her life, still so warm and beautiful, but probably beginning to fade and wither, like his own. Why should she love him so much? He always seemed to women not what he really was, and they loved in him, not himself, but the creature of their imagination, the thing they hankered for in life, and when they had discovered their mistake, still they loved him. And not one of them was happy with him. Time passed; he met women and was friends with them, went further and parted, but never once did he love; there was everything but love.

And now at last when his hair was grey he had fallen in love—real love—for the first time in his life.

Anna Sergueyevna and he loved one another, like dear kindred, like husband and wife, like devoted friends; it seemed to them that Fate had destined them for one another, and it was inconceivable that he should have a wife, she a husband; they were like two birds of passage, a male and a female, which had been caught and forced to live in separate cages. They had forgiven each other all the past of which they were ashamed; they forgave everything in the present, and they felt that their love had changed both of them.

Formerly, when he felt a melancholy compunction, he used to comfort himself with all kinds of arguments, just as they happened to cross his mind, but now he was far removed from any such ideas; he was filled with a profound pity, and he desired to be tender and sincere. . . .

"Don't cry, my darling," he said. "You have cried enough. . . . Now let us talk and see if we can't find some way out."

Then they talked it over, and tried to discover some means of avoiding the necessity for concealment and deception, and the torment of living in different towns, and of not seeing each other for a long time. How could they shake off these intolerable fetters?

"How? How?" he asked, holding his head in his hands. "How?"

And it seemed that but a little while and the solution would be found and there would begin a lovely new life; and to both of them it was clear that the end was still very far off, and that their hardest and most difficult period was only just beginning.

THE WHITE MOTHER
Theodor Sologub

I

EASTER WAS drawing near. Esper Konstantinovitch Saksaulov was in a worried, weary mood. It began, seemingly, from the moment when at the Gorodishchevs' he was asked, "Where are you spending the festival?"

Saksaulov for some reason delayed his reply.

The hostess, a stout, short-sighted, bustling lady, said, "Come to us."

Saksaulov was annoyed. Was it with the girl, who, at her mother's words, glanced at him quickly and instantly withdrew her gaze as she continued her conversation with the young assistant professor?

Saksaulov was eligible in the eyes of mothers of grown-up daughters, and this fact irritated him. He regarded himself as an old bachelor, and he was only thirty-seven. He replied curtly: "Thank you. I always spend this night at home."

The girl glanced at him, smiled, and said, "With whom?"

"Alone," Saksaulov replied, with a slight surprise in his voice.

"What a misanthrope!" said Madame Gorodishchev with a sour smile.

Saksaulov liked his freedom. There were occasions when he wondered how at one time he had nearly come to marry. He was now used to his small flat, furnished in severe style, used to his own valet, the aged, sedate Fedot, and to his no less aged wife, Christine, who cooked his dinner—and was thoroughly convinced that he did not marry because he wished to remain true to his first love. In reality his heart

· 148 ·

had grown cold from indifference resulting from his solitary, aimless life. He had independent means, his father and mother were long since dead, and of near relations he had none. He lived an assured, tranquil life, was attached to some department, intimately acquainted with contemporary literature and art, and took an Epicurean pleasure in the good things of life, while life itself seemed to him empty and meaningless. Were it not for a solitary bright and pure dream that came to him sometimes, he would have grown quite cold, as so many other men have done.

II

His first and only love, that had ended before it had blossomed, in the evening sometimes made him dream sad sweet dreams. Five years ago he had met the young girl who had produced such a lasting impression on him. Pale, delicate, with slender waist, blue-eyed, fair-haired, she had seemed to him an almost celestial creature, a product of air and mist, accidentally cast by fate for a short span into the city din. Her movements were slow; her clear, tender voice sounded soft, like the murmur of a stream rippling gently over stones.

Saksaulov—was it by accident or design?—always saw her in a white dress. The impression of white became to him inseparable from his thought of her. Even her name, Tamara, seemed to him always white, like the snow on the mountain tops. He began to visit Tamara's parents. On more than one occasion had he resolved to speak those words to her that bind the fate of one human being with that of another. But she always eluded him; fear and anguish were reflected in her eyes. Of what was she afraid? Saksaulov saw in her face the signs of girlish love; her eyes lighted up when he appeared, and a faint blush spread over her cheeks.

But on one never-to-be-forgotten evening she listened to him. The time was early spring. It was not long since the river had broken up and the trees had clothed themselves in a soft green gown. In a flat in town Tamara and Saksaulov sat by the open window facing the Neva. Without troubling himself about what to say and how to say it, he spoke sweet, for her terrifying, words. She turned pale, smiled absently, and got up. Her delicate hand trembled on the carved back of the chair.

"To-morrow," Tamara said softly, and went out.

Saksaulov, with a tense expectancy, sat for a long time staring at the door that had hidden Tamara. His head was in a whirl. A sprig of white lilac caught his eye; he took it and went away without bidding good-bye to his hosts.

At night he could not sleep. He stood by the window staring into the dark street that grew lighter towards the morning, smiling and toying with the sprig of white lilac. When it grew light he saw that the floor of the room was littered with petals of white lilac. This struck him as naïve and ridiculous. He took a bath, which made him feel as though he had almost regained his composure, and went to Tamara.

He was told that she was ill, she had caught a chill somewhere. And Saksaulov never saw her again. In two weeks she was dead. He did not go to her funeral. Her death left him almost unshaken. Already he could not tell whether he had loved her or if it were merely a brief passing fascination.

Sometimes in the evening he would dream of her; then her image began to fade. Saksaulov had no portrait of Tamara. It was only after several years had gone by, during last spring, that he was reminded of Tamara by a sprig of white lilac in the window of a restaurant, sadly out of place amidst the rich food. And from that day he again liked to think of Tamara in the evenings. Sometimes when he dozed off, he dreamt that she had come and sat down opposite him and looked at him with a fixed, caressing gaze, seeming to want something. It oppressed and hurt him sometimes to feel Tamara's expectant gaze.

Now, as he left the Gorodishchevs, he thought apprehensively:

"She will come to give me the Easter greeting."

The fear and loneliness were so oppressive that he thought: "Why shouldn't I marry? I need not be alone then on holy mystic nights."

Valeria Michailovna—the Gorodishchev girl—came into his mind. She was not beautiful, but she always dressed well. It seemed to Saksaulov that she liked him and would not refuse him if he proposed.

In the street the noise and crowd distracted his attention; his thoughts of the Gorodishchev girl became tinged with the usual cynicism. Moreover, could he be untrue to Tamara's memory for anyone? The whole world seemed to him so petty and commonplace that he longed for Tamara—and Tamara only—to come and give him the Easter greeting.

"But," he reflected, "she will again fix on me that expectant gaze. Pure, gentle Tamara, what does she want? Will her soft lips kiss mine?"

III

With tormenting thoughts of Tamara, Saksaulov wandered about the streets, peering into the faces of the passers-by; the coarse faces of the men and women disgusted him. He reflected that there was no one with whom he would care to exchange the Easter greeting with any pleasure or love. There would be many kisses on the first day—coarse lips, tangled beards, an odor of wine.

If one had to kiss anyone at all it should be a child. The faces of children became pleasing to Saksaulov.

He walked about for a long time; he grew tired and went into a churchyard off the noisy street. A pale boy, sitting on a seat, glanced up at Saksaulov apprehensively and then sat on motionless, staring straight in front of him. His blue eyes were sad and caressing, like Tamara's. He was so tiny that his feet were not long enough to dangle, but projected straight in front of the seat. Saksaulov sat down beside him and regarded him with a sympathetic curiosity. There was something about this lonely little boy that stirred sweet memories. To look at he was the most ordinary child; in torn, ragged clothes, a white fur cap on his fair little head, and dirty, worn boots on his feet.

For a long time he sat on the seat, then he got up and began to cry pitifully. He ran out of the gate and along the street, stopped, set off in the opposite direction and stopped again. It was clear that he did not know which way to go. He cried softly to himself, the big tears dropping down his cheeks. A crowd gathered. A policeman came up. The boy was asked where he lived.

"Gluikhov House," he lisped in the manner of very young children.

"In what street?" the policeman asked.

But the boy did not know the street, and only repeated, "Gluikhov House."

The policeman, a jolly young fellow, reflected for a moment, and decided that there was no such house in the immediate neighborhood.

"Whom do you live with?" asked a gloomy-looking workman; "have you got a father?"

"I haven't got a father," the boy replied, looking at the crowd with tearful eyes.

"Got no father! dear, dear," the workman said solemnly, shaking his head. "Have you got a mother?"

"Yes, I have a mother," the boy replied.

"What is her name?"

"Mother," the boy replied, then reflecting for a moment added, "Black Mother."

"Black? Is that her name?" the gloomy workman asked.

"First I had a white mother and now I have a black mother," the boy explained.

"Well, my boy, we shall never make head or tail of you," the policeman said decisively. "I had better take you to the police-station. They can find out where you live on the telephone."

He went up to the gate and rang. At this moment a porter, catching sight of the policeman, came out with a broom in his hand. The policeman told him to take the boy to the police-station, but the boy bethought himself and cried, "Let me go; I will find the way myself!"

Was he frightened by the porter's broom, or had he indeed remembered something? At any rate, he ran away so quickly that Saksaulov nearly lost sight of him. Soon, however, the boy slackened his pace. He went up the street, running from one side to the other, trying in vain to find the house he lived in. Saksaulov followed him silently. He did not know how to speak to children.

At last the boy became tired. He stopped by a lamp-post and leant against it. The tears glistened in his eyes.

"Well, my boy," Saksaulov began, "can't you find the house?"

The boy looked at him with his sad, gentle eyes, and suddenly Saksaulov realized what had made him follow the boy so persistently.

In the gaze and mien of the little wanderer there was something very like Tamara.

"What is your name, my dear?" Saksaulov asked gently.

"Lesha," the boy replied.

"Do you live with your mother, Lesha?"

"Yes, with mother—but she is a black mother; I used to have a white mother."

Saksaulov thought that by black mother he must mean a nun.

"How did you get lost?"

"I walked with mother, and we walked and walked. She told me to sit down and wait, and then she went away. And I got frightened."

"Who is your mother?"

"My mother? She is black and angry."

"What does she do?"

The boy thought a while.

"She drinks coffee," he said.

"What else does she do?"

"She quarrels with the lodgers," Lesha replied after a pause.

"And where is your white mother?"

"She was carried away. She was put into a coffin and carried away. And father was carried away, too."

The boy pointed into the distance somewhere and burst into tears.

"What can I do with him?" Saksaulov thought.

Then suddenly the boy began to run again. After having run round a few street-corners he slackened his pace. Saksaulov caught him up a second time. The boy's face expressed a strange mixture of fear and joy.

"Here is the Gluikhov House," he said to Saksaulov, as he pointed to a big, five-storied, ugly building.

At this moment there appeared at the gates of the Gluikhov House a black-haired, black-eyed woman in a black dress, on her head a black kerchief with white spots. The boy shrank back in fear.

"Mother!" he whispered.

His step-mother looked at him in astonishment.

"How did you get here, you rascal?" she cried. "I told you to stop on the seat, didn't I?"

She would have struck him, but observing a gentleman of solemn dignified mien who seemed to be watching them, she lowered her voice.

"Can't you be left for half an hour without running away? I've tired myself out looking for you, you rascal!"

She snatched the boy's little hand in her big one and dragged him within the gate.

Saksaulov made a note of the street and went home.

IV

Saksaulov liked to listen to Fedot's sound judgments. When he reached home he told him about the boy Lesha.

"She had left him on purpose," Fedot announced. "What a wicked woman, to take the boy so far from home!"

"What made her do it?" Saksaulov asked.

"One can't tell. Silly woman—no doubt she thought the boy would wander about the streets until someone or other would pick him up. What can you expect from a step-mother? What use is the child to her?"

"But the police would have found her," Saksaulov said incredulously.

"Perhaps; but she may be leaving the town altogether, and how could they find her then?"

Saksaulov smiled. "Really," he thought, "Fedot should have been an examining magistrate."

However, sitting near the lamp with a book, he dozed off. In his dreams he saw Tamara—gentle and white—she came and sat beside him. Her face was wonderfully like Lesha's. She gazed at him incessantly, persistently, seeming to expect something. It was oppressive for Saksaulov to see her bright, pleading eyes and not to know what it was that she wanted. He got up quickly and walked over to the chair where Tamara appeared to be sitting. Standing before her he implored aloud:

"What do you want? Tell me."

But she was no longer there.

"It was only a dream," Saksaulov thought sadly.

V

Coming out of the Academy exhibition on the following day, Saksaulov met the Gorodishchevs.

He told the girl about Lesha.

"Poor boy!" Valeria Michailovna said softly: "his step-mother simply wants to get rid of him."

"That is by no means certain," Saksaulov replied, annoyed that both Fedot and the girl should take such a tragic view of a simple incident.

"It is quite obvious. The boy has no father and lives with his step-mother. She finds him a nuisance. If she can't get rid of him decently she will cast him off altogether."

"You take too gloomy a view," said Saksaulov with a smile.

"Why don't you adopt him?" Valeria Michailovna suggested.

"I?" Saksaulov asked in surprise.

"You live alone," she persisted; "you have no one belonging to you. Do a good deed at Easter. You will have someone with whom to exchange the greeting, at any rate."

"But what could I do with a child, Valeria Michailovna?"

"Get a nurse for it. Fate seems to have sent the child to you."

Saksaulov looked at the flushed, animated face of the girl in wonder, and with an unconscious gentleness.

When Tamara again appeared to him in his dreams that evening it seemed to him that he knew what she wanted. And in the stillness of his room the words seemed to ring softly: "Do as she has told you."

Saksaulov got up rejoicing, and passed his hand over his sleepy eyes. He caught sight of a sprig of white lilac on the table. Where had it come from? Had Tamara left it in token of her will?

And suddenly it occurred to him that by marrying the Gorodishchev girl and adopting Lesha he would fulfill Tamara's wish. Gladly he breathed in the fragrant perfume of the lilac.

He recollected that he had bought the flower himself that day, but instantly thought, "It makes no difference that I bought it myself. There is an omen in the fact that I wished to buy it and then forgot that I had bought it."

VI

In the morning he set out to find Lesha. The boy met him at the gate and showed him where he lived. Lesha's mother was drinking coffee and quarreling with her red-nosed lodger. This is what Saksaulov was able to learn about Lesha.

His mother had died when he was three years old. His father had married this dark woman and had also died within the year. The dark woman, Irena Ivanovna, had a year-old child of her own. She was about to marry again. The wedding was to take place in a few days, and immediately afterwards they were to go into the "provinces." Lesha was a stranger to her and in her way.

"Give him to me," Saksaulov suggested.

"With pleasure," Irena Ivanovna said with malicious joy. Then after a pause added, "Only you must pay me for his clothes."

And thus Lesha was installed in Saksaulov's home. The Gorodishchev girl helped him to find a nurse and with the other details in connection with Lesha's installment at the flat. For this purpose she had to visit Saksaulov's home. Occupied thus she seemed quite a different being to Saksaulov. The door of her heart seemed to have opened to him. Her eyes became tender and radiant. Altogether she was permeated with the same gentleness that had emanated from Tamara.

VII

Lesha's stories of his white mother touched Fedot and his wife. On Passion Saturday, when putting him to bed, they hung a white sugar egg at the end of his bed.

"This is from your white mother," Christine said. "But you mustn't touch it, dear, until the Lord has risen and the bells are ringing."

Lesha lay down obediently. For a long time he stared at the lovely egg, then he fell asleep.

And Saksaulov on this evening sat at home alone. About midnight an uncontrollable feeling of drowsiness closed his eyes and he was glad, because soon he would see Tamara. And she came, clothed in white, radiant, bringing with her the joyful distant sound of church bells. With a gentle smile she bent over him, and—unutterable joy!—Saksaulov felt a gentle touch on his lips. A gentle voice pronounced softly, "Christ has risen!"

Without opening his eyes Saksaulov stretched out his arms and embraced a tender slim body. This was Lesha, who had climbed on to his knee to give him the Easter greeting.

The church bells had wakened the boy. He had seized the white egg and run in to Saksaulov.

Saksaulov awoke. Lesha laughed and held up his white egg.

"White Mother has sent it," he lisped; "I will give it you and you must give it to Auntie Valeria."

"Very well, dear, I will do as you say," Saksaulov replied.

He put Lesha to bed and then went to Valeria Michailovna with Lesha's white egg, a present from the white mother. But it seemed to Saksaulov at the moment to be a present from Tamara.

TWENTY-SIX MEN AND A GIRL

Maxim Gorky

WE WERE twenty-six men, twenty-six living machines cooped up in a dark hole of a basement where from morn till night we kneaded dough, making pretzels and cracknels. The windows of our basement faced a sunken area lined with bricks that were green with slime; the windows outside were encased in a close-set iron grating, and no ray of sunshine could reach us through the panes which were covered with meal. Our boss had fenced the windows off to prevent any of his bread going to beggars or to those of our comrades who were out of work and starving—our boss called us a bunch of rogues and gave us tainted tripe for dinner instead of meat. . . .

Stuffy and crowded was life in that stony dungeon beneath a low-hanging ceiling covered by soot and cobwebs. Life was hard and sickening within those thick walls smeared with dirt stains and mildew. . . . We got up at five in the morning, heavy with lack of sleep, and at six, dull and listless, we sat down to the table to make pretzels and cracknels out of the dough our comrades had prepared while we were sleeping. And all day long, from morning till ten o'clock at night some of us sat at the table kneading the stiff dough and swaying the body to fight numbness, while others were mixing flour and water. And all day long the simmering water in the cauldron where the pretzels were cooking gurgled pensively and sadly, and the baker's shovel clattered angrily and swiftly on the hearthstone, throwing slippery cooked pieces of dough onto the hot bricks. From morning till night the wood burned at one end of the oven, and the ruddy glow of the flames flickered on the bakery walls, as though grinning at us. The huge oven resembled the ugly head of some fantastic monster thrust up from under the floor, its wide-open jaws ablaze with glowing fire breathing incandescent flames and heat at us, and watching our ceaseless toil through two sunken air-holes over its forehead. These two hollows were like eyes — the pitiless impassive eyes of a monster; they looked at us with an invariable dark scowl, as though weary with looking at slaves of whom nothing human could be expected, and whom they despised with the cold contempt of wisdom.

Day in, day out, amid the meal dust and the grime that we brought in on our feet from the yard, in the smelly stuffiness of the hot basement, we kneaded the dough and made pretzels which were sprinkled with our sweat, and we hated our work with a fierce hatred, and never ate what our hands had made, preferring black rye bread to pretzels. Sitting at a long table facing one another — nine men on each side — our hands and fingers worked mechanically through the long hours, and we had grown so accustomed to our work that we no longer watched our movements. And we had grown so accustomed to one another that each of us knew every furrow on his comrades' faces. We had nothing to talk about, we were used to that, and were silent all the time — unless we swore, for there is always something one can swear at a man for, especially one's comrade. But we rarely swore at each other — is a man to blame if he is half-dead, if he is like a stone image, if all his senses are blunted by the crushing burden of toil? Silence is awful and painful only for those who have said all there is to say; but to people whose words are still unspoken, silence is simple and easy. . . . Sometimes we sang, and this is how our song would begin: during the work somebody would suddenly heave a deep sigh, like a weary horse, and begin softly to sing one of those long-drawn songs whose mournfully tender melody always lightens the heavy burden of the singer's heart. One of the men would sing while we listened in silence to the lonely song, and it would fade and die away beneath the oppressive basement ceiling like the languishing flames of a campfire in the steppe on a wet autumn night, when the grey sky hangs over the earth like a roof of lead. Then another singer would join the first, and two voices would float drearily and softly in the stuffy heat of our crowded pen. And then suddenly several voices at once would take up the song — it would be lashed up like a wave, grow stronger and louder, and seem to break open the damp, heavy walls of our stony prison. . . .

All the twenty-six are singing; loud voices, brought to harmony by long practice, fill the workshop; the song is cramped for room; it breaks against the stone walls, moaning and weeping, and stirs the heart with a gentle prickly pain, reopening old wounds and wakening anguish in the soul. . . . The singers draw deep and heavy sighs; one will suddenly break off and sit listening for a long time to his comrades singing, then his voice will mingle again in the general chorus. Another will cry out dismally: "Ach!" singing with closed eyes, and maybe he sees the broad torrent of sound as a road leading far away, a wide road lit up by the brilliant sun, and he himself walking along it. . . .

The flames in the oven still flicker, the baker's shovel still scrapes on the brick, the water in the cauldron still bubbles and gurgles, the firelight on the wall still flutters in silent laughter. . . . And we chant out, through words not our own, the dull ache within us, the gnawing grief of living men deprived of the sun, the grief of slaves. And so we lived, twenty-six men, in the basement of a big stone house, and so hard was our life, that it seemed as though the three stories of the house were built on our shoulders. . . .

Besides our songs there was something else that we loved and cherished, something that perhaps filled the place of the sun for us. On the second floor of our house there was a gold embroidery workshop, and there, among many girl hands, lived sixteen-year-old Tanya, a housemaid. Every morning a little pink face with blue merry eyes would be pressed to the pane of the little window cut into the door of our workshop leading into the passage, and a sweet ringing voice would call out to us:

"Jail-birdies! Give me some pretzels!"

We would all turn our heads to the sound of that clear voice and look kindly and joyfully at the pure girlish face that smiled at us so sweetly. We liked to see the nose squashed against the glass, the little white teeth glistening from under rosy lips parted in a smile. We would rush to open the door for her, jostling each other, and there she would be, so winsome and sunny, holding out her apron, standing before us with her little head slightly tilted, and her face all wreathed in smiles. A thick long braid of chestnut hair hung over her shoulder on her breast. We grimy, ignorant, ugly men look up at her—the threshold rises four steps above the floor—look up at her with raised heads and wish her good morning, and our words of greeting are special words, found only for her. When we speak to her our voices are softer, our joking lighter. Everything we have for her is special. The baker draws out of the oven a shovelful of the crustiest browned pretzels and shoots them adroitly into Tanya's apron.

"Mind the boss doesn't catch you!" we warn her. She laughs roguishly and cries merrily:

"Good-bye jail-birdies!" and vanishes in a twinkling like a little mouse.

And that is all. . . . But long after she was gone we talk about her—
we say the same things we said the day before and earlier, because she,
and we, and everything around us are the same they were the day
before and earlier. . . . It is very painful and hard when a man lives, and
nothing around him changes, and if it doesn't kill the soul in him, the
longer he lives the more painful does the immobility of things surrounding him become. . . . We always talked of women in a way that
sometimes made us feel disgusted with ourselves and our coarse shameless talk. That is not surprising, since the women we knew did not probably deserve to be talked of in any other way. But of Tanya we never
said a bad word; no one of us ever dared to touch her with his hand and
she never heard a loose joke from any of us. Perhaps it was because she
never stayed long—she would flash before our gaze like a star falling
from the heavens and vanish. Or perhaps it was because she was small
and so very beautiful, and everything that is beautiful inspires respect,
even with rough men. Moreover, though hard labor was turning us into
dumb oxen, we were only human beings, and like all human beings,
could not live without an object of worship. Finer than she there was
nobody about us, and nobody else paid attention to us men living in
the basement—though there were dozens of tenants in the house. And
finally—probably chiefly—we regarded her as something that
belonged to us, something that existed thanks only to our pretzels; we
made it our duty to give her hot pretzels, and this became our daily sacrifice to the idol, almost a holy rite, that endeared her to us ever more
from day to day. Besides pretzels we gave Tanya a good deal of advice—
to dress warmly, not to run quickly upstairs, not to carry heavy bundles
of firewood. She listened to our counsels with a smile, retorted with a
laugh and never obeyed them, but we did not take offense—we were
satisfied to show our solicitude for her.

Often she asked us to do things for her. She would, for instance, ask
us to open a refractory door in the cellar or chop some wood, and we
would gladly and with a peculiar pride do these things for her and anything else she asked.

But when one of us asked her to mend his only shirt, she sniffed
scornfully and said:

"Catch me! Not likely!"

We enjoyed a good laugh at the silly fellow's expense, and never
again asked her to do anything. We loved her—and there all is said. A
man always wants to foist his love on somebody or other, though it frequently oppresses, sometimes sullies, and his love may poison the life
of a fellow creature, for in loving he does not respect the object of his
love. We had to love Tanya, for there was no one else we could love.

At times one of us would suddenly begin to argue something like this:

"What's the idea of making such a fuss over the kid? What's there so remarkable about her anyway?"

We'd soon brusquely silence the fellow who spoke like that—we had to have something we could love: we found it, and loved it, and what we twenty-six loved stood for each of us, it was our holy of holies, and anybody who went against us in this matter was our enemy. We love, perhaps, what is not really good, but then there are twenty-six of us, and we therefore want the object of our adoration to be held sacred by others.

Our love is no less onerous than hate . . . and, perhaps, that is why some stiff-necked people claim that our hate is more flattering than love. . . . But why do they not shun us if that is so?

In addition to the pretzel bakehouse our boss had a bun bakery. It was situated in the same house, and only a wall divided it from our hole. The bun bakers, however, of whom there were four, held themselves aloof from us, considered their work cleaner than ours, and themselves, therefore, better men; they never visited our workshop, and treated us with mocking scorn whenever they met us in the yard. Neither did we visit them—the boss banned such visits for fear we would steal buns. We did not like the bun bakers, because we envied them—their work was easier than ours, they got better wages, they were fed better, they had a roomy, airy workshop, and they were all so clean and healthy, and hence so odious. We, on the other hand, were all a yellow grey-faced lot; three of us were ill with syphilis, some were scabby, and one was crippled by rheumatism. On holidays and off-days they used to dress up in suits and creaking high boots, two of them possessed accordions, and all used to go out for a stroll in the park, whilst we were dressed in filthy tatters, with rags or bast shoes on our feet, and the police wouldn't let us into the park—now, could we love the bun bakers?

And one day we learned that their chief baker had taken to drink, that the boss had dismissed him and taken on another in his place, and that the new man was an ex-soldier who went about in a satin waistcoat and had a watch on a gold chain. We were curious to have a look at that dandy, and every now and then one of us would run out into the yard in the hope of seeing him.

But he came to our workshop himself. Kicking open the door he stood in the doorway, smiling, and said to us:

"Hullo! How do you do, boys!"

The frosty air rushing through the door in a smoky cloud eddied round his feet, while he stood in the doorway looking down at us, his large yellow teeth flashing from under his fair swaggering moustache. His waistcoat was indeed unique—a blue affair, embroidered with flowers, and all glittering, with buttons made of some kind of red stone. The chain was there too. . . .

He was a handsome fellow, was that soldier—tall, strong, with ruddy cheeks and big light eyes that had a nice look in them—a kind, clean look. On his head he wore a white stiffly starched cap, and from under an immaculately clean apron peeped the pointed toes of a highly polished pair of fashionable boots.

Our chief baker politely asked him to close the door. He complied unhurriedly and began questioning us about the boss. We fell over each other telling him that the boss was a skinflint, a crook, a scoundrel and a tormentor—we told him everything there was to tell about the boss that couldn't be put in writing here. The soldier listened, twitching his moustache and regarding us with that gentle, clear look of his.

"You've a lot of girls around here . . ." he said suddenly.

Some of us laughed politely, others pulled sugary faces, and some one informed the soldier that there were nine bits in the place.

"Use 'em?" asked the soldier with a knowing wink.

Again we laughed, a rather subdued, embarrassed laugh. . . . Many of us would have liked to make the soldier believe they were as gay lads as he was, but they couldn't do it, none of us could do it. Somebody confessed as much, saying quietly:

"How comes we. . . ."

"M'yes, you're a long way off!" said the soldier convincedly, subjecting us to a close scrutiny. "You're not . . . er, up to the mark. . . . Ain't got the character . . . the proper shape . . . you know, looks! Looks is what a woman likes about a man! Give her a regular body . . . everything just so! Then of course she likes a bit of muscle. . . . Likes an arm to be an arm, here's the stuff!"

The soldier pulled his right hand out of his pocket, with the sleeve rolled back to the elbow, and held it up for us to see. . . . He had a strong, white arm covered with shining golden hair.

"The leg, the chest—everything must be firm. . . . And then a man's got to be properly dressed . . . in shipshape form. . . . Now, the women just fall for me. Mind you, I don't call 'em or tempt 'em—they hang about my neck five at a time. . . ."

He sat down on a sack of flour and spent a long time in telling us how the women loved him and how dashingly he treated them. Then he took his leave, and when the door closed behind him with a squeak, we sat on in a long silence, meditating over him and his stories. Then suddenly everybody spoke up at once, and it transpired that we had all taken a liking to him. Such a simple, nice fellow, the way he came in, sat down, and chatted. Nobody ever came to see us, nobody talked to us like that, in a friendly way. . . . And we kept on talking about him and his future success with the seamstresses, who, on meeting us in the yard, either steered clear of us with lips offensively pursed, or bore straight down on us as though we did not stand in their path at all. And we only admired them, in the yard or when they passed our windows, dressed in cute little caps and fur coats in the winter, and in flowery hats with bright colored parasols in the summer. But among ourselves we spoke of these girls in a way that, had they heard us, would have made them mad with shame and insult.

"I hope he doesn't . . . spoil little Tanya!" said the chief baker suddenly in a tone of anxiety.

We were all struck dumb by this statement. We had somehow forgotten Tanya—the soldier seemed to have blotted her out with his large, handsome figure. Then a noisy argument broke out: some said that Tanya would not stand for it, some asserted that she would be unable to resist the soldier's charms, and others proposed to break the fellow's bones in the event of him making love to Tanya. Finally, all decided to keep a watch on the soldier and Tanya, and warn the kid to beware of him. . . . That put a stop to the argument.

About a month passed. The soldier baked buns, went out with the seamstresses, frequently dropped in to see us, but never said anything about his victories—all he did was to turn up his moustache and lick his chops.

Tanya came every morning for her pretzels and was invariably gay, sweet and gentle. We tried to broach the subject of the soldier with her—she called him "a pop-eyed dummy" and other funny names and that set our minds at rest. We were proud of our little girl when we saw how the seamstresses clung to the soldier. Tanya's attitude towards him bucked us all up, and under her influence as it were, we ourselves began to evince towards him an attitude of scorn. We loved her more than ever, and greeted her more gladly and kindly in the mornings.

One day, however, the soldier dropped in on us a little the worse for drink, sat down and began to laugh, and when we asked him what he was laughing at, he explained:

"Two of them have had a fight over me. . . . Lida and Grusha. . . . You should have seen what they did to each other! A regular scream, ha-ha! One of 'em grabbed the other by the hair, dragged her all over the floor into the passage, then got on top of her . . . ha-ha-ha! Scratched each other's mugs, tore their clothes. . . . Wasn't that funny! Now, why can't these females have a straight fight? Why do they scratch, eh?"

He sat on a bench, looking so clean and healthy and cheerful, laughing without a stop. We said nothing. Somehow he was odious to us this time.

"Why am I such a lucky devil with the girls? It's a scream! Why, I just wink my eye and the trick's done!"

He raised his white hands covered with glossy hairs and brought them down on his knees with a slap. He surveyed us with a look of pleased surprise, as though himself genuinely astonished at the lucky turn of his affairs with the ladies. His plump ruddy physiognomy shone with smug pleasure and he repeatedly passed his tongue over his lips.

Our chief baker angrily rattled his shovel on the hearth and suddenly said sarcastically:

"It's no great fun felling little fir trees . . . I'd like to see what you'd do with a pine!"

"Eh, what? Were you talking to me?" asked the soldier.

"Yes, you. . . ."

"What did you say?"

"Never mind. . . . Let it lay. . . ."

"Here, hold on! What's it all about? What d'you mean—pine?"

Our baker did not reply. His shovel moved swiftly in the oven, tossing in boiled pretzels and discharging the baked ones noisily onto the floor where boys sat threading them on bast strings. He seemed to have forgotten the soldier. But the latter suddenly got excited. He rose to his feet and stepped up to the oven, exposing himself to the imminent danger of being struck in the chest by the shovel handle that whisked spasmodically in the air.

"Now, look the—who d'you mean? That's an insult. . . . Why, there ain't a girl that could resist me! No fear! And here are you, hinting things against me. . . ."

Indeed, he appeared to be genuinely offended. Evidently the only source of his self-respect was his ability to seduce women: perhaps this ability was the only living attribute he could boast, the only thing that made him feel a human being.

There are some people for whom life holds nothing better or higher than a malady of the soul or flesh. They cherish it throughout life, and it is the sole spring of life to them. While suffering from it they nourish themselves on it. They complain about it to people and in this manner command the interest of their neighbors. They exact a toll of sympathy from people, and this is the only thing in life they have. Deprive them of that malady, cure them of it, and they will be utterly miserable, because they will lose the sole sustenance of their life and become empty husks. Sometimes a man's life is so poor that he is perforce obliged to cultivate a vice and thrive on it. One might say that people are often addicted to vice through sheer boredom.

The soldier was stung to the quick. He bore down on our baker, whining:

"No, you tell me—who is it?"

"Shall I tell you?" said the baker, turning on him suddenly.

"Well?"

"D'you know Tanya?"

"Well?"

"Well, there you are! See what you can do there. . . ."

"Me?"

"Yes, you."

"Her? Easier'n spitting!"

"We'll see!"

"You'll see! Ha-a!"

"Why, she'll. . . ."

"It won't take a month!"

"You're cocky, soldier, ain't you?"

"A fortnight! I'll show you! Who did you say? Tanya? Pshaw!"

"Come on, get out, you're in the way!"

"A fortnight, and the trick's done! Oh, you! . . ."

"Get out!"

The baker suddenly flew into a rage and brandished his shovel. The soldier fell back in amazement, then regarded us all for a while in silence, muttered grimly "All right!" and went out.

All through this argument we had kept our peace, our interest having been engaged in the conversation. But when the soldier left we all broke out into loud and animated speech.

Somebody cried out to the baker:

"That's a bad business you've started, Pavel!"

"Get on with your work!" snapped the baker.

We realized that the soldier had been put on his high ropes and that Tanya was in danger. Yet, while realizing this, we were all gripped by a tense but thrilling curiosity as to what would be the outcome of it. Would Tanya hold her own against the soldier? We almost unanimously voiced the conviction:

"Tanya? She'll hold her ground! She ain't easy prey!"

We were terribly keen on testing our idol; we assiduously tried to convince each other that our idol was a staunch idol and would come out on top in this engagement. We ended up by expressing our doubts as to whether we had sufficiently goaded the soldier, fearing that he would forget the wager and that we would have to prick his conceit some more. Henceforth a new exciting interest had come into our lives, something we had never known before. We argued among ourselves for days on end; we all somehow seemed to have grown cleverer, spoke better and more. It seemed as though we were playing a sort of game with the devil, and the stake on our side was Tanya. And when we had learned from the bun bakers that the soldier had started to "make a dead set for Tanya" our excitement rose to such a furious pitch and life became such a thrilling experience for us that we did not even notice how the boss had taken advantage of our wrought up feelings to throw in extra work by raising the daily knead to fourteen poods of dough. We didn't even seem to tire of the work. Tanya's name was all day long on our lips. And we awaited her morning visits with a peculiar impatience. At times we fancied that when she came in to see us it would be a different Tanya, not the one we always knew.

We told her nothing, however, about the wager. We never asked her any questions and treated her in the same good-natured loving way. But something new had crept into our attitude, something that was alien to our former feelings for Tanya—and that new element was keen curiosity, keen and cold like a blade of steel. . . .

"Boys! Time's up today!" said the baker one morning as he began work.

We were well aware of it without his reminder. Yet we all started.

"You watch her. . . . She'll soon come in!" suggested the baker. Some one exclaimed in a tone of regret:

"It's not a thing the eye can catch!"

And again a lively noisy argument sprang up. Today, at length, we would know how clean and incontaminate was the vessel in which we had laid all the treasure that we possessed. That morning we suddenly realized for the first time that we were gambling for high stakes, that this test of our idol might destroy it for us altogether. All these days we had been hearing that the soldier was doggedly pursuing Tanya with his attentions, but for some reason none of us asked her what her attitude was towards him. She continued regularly to call on us every morning for her pretzels and was always her usual self.

On that day, too, we soon heard her voice:

"Jail-birdies! I've come. . . ."

We hastened to let her in, and when she came in we greeted her, contrary to our custom, with silence. We looked hard at her and were at a loss what to say to her, what to ask her. We stood before her in a silent sullen crowd. She was obviously surprised at the unusual reception, and suddenly we saw her turn pale, look anxious and stir restlessly. Then in a choky voice she asked:

"Why are you all so . . . strange!"

"What about you?" threw in the baker in a grim tone, his eyes fixed on her face.

"What about me?"

"Nothing. . . ."

"Well, give me the pretzels, quick. . . ."

"Plenty of time!" retorted the baker without stirring, his eyes still glued on her face.

She suddenly turned and disappeared through the door.

The baker picked up his shovel, and turning to the oven, let fall calmly:

"Well—she's fixed! The soldier's done it . . . the blighter! . . ."

We shambled back to the table like a herd of jostling sheep, sat down in silence and apathetically set to our work. Presently some one said:

"Maybe it isn't. . . ."

"Shut up! Enough of that!" shouted the baker.

We all knew him for a clever man, cleverer than any of us. And that shout of his we understood as meaning that he was convinced of the soldier's victory. . . . We felt sad and perturbed. . . .

At twelve o'clock—the lunch hour—the soldier came in. He was, as always, clean and spruce and—as always—looked us straight in the eyes. We felt too ill at ease to look at him.

"Well, my dear sirs, d'you want me to show you what a soldier can do?" he said with a proud sneer. "You go out into the passage and peep through the cracks . . . get me?"

We trooped into the passage, and tumbling over each other, pressed our faces to the chinks in the wooden wall looking onto the yard. We did not have to wait long. Soon Tanya came through the yard with a hurried step and anxious look, skipping over puddles of thawed snow and mud. She disappeared through the door of the cellar. Presently the soldier sauntered past whistling, and he went in too. His hands were thrust into his pockets and he twitched his moustache. . . .

It was raining and we saw the drops falling into the puddles which puckered up at the impact. It was a grey wet day—a very bleak day. Snow still lay on the roofs, while on the ground dark patches of slush stood out here and there. On the roofs too the snow was covered with a brownish coating of dirt. It was cold and disagreeable, waiting in that passage. . . .

The first to come out of the cellar was the soldier. He walked leisurely across the yard, twitching his moustache, his hands deep in his pockets—much the same as he always was.

Then Tanya came out. Her eyes . . . her eyes shone with joy and happiness, and her lips smiled. And she walked as though in a dream, swaying, with uncertain gait. . . .

It was more than we could endure. We all made a sudden rush for the door, burst into the yard and began yelling and whistling at her in a fierce, loud, savage uproar.

She started when she saw us and stood stock-still, her feet in a dirty puddle. We surrounded her and cursed her with a sort of malicious glee in a torrent of profanity and shameless taunts.

We did it unhurriedly, quietly, seeing that she had no way of escape from the circle around her and that we could jeer at her to our heart's content. It is strange, but we did not hit her. She stood amid us and turned her head from side to side, listening to our insults. And we never more fiercely, ever more furiously, flung at her the dirt and poison of our wrath.

Her face drained of life. Her blue eyes, which the moment before had looked so happy, were dilated, her breath came in gasps and her lips quivered.

And we, having surrounded her, were wreaking our vengeance on her—for had she not robbed us? She had belonged to us, we had spent our best sentiments on her, and though that best was a mere beggar's pittance, we were twenty-six and she was one, and there was no anguish we could inflict that was fit to meet her guilt! How we insulted her! . . . She said not a word, but simply gazed at us with a look of sheer terror and a long shudder went through her body.

We guffawed, we howled, we snarled. . . . Other people joined us. . . . One of us pulled the sleeve of Tanya's blouse. . . .

Suddenly her eyes blazed; she raised her hands in a slow gesture to put her hair straight, and said loudly but calmly, straight into our faces:

"Oh, you miserable jail-birds! . . ."

And she bore straight down on us, just as if we had not been there, had not stood in her path. Indeed, that is why none of us proved to be in her path.

When she was clear of our circle she added just as loudly without turning round, in a tone of scorn and pride:

"Oh, you filthy swine. . . . You beasts. . . ." And she departed—straight, beautiful, and proud.

We were left standing in the middle of the yard amid the mud, under the rain and a grey sky that had no sun in it. . . .

Then we too shuffled back to our damp stony dungeon. As of old, the sun never peered through our window, and Tanya came never more! . . .

THE OUTRAGE—A TRUE STORY

Aleksandr I. Kuprin

IT WAS five o'clock on a July afternoon. The heat was terrible. The whole of the huge stone-built town breathed out heat like a glowing furnace. The glare of the white-walled house was insufferable. The asphalt pavements grew soft and burned the feet. The shadows of the acacias spread over the cobbled road, pitiful and weary. They too seemed hot. The sea, pale in the sunlight, lay heavy and immobile as one dead. Over the streets hung a white dust.

In the foyer of one of the private theaters a small committee of local barristers who had undertaken to conduct the cases of those who had suffered in the last pogrom against the Jews was reaching the end of its daily task. There were nineteen of them, all juniors, young, progressive and conscientious men. The sitting was without formality, and white suits of duck, flannel and alpaca were in the majority. They sat anywhere, at little marble tables, and the chairman stood in front of an empty counter where chocolates were sold in winter.

The barristers were quite exhausted by the heat which poured in through the windows, with the dazzling sunlight and the noise of the streets. The proceedings went lazily and with a certain irritation.

A tall young man with a fair moustache and thin hair was in the chair. He was dreaming voluptuously how he would be off in an instant on his new-bought bicycle to the bungalow. He would undress quickly, and without waiting to cool, still bathed in sweat, would fling himself into the clear, cold, sweet-smelling sea. His whole body was enervated and tense, thrilled by the thought. Impatiently moving the papers before him, he spoke in a drowsy voice.

"So, Joseph Moritzovich will conduct the case of Rubinchik. . . . Perhaps there is still a statement to be made on the order of the day?"

His youngest colleague, a short, stout Karaite, very black and lively, said in a whisper so that every one could hear: "On the order of the day, the best thing would be iced *kvas*. . . ."

The chairman gave him a stern side-glance, but could not restrain a smile. He sighed and put both his hands on the table to raise himself and declare the meeting closed, when the doorkeeper, who stood at the entrance to the theater, suddenly moved forward and said: "There are seven people outside, sir. They want to come in."

The chairman looked impatiently round the company.

"What is to be done, gentlemen?"

Voices were heard.

"Next time. *Basta!*"

"Let 'em put it in writing."

"If they'll get it over quickly. . . . Decide it at once."

"Let 'em go to the devil. Phew! It's like boiling pitch."

"Let them in." The chairman gave a sign with his head, annoyed. "Then bring me a Vichy, please. But it must be cold."

The porter opened the door and called down the corridor: "Come in. They say you may."

Then seven of the most surprising and unexpected individuals filed into the foyer. First appeared a full-grown, confident man in a smart suit, of the color of dry sea-sand, in a magnificent pink shirt with white stripes and a crimson rose in his buttonhole. From the front his head looked like an upright bean, from the side like a horizontal bean. His face was adorned with a strong, busy, martial moustache. He wore dark blue pince-nez on his nose, on his hands straw-colored gloves. In his left hand he held a black walking-stick with a silver mount, in his right a light blue handkerchief.

The other six produced a strange, chaotic, incongruous impression, exactly as though they had all hastily pooled not merely their clothes, but their hands, feet and heads as well. There was a man with the splendid profile of a Roman senator, dressed in rags and tatters. Another wore an elegant dress waistcoat, from the deep opening of which a dirty Little-Russian shirt leapt to the eye. Here were the unbalanced faces of the criminal type, but looking with a confidence that nothing could shake. All these men, in spite of their apparent youth, evidently possessed a large experience of life, an easy manner, a bold approach, and some hidden, suspicious cunning.

The gentleman in the sandy suit bowed just his head, neatly and easily, and said with a half-question in his voice: "Mr. Chairman?"

"Yes. I am the chairman. What is your business?"

"We—all whom you see before you," the gentleman began in a quiet voice and turned round to indicate his companions, "we come as delegates from the United Rostov-Kharkov-and-Odessa-Nikolayev Association of Thieves."

The barristers began to shift in their seats.

The chairman flung himself back and opened his eyes wide. "Association of *what?*" he said, perplexed.

"The Association of Thieves," the gentleman in the sandy suit coolly repeated. "As for myself, my comrades did me the signal honor of electing me as the spokesman of the deputation."

"Very . . . pleased," the chairman said uncertainly.

"Thank you. All seven of us are ordinary thieves—naturally of different departments. The Association has authorized us to put before your esteemed Committee"—the gentleman again made an elegant bow—"our respectful demand for assistance."

"I don't quite understand . . . quite frankly . . . what is the connection. . . ." The chairman waved his hands helplessly. "However, please go on."

"The matter about which we have the courage and the honor to apply to you, gentlemen, is very clear, very simple, and very brief. It will take only six or seven minutes. I consider it my duty to warn you of this beforehand, in view of the late hour and the 115 degrees that Fahrenheit marks in the shade." The orator expectorated slightly and glanced at his superb gold watch. "You see, in the reports that have lately appeared in the local papers of the melancholy and terrible days of the last pogrom, there have very often been indications that among the instigators of the pogrom who were paid and organized by the police—the dregs of society, consisting of drunkards, tramps, souteneurs, and hooligans from the slums—thieves were also to be found. At first we were silent, but finally we considered ourselves under the necessity of protesting against such an unjust and serious accusation, before the face of the whole of intellectual society. I know well that in the eye of the law we are offenders and enemies of society. But imagine only for a moment, gentlemen, the situation of this enemy of society when he is accused wholesale of an offense which he not only never committed, but which he is ready to resist with the whole strength of his soul. It goes without saying that he will feel the outrage of such an injustice more keenly than a normal, average, fortunate citizen. Now, we declare that the accusation brought against us is utterly devoid of all basis, not merely of fact but even of logic. I intend to prove this in a few words if the honorable committee will kindly listen."

"Proceed," said the chairman.

"Please do . . . Please . . ." was heard from the barristers, now animated.

"I offer you my sincere thanks in the name of all my comrades. Believe me, you will never repent your attention to the representatives of our . . . well, let us say, slippery, but nevertheless difficult, profession. 'So we begin,' as Giraldoni sings in the prologue to *Pagliacci*.

"But first I would ask your permission, Mr. Chairman, to quench my thirst a little. . . . Porter, bring me a lemonade and a glass of English bitter, there's a good fellow. Gentlemen, I will not speak of the moral aspect of our profession nor of its social importance. Doubtless you know better than I the striking and brilliant paradox of Proudhon: *La propriété c'est le vol*—a paradox if you like, but one that has never yet been refuted by the sermons of cowardly bourgeois or fat priests. For instance: a father accumulates a million by energetic and clever exploitation, and leaves it to his son—a rickety, lazy, ignorant, degenerate idiot, a brainless maggot, a true parasite. Potentially a million rubles is a million working days, the absolutely irrational right to labor, sweat, life, and blood of a terrible number of men. Why? What is the ground of reason? Utterly unknown. Then why not agree with the proposition, gentlemen, that our profession is to some extent as it were a correction of the excessive accumulation of values in the hands of individuals, and serves as a protest against all the hardships, abominations, arbitrariness, violence, and negligence of the human personality, against all the monstrosities created by the bourgeois capitalistic organization of modern society? Sooner or later, this order of things will assuredly be overturned by the social revolution. Property will pass away into the limbo of melancholy memories and with it, alas! we will disappear from the face of the earth, we, *les braves chevaliers d'industrie*."

The orator paused to take the tray from the hands of the porter, and placed it near to his hand on the table.

"Excuse me, gentlemen. . . . Here, my good man, take this, . . . and by the way, when you go out shut the door close behind you."

"Very good, your Excellency!" the porter bawled in jest.

The orator drank off half a glass and continued: "However, let us leave aside the philosophical, social, and economic aspects of the question. I do not wish to fatigue your attention. I must nevertheless point out that our profession very closely approaches the idea of that which is called art. Into it enter all the elements which go to form art—vocation, inspiration, fantasy, inventiveness, ambition, and a long and arduous apprenticeship to the science. From it is absent virtue alone, concerning which the great Karamzin wrote with such stupendous and fiery fascination. Gentlemen, nothing is further from my intention than to trifle with you and waste your precious time with idle paradoxes; but I cannot avoid expounding my idea briefly. To an outsider's ear it sounds absurdly wild and ridiculous to speak of the vocation of a thief. However, I venture to assure you that this vocation is a reality. There are men who possess a peculiarly strong visual memory, sharpness and accuracy of eye, presence of mind, dexterity of hand, and above all a subtle sense of touch, who are as it were born into God's world for the sole and special purpose of becoming distinguished card-sharpers. The pickpockets' profession demands extraordinary nimbleness and agility, a terrific certainty of movement, not to mention a ready wit, a talent for observation and strained attention. Some have a positive vocation for breaking open safes: from their tenderest childhood they are attracted by the mysteries of every kind of complicated mechanism—bicycles, sewing machines, clock-work toys and watches. Finally, gentlemen, there are people with an hereditary animus against private property. You may call this phenomenon degeneracy. But I tell you that you cannot entice a true thief, and thief by vocation, into the prose of honest vegetation by any gingerbread reward, or by the offer of a secure position, or by the gift of money, or by a woman's love: because there is here a permanent beauty of risk, a fascinating abyss of danger, the delightful sinking of the heart, the impetuous pulsation of life, the ecstasy! You are armed with the protection of the law, by locks, revolvers, telephones, police and soldiery; but we only by our own dexterity, cunning and fearlessness. We are the foxes, and society—is a chicken-run guarded by dogs. Are you aware that the most artistic and gifted natures in our villages become horse-thieves and poachers? What would you have? Life is so meager, so insipid, so intolerably dull to eager and high-spirited souls!

"I pass on to inspiration. Gentlemen, doubtless you have had to read of thefts that were supernatural in design and execution. In the headlines of the newspapers they are called 'An Amazing Robbery,' or 'An Ingenious Swindle,' or again 'A Clever Ruse of the Gangsters.' In such cases our bourgeois paterfamilias waves his hands and exclaims: 'What a terrible thing! If only their abilities were turned to good—their inventivness, their amazing knowledge of human psychology, their self-possession, their fearlessness, their incomparable histrionic powers! What extraordinary benefits they would bring to the country!' But it is well known that the bourgeois paterfamilias was specially devised by Heaven to utter commonplaces and trivialities. I myself sometimes— we thieves are sentimental people, I confess—I myself sometimes admire a beautiful sunset in Aleksandra Park or by the sea-shore. And I am always certain beforehand that some one near me will say with infallible *aplomb*: 'Look at it. If it were put into picture no one would ever believe it!' I turn round and naturally I see a self-satisfied, full-fed paterfamilias, who delights in repeating some one else's silly statement as though it were his own. As for our dear country, the bourgeois pater-familias looks upon it as though it were a roast turkey. If you've managed to cut the best part of the bird for yourself, eat it quietly in a comfortable corner and praise God. But he's not really the important person. I was led away by my detestation of vulgarity and I apologize for the digression. The real point is that genius and inspiration, even when they are not devoted to the service of the Orthodox Church, remain rare and beautiful things. Progress is a law—and theft too has its creation.

. "Finally, our profession is by no means as easy and pleasant as it seems to the first glance. It demands long experience, constant prac-tice, slow and painful apprenticeship. It comprises in itself hundreds of supple, skilful processes that the cleverest juggler cannot compass. That I may not give you only empty words, gentlemen, I will perform a few experiments before you now. I ask you to have every confidence in the demonstrators. We are all at present in the enjoyment of legal freedom, and though we are usually watched, and every one of us is known by face, and our photographs adorn the albums of all detective departments, for the time being we are not under the necessity of hid-ing ourselves from anybody. If any one of you should recognize any of us in the future under different circumstances, we ask you earnestly always to act in accordance with your professional duties and your obligations as citizens. In grateful return for your kind attention we have decided to declare your property inviolable, and to invest it with a thieves' taboo. However, I proceed to business."

The orator turned round and gave an order: "Sesoi the Great, will you come this way!"

An enormous fellow with a stoop, whose hands reached to his knees, without a forehead or a neck, like a big, fair Hercules, came forward. He grinned stupidly and rubbed his left eyebrow in his confusion.

"Can't do nothin' here," he said hoarsely.

The gentleman in the sandy suit spoke for him, turning to the com-mittee.

"Gentlemen, before you stands a respected member of our associa-tion. His specialty is breaking open safes, iron strong boxes, and other receptacles for monetary tokens. In his night work he sometimes avails himself of the electric current of the lighting installation for fusing metals. Unfortunately he has nothing on which he can demonstrate the best items of his repertoire. He will open the most elaborate lock irreproachably. . . . By the way, this door here, it's locked, is it not?"

Every one turned to look at the door, on which a printed notice hung: "Stage Door. Strictly Private."

"Yes, the door's locked, evidently," the chairman agreed.

"Admirable. Sesoi the Great, will you be so kind?"

"'Tain't nothin' at all," said the giant leisurely.

He went close to the door, shook it cautiously with his hand, took out of his pocket a small bright instrument, bent down to the keyhole, made some almost imperceptible movements with the tool, suddenly straightened and flung the door wide in silence. The chairman had his watch in his hands. The whole affair took only ten seconds.

"Thank you, Sesoi the Great," said the gentleman in the sandy suit politely. "You may go back to your seat."

But the chairman interrupted in some alarm: "Excuse me. This is all very interesting and instructive, but . . . is it included in your esteemed colleague's profession to be able to lock the door again?"

"Ah, *mille pardons.*" The gentleman bowed hurriedly. "It slipped my mind. Sesoi the Great, would you oblige?"

The door was locked with the same adroitness and the same silence. The esteemed colleague waddled back to his friends, grinning.

"Now I will have the honor to show you the skill of one of our comrades who is in the line of picking pockets in theaters and railway-stations," continued the orator. "He is still very young, but you may to some extent judge from the delicacy of his present work of the heights he will attain by diligence. Yasha!" A swarthy youth in a blue silk blouse and long glacé boots, like a gipsy, came forward with a swagger, fingering the tassels of his belt, and merrily screwing up his big, impudent black eyes with yellow whites.

"Gentlemen," said the gentleman in the sandy suit persuasively, "I must ask if one of you would be kind enough to submit himself to a little experiment. I assure you this will be an exhibition only, just a game."

He looked round over the seated company.

The short plump Karaite, black as a beetle, came forward from his table.

"At your service," he said amusedly.

"Yasha!" The orator signed with his head.

Yasha came close to the solicitor. On his left arm, which was bent, hung a bright-colored, figured scarf.

"Suppose yer in church or at the bar in one of the halls,—or watchin' a circus," he began in a sugary, fluent voice. "I see straight off—there's a toff. . . . Excuse me, sir. Suppose you're the toff. There's no offense — just means a rich gent, decent enough, but don't know his way about. First—what's he likely to have about 'im? All sorts. Mostly, a ticker and a chain. Whereabouts does he keep 'em? Somewhere in his top vest pocket—here. Others have 'em in the bottom pocket. Just here. Purse—most always in the trousers, except when a greeny keeps it in his jacket. Cigar-case. Have a look first what it is—gold, silver—with a monogram. Leather—what decent man'd soil his hands? Cigar-case.

Seven pockets: here, here, here, up there, there, here and here again. That's right, ain't it? That's how you go to work."

As he spoke the young man smiled. His eyes shone straight into the barrister's. With a quick, dexterous movement of his right hand he pointed to various portions of his clothes.

"Then again you might see a pin here in the tie. However we do not appropriate. Such *gents* nowadays—they hardly ever wear a real stone. Then I comes up to him. I begin straight off to talk to him like a gent: 'Sir, would you be so kind as to give me a light from your cigarette'— or something of the sort. At any rate, I enter into conversation. What's next? I look him straight in the peepers, just like this. Only two of me fingers are at it—just this and this." Yasha lifted two fingers of his right hand on a level with the solicitor's face, the forefinger and the middle finger and moved them about.

"D' you see? With these two fingers I run over the whole pianner. Nothin' wonderful in it: one, two, three—ready. Any man who wasn't stupid could learn easily. That's all it is. Most ordinary business. I thank you."

The pickpocket swung on his heel as if to return to his seat.

"Yasha!" The gentleman in the sandy suit said with meaning weight. "Yasha!" he repeated sternly.

Yasha stopped. His back was turned to the barrister, but he evidently gave his representative an imploring look, because the latter frowned and shook his head.

"Yasha!" he said for the third time, in a threatening tone.

"Huh!" The young thief grunted in vexation and turned to face the solicitor. "Where's your little watch, sir?" he said in a piping voice.

"Oh!" the Karaite brought himself up sharp.

"You see—now you say 'Oh!'" Yasha continued reproachfully. "All the while you were admiring me right hand, I was operatin' yer watch with my left. Just with these two little fingers, under the scarf. That's why we carry a scarf. Since your chain's not worth anything—a present from some *mamselle* and the watch is a gold one, I've left you the chain as a keepsake. Take it," he added with a sigh, holding out the watch.

"But . . . That is clever," the barrister said in confusion. "I didn't notice it at all."

"That's our business," Yasha said with pride.

He swaggered back to his comrades. Meantime the orator took a drink from his glass and continued.

"Now, gentlemen, our next collaborator will give you an exhibition of some ordinary card tricks, which are worked at fairs, on steamboats and railways. With three cards, for instance, an ace, a queen, and a six, he can quite easily. . . . But perhaps you are tired of these demonstrations, gentlemen. . . ."

"Not at all. It's extremely interesting," the chairman answered affably. "I should like to ask one question—that is if it is not too indiscreet—what is your own specialty?"

"Mine . . . H'm. . . . No, how could it be an indiscretion? . . . I work the big diamond shops . . . and my other business is banks," answered the orator with a modest smile. "Don't think this occupation is easier than others. Enough that I know four European languages, German, French, English, and Italian, not to mention Polish, Ukrainian, and Yiddish. But shall I show you some more experiments, Mr. Chairman?"

The chairman looked at his watch.

"Unfortunately the time is too short," he said. "Wouldn't it be better to pass on to the substance of your business? Besides, the experiments we have just seen have amply convinced us of the talent of your esteemed associates. . . . Am I not right, Isaac Abramovich?"

"Yes, yes . . . absolutely," the Karaite barrister readily confirmed.

"Admirable," the gentleman in the sandy suit kindly agreed. "My dear Count"—he turned to a blond, curly-haired man, with a face like a billiard-maker on a bank-holiday—"put your instruments away. They will not be wanted. I have only a few words more to say, gentlemen. Now that you have convinced yourselves that our art, although it does not enjoy the patronage of high-placed individuals, is nevertheless an art; and you have probably come to my opinion that this art is one which demands many personal qualities besides constant labor, danger, and unpleasant misunderstandings—you will also, I hope, believe that it is possible to become attached to its practice and to love and esteem it, however strange that may appear at first sight. Picture to yourselves that a famous poet of talent, whose tales and poems adorn the pages of our best magazines, is suddenly offered the chance of writing verses at a penny a line, signed into the bargain, as an advertisement for 'Cigarettes Jasmine'—or that a slander was spread about one of you distinguished barristers, accusing you of making a business of concocting evidence for divorce cases, or of writing petitions from the cabmen to the governor in public-houses! Certainly your relatives, friends and acquaintances wouldn't believe it. But the rumor has already done its poisonous work, and you have to live through minutes of torture. Now picture to yourselves that such a disgraceful and vexatious slander, started by God knows whom, begins to threaten not only your good name and your quiet digestion, but your freedom, your health, and even your life!

"This is the position of us thieves, now being slandered by the newspapers. I must explain. There is in existence a class of scum—*passez-moi le mot*—whom we call their 'Mothers' Darlings.' With these we are unfortunately confused. They have neither shame nor conscience, a dissipated riff-raff, mothers' useless darlings, idle, clumsy drones, shop assistants who commit unskilful thefts. He thinks nothing of living on his mistress, a prostitute, like the male mackerel, who always swims after the female and lives on her excrements. He is capable of robbing a child with violence in a dark alley, in order to get a penny; he will kill a man in his sleep and torture an old woman. These men are the pests of our profession. For them the beauties and the traditions of the art have no existence. They watch us real, talented thieves like a pack of jackals after a lion. Suppose I've managed to bring off an important job—we won't mention the fact that I have to leave two-thirds of what I get to the receivers who sell the goods and discount the notes, or the customary subsidies to our incorruptible police—I still have to share out something to each one of these parasites, who have got wind of my job, by accident, hearsay, or a casual glance.

"So we call them *Motients*, which means 'half,' a corruption of *moitié* . . . Original etymology. I pay him only because he knows and may inform against me. And it mostly happens that even when he's got his share he runs off to the police in order to get another dollar. We, honest thieves. . . . Yes, you may laugh, gentlemen, but I repeat it: we honest thieves detest these reptiles. We have another name for them, a stigma of ignominy; but I dare not utter it here out of respect for the place and for my audience. Oh, yes, they would gladly accept an invitation to a pogrom. The thought that we may be confused with them is a hundred times more insulting to us even than the accusation of taking part in a pogrom.

"Gentlemen! While I have been speaking I have often noticed smiles on your faces. I understand you. Our presence here, our application for your assistance, and above all the unexpectedness of such a phenomenon as a systematic organization of thieves, with delegates who are thieves, and a leader for the deputation, also a thief by profession—it is all so original that it must inevitably arouse a smile. But now I will speak from the depth of my heart. Let us be rid of our outward wrappings, gentlemen, let us speak as men to men.

"Almost all of us are educated, and all love books. We don't only read the adventures of Roqueambole, as the realistic writers say of us. Do you think our hearts did not bleed and our cheeks did not burn from shame, as though we had been slapped in the face, all the time that this unfortunate, disgraceful, accursed, cowardly war lasted. Do you really think that our souls do not flame with anger when our country is lashed with Cossack-whips, and trodden under foot, shot and spit at by mad, exasperated men? Will you not believe that we thieves meet every step towards the liberation to come with a thrill of ecstasy?

"We understand, every one of us—perhaps only a little less than you barristers, gentlemen—the real sense of the pogroms. Every time that some dastardly event or some ignominious failure has occurred, after executing a martyr in a dark corner of a fortress, or after deceiving public confidence, some one who is hidden and unapproachable gets frightened of the people's anger and diverts its vicious element upon the heads of innocent Jews. Whose diabolical mind invents these pogroms—these titanic blood-lettings, these cannibal amusements for the dark, bestial souls?

"We all see with certain clearness that the last convulsions of the bureaucracy are at hand. Forgive me if I present it imaginatively. There was a people that had a chief temple, wherein dwelt a bloodthirsty deity, behind a curtain, guarded by priests. Once fearless hands tore the curtain away. Then all the people saw, instead of a god, a huge, shaggy, voracious spider, like a loathsome cuttlefish. They beat it and shoot at it: it is dismembered already; but still in the frenzy of its final agony it stretches over all the ancient temple its disgusting, clawing tentacles. And the priests, themselves under sentence of death, push into the monster's grasp all whom they can seize in their terrified, trembling fingers.

"Forgive me. What I have said is probably wild and incoherent. But I am somewhat agitated. Forgive me. I continue. We thieves by profession know better than any one else how these programs were organized. We wander everywhere: into public houses, markets, tea-shops, doss-houses, public places, the harbor. We can swear before God and man and posterity that we have seen how the police organize the massacres, without shame and almost without concealment. We know them all by face, in uniform or disguise. They invited many of us to take part; but there was none so vile among us as to give even the outward consent that fear might have extorted.

"You know, of course, how the various strata of Russian society behave towards the police? It is not even respected by those who avail themselves of its dark services. But we despise and hate it three, ten times more—not because many of us have been tortured in the detective departments, which are just chambers of horror, beaten almost to death, beaten with whips of ox-hide and of rubber in order to extort a confession or to make us betray a comrade. Yes, we hate them for that too. But we thieves, all of us who have been in prison, have a mad passion for freedom. Therefore we despise our gaolers with all the hatred that a human heart can feel. I will speak for myself. I have been tortured three times by police detectives till I was half dead. My lungs and liver have been shattered. In the mornings I spit blood until I can breathe no more. But if I were told that I will be spared a fourth flogging only by shaking hands with a chief of the detective police, I would refuse to do it!

"And then the newspapers say that we took from these hands Judasmoney, dripping with human blood. No, gentlemen, it is a slander which stabs our very soul, and inflicts insufferable pain. Not money, nor threats, nor promises will suffice to make us mercenary murderers of our brethren, nor accomplices with them."

"Never . . . No . . . No . . .," his comrades standing behind him began to murmur.

"I will say more," the thief continued. "Many of us protected the victims during this progrom. Our friend, called Sesoi the Great—you have just seen him, gentlemen—was then lodging with a Jewish braid-maker on the Moldavanka. With a poker in his hands he defended his landlord from a great horde of assassins. It is true, Sesoi the Great is a man of enormous physical strength, and this is well known to many of the inhabitants of the Moldavanka. But you must agree, gentlemen, that in these moments Sesoi the Great looked straight into the face of death. Our comrade Martin the Miner—this gentleman here"—the orator pointed to a pale, bearded man with beautiful eyes who was holding himself in the background—"saved an old Jewess, whom he had never seen before, who was being pursued by a crowd of these *canaille*. They broke his head with a crowbar for his pains, smashed his arm in two places and splintered a rib. He is only just out of hospital. That is the way our most ardent and determined members acted. The others trembled for anger and wept for their own impotence.

"None of us will forget the horrors of those bloody days and bloody nights lit up by the glare of fires, those sobbing women, those little children's bodies torn to pieces and left lying in the street. But for all that not one of us thinks that the police and the mob are the real origin of the evil. These tiny, stupid, loathsome vermin are only a senseless fist that is governed by a vile, calculating mind, moved by a diabolical will.

"Yes, gentlemen," the orator continued, "we thieves have nevertheless merited your legal contempt. But when you, noble gentlemen, need the help of clever, brave, obedient men at the barricades, men who will be ready to meet death with a song and a jest on their lips for the most glorious word in the world—Freedom—will you cast us off then and order us away because of an inveterate revulsion? Damn it all, the first victim in the French Revolution was a prostitute. She jumped up on to a barricade, with her skirt caught elegantly up into her hand and called out: 'Which of you soldiers will dare to shoot a woman?' Yes, by God." The orator exclaimed aloud and brought down his fist on to the marble table top: "They killed her, but her action was magnificent, and the beauty of her words immortal.

"If you should drive us away on the great day, we will turn to you and say: 'You spotless Cherubim—if human thoughts had the power to wound, kill, and rob man of honor and property, then which of you innocent doves would not deserve the knout and imprisonment for life?' Then we will go away from you and build our own gay, sporting, desperate thieves' barricade, and will die with such united songs on our lips that you will envy us, you who are whiter than snow!

"But I have been once more carried away. Forgive me. I am at the end. You now see, gentlemen, what feelings the newspaper slanders have excited in us. Believe in our sincerity and do what you can to remove the filthy stain which has so unjustly been cast upon us. I have finished."

He went away from the table and joined his comrades. The barristers were whispering in an undertone, very much as the magistrates of the bench at sessions. Then the chairman rose.

"We trust you absolutely, and we will make every effort to clear your association of this most grievous charge. At the same time my colleagues have authorized me, gentlemen, to convey to you their deep respect for your passionate feelings as citizens. And for my own part I ask the leader of the deputation for permission to shake him by the hand."

The two men, both tall and serious, held each other's hands in a strong, masculine grip.

The barristers were leaving the theater; but four of them hung back a little beside the clothes rack in the hall. Isaac Abramovich could not find his new, smart grey hat anywhere. In its place on the wooden peg hung a cloth cap jauntily flattened in on either side.

"Yasha!" The stern voice of the orator was suddenly heard from the other side of the door. "Yasha! It's the last time I'll speak to you, curse you! . . . Do you hear?"

The heavy door opened wide. The gentleman in the sandy suit entered. In his hands he held Isaac Abramovich's hat; on his face was a well-bred smile.

"Gentlemen, for Heaven's sake forgive us—an odd little misunderstanding. One of our comrades exchanged his hat by accident. . . . Oh, it is yours! A thousand pardons. Doorkeeper! Why don't you keep an eye on things, my good fellow, eh? Just give me that cap, there. Once more, I ask you to forgive me, gentlemen."

With a pleasant bow and the same well-bred smile he made his way quickly into the street.

LAZARUS

Leonid Andreyev

I

WHEN LAZARUS rose from the grave, after three days and nights in the mysterious thraldom of death, and returned alive to his home, it was a long time before any one noticed the evil peculiarities in him that were later to make his very name terrible. His friends and relatives were jubilant that he had come back to life. They surrounded him with tenderness, they were lavish of their eager attentions, spending the greatest care upon his food and drink and the new garments they made for him. They clad him gorgeously in the glowing colors of hope and laughter, and when, arrayed like a bridegroom, he sat at table with them again, ate again, and drank again, they wept fondly and summoned the neighbors to look upon the man miraculously raised from the dead.

The neighbors came and were moved with joy. Strangers arrived from distant cities and villages to worship the miracle. They burst into stormy exclamations, and buzzed around the house of Mary and Martha, like so many bees.

That which was new in Lazarus' face and gestures they explained naturally, as the traces of his severe illness and the shock he had passed through. It was evident that the disintegration of the body had been halted by a miraculous power, but that the restoration had not been complete; that death had left upon his face and body the effect of an artist's unfinished sketch seen through a thin glass. On his temples, under his eyes, and in the hollow of his cheek lay a thick, earthly blue.

His fingers were blue, too, and under his nails, which had grown long in the grave, the blue had turned livid. Here and there on his lips and body, the skin, blistered in the grave, had burst open and left reddish glistening cracks, as if covered with a thin, glassy slime. And he had grown exceedingly stout. His body was horribly bloated and suggested the fetid, damp smell of putrefaction. But the cadaverous, heavy odor that clung to his burial garments and, as it seemed, to his very body, soon wore off, and after some time the blue of his hands and face softened, and the reddish cracks of his skin smoothed out, though they never disappeared completely. Such was the aspect of Lazarus in his second life. It looked natural only to those who had seen him buried.

Not merely Lazarus' face, but his very character, it seemed, had changed; though it astonished no one and did not attract the attention it deserved. Before his death Lazarus had been cheerful and careless, a lover of laughter and harmless jest. It was because of his good humor, pleasant and equable, his freedom from meanness and gloom, that he had been so beloved by the Master. Now he was grave and silent; neither he himself jested nor did he laugh at the jests of others; and the words he spoke occasionally were simple, ordinary and necessary words—words as much devoid of sense and depth as are the sounds with which an animal expresses pain and pleasure, thirst and hunger. Such words a man may speak all his life and no one would ever know the sorrows and joys that dwelt within him.

Thus it was that Lazarus sat at the festive table among his friends and relatives—his face the face of a corpse over which, for three days, death had reigned in darkness, his garments gorgeous and festive, glittering with gold, bloody-red and purple; his mien heavy and silent. He was horribly changed and strange, but as yet undiscovered. In high waves, now mild, now stormy, the festivities went on around him. Warm glances of love caressed his face, still cold with the touch of the grave; and a friend's warm hand patted his bluish, heavy hand. And the music played joyous tunes mingled of the sounds of the tympanum, the pipe, the zither and the dulcimer. It was as if bees were humming, locusts buzzing and birds singing over the happy home of Mary and Martha.

II

Some one recklessly lifted the veil. By one breath of an uttered word he destroyed the serene charm, and uncovered the truth in its ugly nakedness. No thought was clearly defined in his mind, when his lips smilingly asked: "Why do you not tell us, Lazarus, what was There?" And all became silent, struck with the question. Only now it seemed to have occurred to them that for three days Lazarus had been dead; and they looked with curiosity, awaiting an answer. But Lazarus remained silent.

"You will not tell us?" wondered the inquirer. "Is it so terrible There?"

Again his thought lagged behind his words. Had it preceded them, he would not have asked the question, for, at the very moment he uttered it, his heart sank with a dread fear. All grew restless; they awaited the words of Lazarus anxiously. But he was silent, cold and severe, and his eyes were cast down. And now, as if for the first time, they perceived the horrible bluishness of his face and the loathsome corpulence of his body. On the table, as if forgotten by Lazarus, lay his livid blue hand, and all eyes were riveted upon it, as though expecting the desired answer from that hand. The musicians still played; then silence fell upon them, too, and the gay sounds died down, as scattered coals are extinguished by water. The pipe became mute, and the ringing tympanum and the murmuring dulcimer; and as though a chord were broken, as though song itself were dying, the zither echoed a trembling broken sound. Then all was quiet.

"You will not?" repeated the inquirer, unable to restrain his babbling tongue. Silence reigned, and the livid blue hand lay motionless. It moved slightly, and the company sighed with relief and raised their eyes. Lazarus, risen from the dead, was looking straight at them, embracing all with one glance, heavy and terrible.

This was on the third day after Lazarus had arisen from the grave. Since then many had felt that his gaze was the gaze of destruction, but neither those who had been forever crushed by it, nor those who in the prime of life (mysterious even as death) had found the will to resist his glance, could ever explain the terror that lay immovable in the depths of his black pupils. He looked quiet and simple. One felt that he had no intention to hide anything, but also no intention to tell anything. His look was cold, as of one who is entirely indifferent to all that is alive. And many careless people who pressed around him, and did not notice him, later learned with wonder and fear the name of this stout, quiet man who brushed against them with his sumptuous, gaudy garments. The sun did not stop shining when he looked, neither did the fountain cease playing, and the Eastern sky remained cloudless and blue as always; but the man who fell under his inscrutable gaze could no longer feel the sun, nor hear the fountain, nor recognize his native sky. Sometimes he would cry bitterly, sometimes tear his hair in despair and madly call for help; but generally it happened that the men thus stricken by the gaze of Lazarus began to fade away listlessly and quietly and pass into a slow death lasting many long years. They died in the presence of everybody, colorless, haggard and gloomy, like trees withering on rocky ground. Those who screamed in madness sometimes came back to life; but the others, never.

"So you will not tell us, Lazarus, what you saw There?" the inquirer repeated for the third time. But now his voice was dull, and a dead, grey weariness looked stupidly from out his eyes. The faces of all present were also covered by the same dead grey weariness like a mist. The guests stared at one another stupidly, not knowing why they had come together or why they sat around this rich table. They stopped talking, and vaguely felt it was time to leave; but they could not overcome the lassitude that spread through their muscles. So they continued to sit there, each one isolated, like little dim lights scattered in the darkness of night.

The musicians were paid to play, and they again took up the instruments, and again played gay or mournful airs. But it was music made to order, always the same tunes, and the guests listened wonderingly. Why was this music necessary, they thought, why was it necessary and what good did it do for people to pull at strings and blow their cheeks into thin pipes, and produce varied and strange-sounding noises?

"How badly they play!" said some one.

The musicians were insulted and left. Then the guests departed one by one, for it was nearing night. And when the quiet darkness enveloped them, and it became easier to breathe, the image of Lazarus suddenly arose before each one in stern splendor. There he stood, with the blue face of a corpse and the raiment of a bridegroom, sumptuous and resplendent, in his eyes that cold stare in the depths of which lurked *The Horrible!* They stood still as if turned into stone. The darkness surrounded them, and in the midst of this darkness flamed up the horrible apparition, the supernatural vision, of the one who for three days had lain under the measureless power of death. Three days he had been dead. Thrice had the sun risen and set—and he had lain dead. The children had played, the water had murmured as it streamed over the rocks, the hot dust had clouded the highway—and he had been dead. And now he was among men again—touched them—looked at them—*looked at them!* And through the black rings of his pupils, as through dark glasses, the unfathomable *There* gazed upon humanity.

III

No one took care of Lazarus, and no friends or kindred remained with him. Only the great desert, enfolding the Holy City, came close to the threshold of his abode. It entered his home, and lay down on his couch like a spouse, and put out all the fires. No one cared for Lazarus. One after the other went away, even his sisters, Mary and Martha. For a long while Martha did not want to leave him, for she knew not who would nurse him or take care of him; and she cried and prayed. But one night, when the wind was roaming about the desert, and the rustling cypress trees were bending over the roof, she dressed herself quietly, and quietly went away. Lazarus probably heard how the door was slammed — it had not shut properly and the wind kept knocking it continually against the post — but he did not rise, did not go out, did not try to find out the reason. And the whole night until the morning the cypress trees hissed over his head, and the door swung to and fro, allowing the cold, greedily prowling desert to enter his dwelling. Everybody shunned him as though he were a leper. They wanted to put a bell on his neck to avoid meeting him. But some one, turning pale, remarked it would be terrible if at night, under the windows, one should happen to hear Lazarus' bell, and all grew pale and assented.

Since he did nothing for himself, he would probably have starved had not his neighbors, in trepidation, saved some food for him. Children brought it to him. They did not fear him, neither did they laugh at him in the innocent cruelty in which children often laugh at unfortunates. They were indifferent to him, and Lazarus showed the same indifference to them. He showed no desire to thank them for their services; he did not try to pat the dark hands and look into the simple shining little eyes. Abandoned to the ravages of time and the desert, his house was falling to ruins, and his hungry, bleating goats had long been scattered among his neighbors. His wedding garments had grown old. He wore them without changing them, as he had donned them on that happy day when the musicians played. He did not see the difference between old and new, between torn and whole. The brilliant colors were burnt and faded; the vicious dogs of the city and the sharp thorns of the desert had rent the fine clothes to shreds.

During the day, when the sun beat down mercilessly upon all living things, and even the scorpions hid under the stones, convulsed with a mad desire to sting, he sat motionless in the burning rays, lifting high his blue face and shaggy wild beard.

While yet the people were unafraid to speak to him, some one had asked him: "Poor Lazarus! Do you find it pleasant to sit so, and look at the sun?" And he answered: "Yes, it is pleasant."

The thought suggested itself to people that the cold of the three days in the grave had been so intense, its darkness so deep, that there was not in all the earth enough heat or light to warm Lazarus and lighten the gloom of his eyes; and inquirers turned away with a sigh.

And when the setting sun, flat and purple-red, descended to earth, Lazarus went into the desert and walked straight toward it, as though intending to reach it. Always he walked directly toward the sun, and those who tried to follow him and find out what he did at night in the desert had indelibly imprinted upon their mind's vision the black silhouette of a tall, stout man against the red background of an immense disk. The horrors of the night drove them away, and so they never found out what Lazarus did in the desert; but the image of the black form against the red was burned forever into their brains. Like an animal with a cinder in its eye which furiously rubs its muzzle against its paws, they foolishly rubbed their eyes; but the impression left by Lazarus was ineffaceable, forgotten only in death.

There were people living far away who never saw Lazarus and only heard of him. With an audacious curiosity which is stronger than fear and feeds on fear, with a secret sneer in their hearts, some of them came to him one day as he basked in the sun, and entered into conversation with him. At that time his appearance had changed for the better and was not so frightful. At first the visitors snapped their fingers and thought disapprovingly of the foolish inhabitants of the Holy City. But when the short talk came to an end and they went home, their expression was such that the inhabitants of the Holy City at once knew their errand and said: "Here go some more madmen at whom Lazarus has looked." The speakers raised their hands in silent pity.

Other visitors came, among them brave warriors in clinking armor, who knew not fear, and happy youths who made merry with laughter and song. Busy merchants, jingling their coins, ran in for awhile, and proud attendants at the Temple placed their staffs at Lazarus' door. But no one returned the same as he came. A frightful shadow fell upon their souls, and gave a new appearance to the old familiar world.

Those who felt any desire to speak, after they had been stricken by the gaze of Lazarus, described the change that had come over them somewhat like this:

All objects seen by the eye and palpable to the hand became empty, light and transparent, as though they were light shadows in the darkness; and this darkness enveloped the whole universe. It was dispelled neither by the sun, nor by the moon, nor by the stars, but embraced the earth like a mother, and clothed it in a boundless black veil.

Into all bodies it penetrated, even into iron and stone; and the particles of the body lost their unity and became lonely. Even to the heart of the particles it penetrated, and the particles of the particles became lonely.

The vast emptiness which surrounds the universe, was not filled with things seen, with sun or moon or stars; it stretched boundless, penetrating everywhere, disuniting everything, body from body, particle from particle.

In emptiness the trees spread their roots, themselves empty; in emptiness rose phantom temples, palaces and houses—all empty; and in the emptiness moved restless Man, himself empty and light, like a shadow.

There was no more a sense of time; the beginning of all things and their end merged into one. In the very moment when a building was

*being erected and one could hear the builders striking with their ham-
mers, one seemed already to see its ruins, and then emptiness where the
ruins were.*

*A man was just born, and funeral candles were already lighted at his
head, and then were extinguished; and soon there was emptiness where
before had been the man and the candles.*

*And surrounded by Darkness and Empty Waste, Man trembled hope-
lessly before the dread of the Infinite.*

So spoke those who had a desire to speak. But much more could
probably have been told by those who did not want to talk, and who
died in silence.

IV

At that time there lived in Rome a celebrated sculptor by the name of
Aurelius. Out of clay, marble and bronze he created forms of gods and
men of such beauty that this beauty was proclaimed immortal. But he
himself was not satisfied, and said there was a supreme beauty that he
had never succeeded in expressing in marble or bronze. "I have not yet
gathered the radiance of the moon," he said; "I have not yet caught the
glare of the sun. There is no soul in my marble, there is no life in my
beautiful bronze." And when by moonlight he would slowly wander
along the roads, crossing the black shadows of the cypress-trees, his
white tunic flashing in the moonlight, those he met used to laugh
good-naturedly and say: "Is it moonlight that you are gathering,
Aurelius? Why did you not bring some baskets along?"

And he, too, would laugh and point to his eyes and say: "Here are the baskets in which I gather the light of the moon and the radiance of the sun."

And that was the truth. In his eyes shone moon and sun. But he
could not transmit the radiance to marble. Therein lay the greatest
tragedy of his life. He was a descendant of an ancient race of patricians,
had a good wife and children, and except in this one respect, lacked
nothing.

When the dark rumor about Lazarus reached him, he consulted his
wife and friends and decided to make the long voyage to Judea, in order
that he might look upon the man miraculously raised from the dead. He
felt lonely in those days and hoped on the way to renew his jaded
energies. What they told him about Lazarus did not frighten him. He
had meditated much upon death. He did not like it, nor did he like
those who tried to harmonize it with life. On this side, beautiful life; on
the other, mysterious death, he reasoned, and no better lot could befall
a man than to live—to enjoy life and the beauty of living. And he

already had conceived a desire to convince Lazarus of the truth of this view and to return his soul to life even as his body had been returned. This task did not appear impossible, for the reports about Lazarus, fearsome and strange as they were, did not tell the whole truth about him, but only carried a vague warning against something awful.

Lazarus was getting up from a stone to follow in the path of the setting sun, on the evening when the rich Roman, accompanied by an armed slave, approached him, and in a ringing voice called to him: "Lazarus!"

Lazarus saw a proud and beautiful face, made radiant by fame, and white garments and precious jewels shining in the sunlight. The ruddy rays of the sun lent to the head and face a likeness to dimly shining bronze—that was what Lazarus saw. He sank back to his seat obediently, and wearily lowered his eyes.

"It is true you are not beautiful, my poor Lazarus," said the Roman quietly, playing with his gold chain. "You are even frightful, my poor friend; and death was not lazy the day when you so carelessly fell into its arms. But you are as fat as a barrel, and 'Fat people are not bad,' as the great Cæsar said. I do not understand why people are so afraid of you. You will permit me to stay with you over night? It is already late, and I have no abode."

Nobody had ever asked Lazarus to be allowed to pass the night with him.

"I have no bed," said he.

"I am somewhat of a warrior and can sleep sitting," replied the Roman. "We shall make a light."

"I have no light."

"Then we will converse in the darkness like two friends. I suppose you have some wine?"

"I have no wine."

The Roman laughed.

"Now I understand why you are so gloomy and why you do not like your second life. No wine? Well, we shall do without. You know there are words that go to one's head even as Falernian wine."

With a motion of his head he dismissed the slave, and they were alone. And again the sculptor spoke, but it seemed as though the sinking sun had penetrated into his words. They faded, pale and empty, as if trembling on weak feet, as if slipping and falling, drunk with the wine of anguish and despair. And black chasms appeared between the two men—like remote hints of vast emptiness and vast darkness.

"Now I am your guest and you will not ill-treat me, Lazarus!" said the Roman. "Hospitality is binding even upon those who have been three days dead. Three days, I am told, you were in the grave. It must have been cold there . . . and it is from there that you have brought this bad habit of doing without light and wine. I like a light. It gets dark so quickly here. Your eyebrows and forehead have an interesting line: even as the ruins of castles covered with the ashes of an earthquake. But why in such strange, ugly clothes? I have seen the bridegrooms of your country, they wear clothes like that—such ridiculous clothes—such awful garments. . . . Are you a bridegroom?"

Already the sun had disappeared. A gigantic black shadow was approaching fast from the west, as if prodigious bare feet were rustling over the sand. And the chill breezes stole up behind.

"In the darkness you seem even bigger, Lazarus, as though you had grown stouter in these few minutes. Do you feed on darkness, perchance? . . . And I would like a light . . . just a small light . . . just a small light. And I am cold. The nights here are so barbarously cold. . . . If it were not so dark, I should say you were looking at me, Lazarus. Yes, it seems, you are looking. You are looking. *You are looking at me!* . . . I feel it—now you are smiling."

The night had come, and a heavy blackness filled the air.

"How good it will be when the sun rises again to-morrow. . . . You know I am a great sculptor . . . so my friends call me. I create, yes, they say I create, but for that daylight is necessary. I give life to cold marble. I melt the ringing bronze in the fire, in a bright, hot fire. Why did you touch me with your hand?"

"Come," said Lazarus, "you are my guest." And they went into the house. And the shadows of the long evening fell on the earth. . . .

The slave at last grew tired waiting for his master, and when the sun stood high he came to the house. And he saw, directly under its burning rays, Lazarus and his master sitting close together. They looked straight up and were silent.

The slave wept and cried aloud: "Master, what ails you, Master!"

The same day Aurelius left for Rome. The whole way he was thoughtful and silent, attentively examining everything, the people, the ship, and the sea, as though endeavoring to recall something. On the sea a great storm overtook them, and all the while Aurelius remained on deck and gazed eagerly at the approaching and falling waves. When he reached home his family were shocked at the terrible change in his demeanor, but he calmed them with the words: "I have found it!"

In the dusty clothes which he had worn during the entire journey and had not changed, he began his work, and the marble ringingly responded to the resounding blows of the hammer. Long and eagerly he worked, admitting no one. At last, one morning, he announced that the work was ready, and gave instructions that all his friends, and the severe critics and judges of art, be called together. Then he donned gorgeous garments, shining with gold, glowing with the purple of the byssin.

"Here is what I have created," he said thoughtfully.

His friends looked, and immediately the shadow of deep sorrow covered their faces. It was a thing monstrous, possessing none of the forms familiar to the eye, yet not devoid of a hint of some new unknown form. On a thin tortuous little branch, or rather an ugly likeness of one, lay crooked, strange, unsightly, shapeless heaps of something turned outside in, or something turned inside out—wild fragments which seemed to be feebly trying to get away from themselves. And, accidentally, under one of the wild projections, they noticed a wonderfully sculptured butterfly, with transparent wings, trembling as though with a weak longing to fly.

"Why that wonderful butterfly, Aurelius?" timidly asked some one.

"I do not know," answered the sculptor.

The truth had to be told, and one of his friends, the one who loved Aurelius best, said: "This is ugly, my poor friend. It must be destroyed. Give me the hammer." And with two blows he destroyed the monstrous mass, leaving only the wonderfully sculptured butterfly.

After that Aurelius created nothing. He looked with absolute indifference at marble and at bronze and at his own divine creations, in which dwelt immortal beauty. In the hope of breathing into him once again the old flame of inspiration, with the idea of awakening his dead soul, his friends led him to see the beautiful creations of others, but he remained indifferent and no smile warmed his closed lips. And only after they spoke to him much and long of beauty, he would reply wearily:

"But all this is—a lie."

And in the daytime, when the sun was shining, he would go into his rich and beautifully laid-out garden, and finding a place where there was no shadow, would expose his bare head and his dull eyes to the glitter and burning heat of the sun. Red and white butterflies fluttered around; down into the marble cistern ran splashing water from the crooked mouth of a blissfully drunken Satyr; but he sat motionless, like a pale shadow of that other one who, in a far land, at the very gates of the stony desert, also sat motionless under the fiery sun.

V

And it came about finally that Lazarus was summoned to Rome by the great Augustus.

They dressed him in gorgeous garments as though it had been ordained that he was to remain a bridegroom to an unknown bride until the very day of his death. It was as if an old coffin, rotten and falling apart, were regilded over and over, and gay tassels were hung on it. And solemnly they conducted him in gala attire, as though in truth it were a bridal procession, the runners loudly sounding the trumpet that the way be made for the the ambassadors of the Emperor. But the roads along which he passed were deserted. His entire native land cursed the execrable name of Lazarus, the man miraculously brought to life, and the people scattered at the mere report of his horrible approach. The trumpeters blew lonely blasts, and only the desert answered with a dying echo.

Then they carried him across the sea on the saddest and most gorgeous ship that was ever mirrored in the azure waves of the Mediterranean. There were many people aboard, but the ship was silent and still as a coffin, and the water seemed to moan as it parted before the short curved prow. Lazarus sat lonely, baring his head to the sun, and listening in silence to the splashing of the waters. Further away the seamen and the ambassadors gathered like a crowd of distressed shadows. If a thunderstorm had happened to burst upon them at that time or the wind had overwhelmed the red sails, the ship would probably have perished, for none of those who were on her had strength or desire enough to fight for life. With supreme effort some went to the side of the ship and eagerly gazed at the blue, transparent abyss. Perhaps they imagined they saw a naiad flashing a pink shoulder through the waves, or an insanely joyous and drunken centaur galloping by, splashing up the water with his hoofs. But the sea was deserted and mute, and so was the watery abyss.

Listlessly Lazarus set foot on the streets of the Eternal City, as though all its riches, all the majesty of its gigantic edifices, all the luster and beauty and music of refined life, were simply the echo of the wind in the desert, or the misty images of hot running sand. Chariots whirled by; the crowd of strong, beautiful, haughty men passed on, builders of the Eternal City and proud partakers of its life; songs rang out; fountains laughed; pearly laughter of women filled the air, while the drunkard philosophized and the sober ones smilingly listened; horseshoes rattled on the pavement. And surrounded on all sides by glad sounds, a fat, heavy man moved through the center of the city like a cold spot of silence, sowing in his path grief, anger and vague, carking distress. Who dared to be sad in Rome? indignantly demanded frowning citizens; and in two days the swift-tongued Rome knew of Lazarus, the man miraculously raised from the grave, and timidly evaded him.

There were many brave men ready to try their strength, and at their senseless call Lazarus came obediently. The Emperor was so engrossed with state affairs that he delayed receiving the visitor, and for seven days Lazarus moved among the people.

A jovial drunkard met him with a smile on his red lips. "Drink, Lazarus, drink!" he cried, "Would not Augustus laugh to see you drink!" And naked, besotted women laughed, and decked the blue hands of Lazarus with rose-leaves. But the drunkard looked into the eyes of Lazarus—and his joy ended forever. Thereafter he was always drunk. He drank no more, but was drunk all the time, shadowed by fearful dreams, instead of the joyous reveries that wine gives. Fearful dreams became the food of his broken spirit. Fearful dreams held him day and night in the mists of monstrous fantasy, and death itself was no more fearful than the apparition of its fierce precursor.

Lazarus came to a youth and his lass who loved each other and were beautiful in their love. Proudly and strongly holding in his arms his beloved one, the youth said, with gentle pity: "Look at us, Lazarus, and rejoice with us. Is there anything stronger than love?"

And Lazarus looked at them. And their whole life they continued to love one another, but their love became mournful and gloomy, even as those cypress trees over the tombs that feed their roots on the putrescence of the grave, and strive in vain in the quiet evening hour to touch the sky with their pointed tops. Hurled by fathomless life-forces into each other's arms, they mingled their kisses with tears, their joy with pain, and only succeeded in realizing the more vividly a sense of their slavery to the silent Nothing. Forever united, forever parted, they flashed like sparks, and like sparks went out in boundless darkness.

Lazarus came to a proud sage, and the sage said to him: "I already know all the horrors that you may tell me, Lazarus. With what else can you terrify me?"

Only a few moments passed before the sage realized that the knowledge of the horrible is not the horrible, and that the sight of death is not death. And he felt that in the eyes of the Infinite wisdom and folly are the same, for the Infinite knows them not. And the boundaries between knowledge and ignorance, between truth and falsehood, between top and bottom, faded and his shapeless thought was suspended in emptiness. Then he grasped his grey head in his hands and cried out insanely: "I cannot think! I cannot think!"

Thus it was that under the cool gaze of Lazarus, the man miraculously raised from the dead, all that serves to affirm life, its sense and its joys, perished. And people began to say it was dangerous to allow him to see the Emperor; that it were better to kill him and bury him secretly, and swear he had disappeared. Swords were sharpened and youths devoted to the welfare of the people announced their readiness to become assassins, when Augustus upset the cruel plans by demanding that Lazarus appear before him.

Even though Lazarus could not be kept away, it was felt that the heavy impression conveyed by his face might be somewhat softened. With that end in view expert painters, barbers and artists were secured who worked the whole night on Lazarus' head. His beard was trimmed

and curled. The disagreeable and deadly bluishness of his hands and
face was covered up with paint; his hands were whitened, his cheeks
rouged. The disgusting wrinkles of suffering that ridged his old face
were patched up and painted, and on the smooth surface, wrinkles of
good-nature and laughter, and of pleasant, good-humored cheeriness,
were laid on artistically with fine brushes.

Lazarus submitted indifferently to all they did with him, and soon
was transformed into a stout, nice-looking old man, for all the world a
quiet and good-humored grandfather of numerous grandchildren. He
looked as though the smile with which he told funny stories had not left
his lips, as though a quiet tenderness still lay hidden in the corner of
his eyes. But the wedding-dress they did not dare to take off; and they
could not change his eyes—the dark, terrible eyes from out of which
stared the incomprehensible *There*.

VI

Lazarus was untouched by the magnificence of the imperial apart-
ments. He remained stolidly indifferent, as though he saw no contrast
between his ruined house at the edge of the desert and the solid, beautiful palace of stone. Under his feet the hard marble of the floor took
on the semblance of the moving sands of the desert, and to his eyes the
throngs of gaily dressed, haughty men were as unreal as the emptiness
of the air. They looked not into his face as he passed by, fearing to come
under the awful bane of his eyes; but when the sound of his heavy steps
announced that he had passed, heads were lifted, and eyes examined
with timid curiosity the figure of the corpulent, tall, slightly stooping
old man, as he slowly passed into the heart of the imperial palace. If
death itself had appeared men would not have feared it so much; for
hitherto death had been known to the dead only, and life to the living
only, and between these two there had been no bridge. But this strange
being knew death, and that knowledge of his was felt to be mysterious
and cursed. "He will kill our great, divine Augustus," men cried with
horror, and they hurled curses after him. Slowly and stolidly he passed
them by, penetrating ever deeper into the palace.

Cæsar knew already who Lazarus was, and was prepared to meet
him. He was a courageous man; he felt his power was invincible, and
in the fateful encounter with the man "wonderfully raised from the
dead" he refused to lean on other men's weak help. Man to man, face
to face, he met Lazarus.

"Do not fix your gaze on me, Lazarus," he commanded. "I have
heard that your head is like the head of Medusa, and turns into stone

all upon whom you look. But I should like to have a close look at you, and to talk to you before I turn into stone," he added in a spirit of playfulness that concealed his real misgivings.

Approaching him, he examined closely Lazarus' face and his strange festive clothes. Though his eyes were sharp and keen, he was deceived by the skilful counterfeit.

"Well, your appearance is not terrible, venerable sir. But all the worse for men, when the terrible takes on such a venerable and pleasant appearance. Now let us talk."

Augustus sat down, and as much by glance as by words began the discussion. "Why did you not salute me when you entered?"

Lazarus answered indifferently: "I did not know it was necessary."

"You are a Christian?"

"No."

Augustus nodded approvingly. "That is good. I do like not the Christians. They shake the tree of life, forbidding it to bear fruit, and they scatter to the wind its fragrant blossoms. But who are you?"

With some effort Lazarus answered: "I was dead."

"I heard about that. But who are you now?"

Lazarus' answer came slowly. Finally he said again, listlessly and indistinctly: "I was dead."

"Listen to me, stranger," said the Emperor sharply, giving expression to what had been in his mind before. "My empire is an empire of the living; my people are a people of the living and not of the dead. You are superfluous here. I do not know who you are, I do not know what you have seen There, but if you lie, I hate your lies, and if you tell the truth, I hate your truth. In my heart I feel the pulse of life; in my hands I feel power, and my proud thoughts, like eagles, fly through space. Behind my back, under the protection of my authority, under the shadow of the laws I have created, men live and labor and rejoice. Do you hear this divine harmony of life? Do you hear the war cry that men hurl into the face of the future, challenging it to strife?"

Augustus extended his arms reverently and solemnly cried out: "Blessed art thou, Great Divine Life!"

But Lazarus was silent, and the Emperor continued more severely: "You are not wanted here. Pitiful remnant, half devoured of death, you fill men with distress and aversion to life. Like a caterpillar on the fields, you are gnawing away at the full seed of joy, exuding the slime of despair and sorrow. Your truth is like a rusted sword in the hands of a night assassin, and I shall condemn you to death as an assassin. But first I want to look into your eyes. Mayhap only cowards fear them, and brave men are spurred on to struggle and victory. Then will you merit not death but a reward. Look at me, Lazarus."

At first it seemed to divine Augustus as if a friend were looking at him, so soft, so alluring, so gently fascinating was the gaze of Lazarus. It promised not horror but quiet rest, and the Infinite dwelt there as a fond mistress, a compassionate sister, a mother. And ever stronger grew its gentle embrace, until he felt, as it were, the breath of a mouth hungry for kisses. . . . Then it seemed as if iron bones protruded in a ravenous grip, and closed upon him in an iron band; and cold nails touched his heart, and slowly, slowly sank into it.

"It pains me," said divine Augustus, growing pale; "but look, Lazarus, look!"

Ponderous gates, shutting off eternity, appeared to be slowly swinging open, and through the growing aperture poured in, coldly and calmly, the awful horror of the Infinite. Boundless Emptiness and Boundless Gloom entered like two shadows, extinguishing the sun, removing the ground from under the feet, and the cover from over the head. And the pain in his icy heart ceased.

"Look at me, look at me, Lazarus!" commanded Augustus, staggering. . . .

Time ceased and the beginning of things came perilously near to the end. The throne of Augustus, so recently erected, fell to pieces, and emptiness took the place of the throne and of Augustus. Rome fell silently into ruins. A new city rose in its place, and it too was erased by emptiness. Like phantom giants, cities, kingdoms, and countries swiftly fell and disappeared into emptiness—swallowed up in the black maw of the Infinite. . . .

"Cease," commanded the Emperor. Already the accent of indifference was in his voice. His arms hung powerless, and his eagle eyes flashed and were dimmed again, struggling against overwhelming darkness.

"You have killed me, Lazarus," he said drowsily.

These words of despair saved him. He thought of the people, whose shield he was destined to be, and a sharp, redeeming pang pierced his dull heart. He thought of them doomed to perish, and he was filled with anguish. First they seemed bright shadows in the gloom of the Infinite.—How terrible! Then they appeared as fragile vessels with life-agitated blood, and hearts that knew both sorrow and great joy.—And he thought of them with tenderness.

And so thinking and feeling, inclining the scales now to the side of life, now to the side of death, he slowly returned to life, to find in its suffering and joy a refuge from the gloom, emptiness and fear of the Infinite.

"No, you did not kill me, Lazarus," said he firmly. "But I will kill you. Go!"

Evening came and divine Augustus partook of food and drink with great joy. But there were moments when his raised arm would remain suspended in the air, and the light of his shining, eager eyes was dimmed. It seemed as if an icy wave of horror washed against his feet. He was vanquished but not killed, and coldly awaited his doom, like a black shadow. His nights were haunted by horror, but the bright days still brought him the joys, as well as the sorrows, of life.

Next day, by order of the Emperor, they burned out Lazarus' eyes with hot irons and sent him home. Even Augustus dared not kill him.

* * *

Lazarus returned to the desert and the desert received him with the breath of the hissing wind and the ardor of the glowing sun. Again he sat on the stone with matted beard uplifted; and two black holes, where the eyes had once been, looked dull and horrible at the sky. In the distance the Holy City surged and roared restlessly, but near him all was deserted and still. No one approached the place where Lazarus, miraculously raised from the dead, passed his last days, for his neighbors had long since abandoned their homes. His cursed knowledge, driven by the hot irons from his eyes deep into the brain, lay there in ambush; as if from ambush it might spring out upon men with a thousand unseen eyes. No one dared to look at Lazarus.

And in the evening, when the sun, swollen crimson and growing larger, bent its way toward the west, blind Lazarus slowly groped after it. He stumbled against stones and fell; corpulent and feeble, he rose heavily and walked on; and against the red curtain of sunset his dark form and outstretched arms gave him the semblance of a cross.

It happened once that he went and never returned. Thus ended the second life of Lazarus, who for three days had been in the mysterious thraldom of death and then was miraculously raised from the dead.